A LIKELY STORY

A LIKELY STORY

Jenn McKinlay

BERKLEY PRIME CRIME, NEW YORK

**BERKLEY
PRIME
CRIME**

**An imprint of Penguin Random House LLC
375 Hudson Street, New York, New York 10014**

This book is an original publication of Penguin Random House LLC.

Library of Congress Cataloging-in-Publication Data

McKinlay, Jenn.
A likely story / Jenn McKinlay.—First edition.
pages ; cm
ISBN 978-0-425-26074-6
I. Title.
PS3612.A948L55 2015
813'.6—dc23
2015020873

FIRST EDITION: November 2015

PRINTED IN THE UNITED STATES OF AMERICA

10 9 8 7 6 5 4 3 2 1

Cover illustration by Julia Green.
Cover design by Rita Frangie.
Interior text design by Laura K. Corless.

Penguin
Random
House

*For the Hub, Chris Hansen Orf, being married to you
has been the best time I've ever had. You've given me the two
greatest gifts of my life, our sons, Beckett and Wyatt, for which I
am ever grateful. Our family is and always will be our greatest
achievement, and I'm so glad we're in it together. And if all
that isn't enough, you gave me the opening line to this book.
I simply couldn't do this without you, Hub. Love you forever.*

Acknowledgments

I remember the day that my fabulous editor, Kate Seaver, met me for lunch and told me that *A Likely Story* was going to be released in hardcover. I was speechless. Anyone who knows me knows that this *never* happens. With a waiter hovering nearby, I finally managed to choke out, "We're going to need a minute." This might be my most favorite moment in time during my whole writing journey, and I am so pleased that I got to share it with my editor, Kate. She has been with me for all three of my series with endless encouragement, support and brilliant insight. There really aren't enough words to thank her for all that she has done for me, so I'll just keep saying, "Thank you so much, Kate!" until she gets tired of hearing it.

In addition to Kate, there are so many people involved in the publication of a book who I never get to see that I have to say a blanket thank-you to everyone at Berkley Prime Crime who has worked on my different series. I feel very fortunate to have such a terrific publishing house working to help make my books the best they can be. And here's a special shout-out to

Danielle Dill in PR for tirelessly arranging signings, interviews and everything else my crazy head cooks up. You are a wonder!

Lastly, I want to thank my mom, Susan McKinlay; my dad, Don McKinlay; my brother, Jed McKinlay; my husband, Chris Hansen Orf; and my sons, Beckett Orf and Wyatt Orf—the family I started from and the family I made. You people are my cornerstones and you have never let me crack and crumble, not even when the going got really rough. I feel so very lucky to have you all in my life. Love you always.

A LIKELY STORY

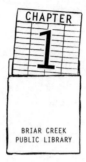

CHAPTER
1

BRIAR CREEK
PUBLIC LIBRARY

66 I need a plunger and a mop stat!" Lindsey Norris cried
from the family restroom in the children's area of the
Briar Creek Public Library. There was an inch of water on
the floor, and the water spilling over the toilet bowl showed
no signs of slowing.

The harried mother and daughter who had just been in
the restroom stood by the door, with the young girl giving
Lindsey big worried looks while the mother gushed apologies
almost as fast as the toilet spilled water.

"I'm so sorry, so sorry, so very, very sorry," Kimberly Curtis said.

"It's fine," Lindsey lied. "Happens all the time."

She glanced down at the young girl, Madison Curtis, who
was pulling her winter hat over her face as if to hide. She
peeked at Lindsey from under the edge and said, "I sorry.
Ducky wanted to swim."

Lindsey felt her lips turn up in spite of the situation. She
glanced at Kimberly and said, "It does make sense on one level."

Kimberly hugged her daughter and gave Lindsey an appreciative glance. "You're very kind, but there is nothing logical about flushing a stuffed duck down the toilet."

"Here's the mop!"

Lindsey glanced past Kimberly and Madison at her second in command. Her longtime friend Beth Stanley was coming at her with a mop in one hand and a plunger in the other, or more accurately, a mop under one wing and a plunger under the other.

"Wild guess here," Lindsey said as she took in Beth's bright yellow hooded sweatshirt with wings on the sleeves and an orange beak and two large eyes sewn onto the hood. *"Make Way for Ducklings* for story time?"

"McCloskey is the man!" Beth said. "Yes, we read all the feathered faves: *The Story about Ping*; *Come Along, Daisy!* and *The Ugly Duckling*, natch."

"Well, you inspired little Madison here to set one free," Lindsey said.

"Uh-oh," Beth said. She looked past Lindsey at the bathroom floor.

"It's fine. I changed into my boots," Lindsey said. She pointed to her L.L.Bean snow boots. "I'll just waddle on in there and shut the water off."

"I'll help. I'm in boots, too. They look like duck feet, don't you think?" Beth asked.

"They do," Lindsey agreed. She looked at Kimberly and Madison. "We're going to start cleaning, and then I'm going to call our maintenance people from the town and see if they can get your duck out of the pipes."

Madison's face crumpled, and she looked like she was going to have a complete meltdown. Beth, ever in touch with her story timers, saw the brewing storm and started having a conversation with Madison's duck.

"You're going where? Oh, sorry," she called into the toilet.

She glanced at them with a chagrined look. "I forgot to speak in duck." She turned back to the toilet and said, "Quack, quack quackety quackers."

Madison's face went from distraught to hopeful. Beth kept up the conversation, making Madison laugh while Kimberly leaned close to Lindsey and said, "We won't need Fluffy back. When Madison made it her go-to stuffie, Beth advised me to buy more of the same. I bought three of them, and I rotate them in and out so they have the same amount of wear."

"Brilliant," Lindsey whispered back. Then she hurried into the bathroom to shut the water off.

"Where did Fluffy go?" Madison asked Beth. Her four-year-old voice was so pitiful that Lindsey wanted to hug her.

"Fluffy says she's going to visit her sister and she'll be back"—Beth paused to look at Kimberly, who nodded—"after dinner."

Madison beamed and clapped her hands as Beth and Lindsey sloshed back toward them.

"What do you say, Madison?" Kimberly asked her daughter.

"Thank you," Madison hugged Beth around the knees and then did the same to Lindsey.

"You're welcome," they said together. They waved as the mother and daughter bundled up to go out into the February cold.

"Maintenance is never going to get that duck out of there, are they?" Lindsey asked.

"Not a chance," Beth said. "But it's okay. Kim is smart and has backups."

"So she said. Great advice you gave her there."

"Sometimes I pull a good one out of my beak," Beth joked. "Quack."

"Clark from maintenance just called. They are fixing an electrical issue with the town garage and can't get back here until late this afternoon," Ms. Cole said as she joined them. She looked at the bathroom with disapproval and added, "When Mr. Tupper was director we never had plumbing issues."

"That's ridicu—" Beth protested, but Lindsey interrupted her.

"Thank you for calling them, Ms. Cole," Lindsey said.

When she had taken the job as director of the small town library a couple of years ago, she'd had no idea that her skill set would expand to include basic plumbing, but then there were a lot of things she hadn't expected when she took this job. She supposed the unexpected was what kept it interesting.

She glanced at her watch; speaking of interesting, she had a meeting to attend. Her weekly crafternoon group was scheduled for one hour from now, and she knew what she had to do. Mop.

"Hurry!" Beth said as she and Lindsey hustled down the hallway.

Lindsey was surprised at how much of an important part of her life their weekly crafternoon meetings had become for her over the past couple of years.

Briar Creek was a small town nestled on the coast of Connecticut. Its claim to fame was that Captain Kidd had once buried treasure out in the Thumb Islands, which numbered into the hundreds if you counted big rocks in the bay. As of yet, no one had found the treasure, although plenty had tried.

When Lindsey had become the director of the library, she knew that in order to survive, she had to make the library a place where people really enjoyed spending time. One of her very first ideas had been to form a crafternoon club, a group of women who met every Thursday for lunch, book talk and crafting. Men were welcome, too, but so far they'd had no takers.

Instead of a program for the library, what Lindsey had

gotten was a close-knit group of friends who shared her love of food and books and tolerated her inability to craft. She adored each and every one of them.

She and Beth skidded into the room to find the lunchtime meeting already under way. Nancy Peyton, Lindsey's landlord, was leading the discussion.

"Inspector Grant," Nancy said. "What do we think of him, ladies?"

Her short gray hair was cut to flatter her large sparkling blue eyes. She was dressed in her usual turtleneck sweater and slacks with a heavy chambray shirt over the sweater to keep out the winter chill.

"I like him," Violet La Rue said. "He has spunk."

Lindsey smiled as she and Beth hit the buffet spread and loaded up their plates. Violet would know a spunky personality since she had one herself. A retired star of the Broadway theater scene, Violet dressed in long flowing caftans in brilliant jewel tones. She wore her thick gray hair in a knot on the back of her head. While about the same age as Nancy, Violet's brown complexion was wrinkle free except for several tiny lines at the corners of her eyes, which only showed when she laughed, which she did quite often.

Given both Violet's and Nancy's feisty ways, it was no surprise to Lindsey that they approved of Inspector Grant, the hero of this week's book under discussion, *The Daughter of Time* by Josephine Tey.

"Hurry up, you two, before we get to the good stuff," Charlene La Rue ordered.

Charlene was Violet's daughter and just as lovely as her mother. Charlene worked in New Haven as a newscaster but spent her off time in Briar Creek with her husband and children, as her children loved to help their grandmother with whatever community theater project she had under way.

Charlene had been in charge of the food this week, and it consisted of a large casserole dish filled with shepherd's pie, an arugula salad, sweet tea and chocolate cream pie for dessert. The shepherd's pie was still hot, and Lindsey felt her mouth begin to water. She'd had no idea that swabbing a bathroom floor could cause such an appetite.

"The good stuff?" Mary Murphy asked. "Are we talking about the food or the book?"

Mary Murphy was a pretty brunette who owned the local café the Blue Anchor with her husband, Ian Murphy. She was also the younger sister of Lindsey's ex-boyfriend Captain Mike Sullivan, known to everyone locally as Sully.

Lindsey always appreciated that Mary was able to separate their friendship from Lindsey's relationship with her brother, although Mary did lobby on her brother's behalf every chance she got.

"The book, definitely the book," Charlene said.

"Speaking of which," Nancy paused and her eyes twinkled as she looked at Lindsey. "Can you imagine trying to solve the mystery of whether King Richard III murdered the princes in the tower just because you were hospitalized with a broken leg and were bored? Who does that sort of thing, solve mysteries just because?"

Lindsey shoved a forkful of salad into her mouth and then pointed to her lips to indicate she couldn't talk right now because she was chewing.

Charlene laughed. She scooted over on the couch so that Lindsey could sit next to her. Then she looked at Lindsey and said, "She's teasing you."

Lindsey swallowed. "You think?"

Beth took a seat on the other couch next to Mary and said to Lindsey, "We could always talk about who you're dating if that would be more comfortable than your inclination for amateur sleuthing."

"Did you know that *The Daughter of Time* was written in nineteen fifty-one, shortly before Tey's death? It was her last novel and was voted number one on the list of top one hundred crime novels of all time by the UK Crime Writers' Association in nineteen ninety."

Mary shook her head at her. "That was the worst attempt at a subject change ever in the history of our meetings."

"Obviously, Lindsey does not wish to discuss her personal life," Violet said. "We should respect that."

"We should," Nancy agreed. "But we're not going to, are we?"

"Of course not," Mary said. "So, how is the old love life?"

Lindsey gave her a stubborn look. "I'm not dating anyone right now, so it's steady as she goes, thank you very much."

"Really?" Mary asked. She sounded disappointed. "Not even a lunch date?"

"No breakfast, lunch or dinner dates," Lindsey said. "Or any other kind of date, for that matter."

"So, you're not dating at all?" Violet clarified. She caught Lindsey with her hawklike stare, and Lindsey turned to Charlene.

"I bet you never lie to her," she said. "She'd catch you in a nanosecond."

"That stare is like getting blasted with a laser gun," Charlene agreed. "It's kept me on my toes my whole life."

"It's sort of like Tey's hero Inspector Grant and his ability to judge a person's character by their face," Lindsey said.

"It doesn't keep you from changing the subject though, does it?" Violet asked, looking a bit put out.

Lindsey grinned. Violet had a horse in the race for Lindsey's affections, an actor friend of hers named Robbie Vine, who was ridiculously charming and also married, adding to what was already a complicated situation.

"Speaking of Inspector Grant's uncanny ability," Lindsey said. "Do you think it's possible?"

"To read a person's character from their face? I wish," Beth said. She pushed her salad around her plate with her fork. "Every time I think I've nailed it, the guy turns out to be a toad. I've dated more than my share of toads. I'm surprised I don't have warts."

"But I thought you had a nice time with that young banker you went out to dinner with last week," Nancy said.

"Ugh," Beth grunted. "He's all about conspicuous consumption, you know, the big house, expensive car, designer label life. So shallow."

"That's too bad," Violet said. She patted Beth's shoulder. "Don't you worry, the right one will come along."

"Speaking of the right *one*," Charlene said.

She turned her reporter's gaze on Lindsey, who immediately hopped up from her seat before the conversation could veer back to her personal life.

"Do we have enough paper for the paper flowers we're making?" she asked. "Maybe I should go check on that."

She crossed the room to their crafting table. Today they we making bouquets of paper roses out of recycled office paper. Lindsey planned to use the bouquets to decorate the library and help fight off the winter doldrums.

Starting with scrap paper with words printed on them, they employed a template to cut the petals out, then they colored just the edges of the paper to give the flowers some pop. Next they would use a glue gun to layer the petals from biggest to smallest. Once the flowers were done they would attach green florist wire for the stem and then put them in vases all over the library.

She heard the women resume talking about the novel, and she heaved a sigh of relief. She loved them all dearly, but she didn't want to talk about her love life, since she barely had a handle on it herself. In truth, it wasn't complicated so much as it was none of their business, but that seemed rude to say.

"Lindsey, can I talk to you for a sec?"

Lindsey glanced up at the door to see their library clerk Ann Marie Martin standing there. The ladies all greeted Ann Marie warmly, and Nancy promised to bake a batch of molasses cookies for Ann Marie to bring home to her two precocious boys.

When Lindsey had started at the library, Ann Marie had dressed in the standard-issue mom ponytail and corduroy jumper, but as the boys had gotten older and were more occupied in school, Ann Marie was letting her dark brown hair down and dressing in tailored slacks and pretty sweaters. Still, she always smelled like cinnamon and apples, which Lindsey found comforting.

There was no question that Ann Marie was looking much more professional these days. An idea wriggled in the back of Lindsey's brain, but she pushed it aside for the moment, focusing instead on her employee.

"What can I do for you?" Lindsey asked.

"We finally got that book in for Stewart Rosen," Ann Marie said. She held up the book in question. It was a medical text that they'd borrowed from a university for him. "They're giving us a very short turnaround on it. Just two weeks."

Lindsey glanced at the title and nodded. "Stewart will want this right away, then."

"That's what I was thinking," Ann Marie said. "Do you want me to put a call in to Sully to see if the water taxi is available?"

"That'd be great," Lindsey said. She felt her heart kick up a notch at the thought of spending the afternoon with Sully.

"I think Stewart and Peter have some other books put aside for them on the hold shelf as well. Could you check this one out to them and put it with the others?"

"You got it, boss," Ann Marie said. "Make sure you dress warm. The wind out on the water today is brutal."

"Will do," Lindsey said.

In her previous occupation as an academic librarian, Lindsey had never mopped up after overflowing toilets, but she'd never gotten to go on boat rides either. Even though it was a chilly day in February, she couldn't help but be pleased that she was going out to the islands to deliver books to two of their homebound patrons. It was one of the parts of her job that made her feel as if she really was making a difference in her patrons' lives.

When Lindsey had become the library director, she had made it her mission to reach out to the residents of the Thumb Islands and provide them with borrowing privileges, and they had responded with great enthusiasm. Stewart and Peter Rosen were elderly brothers who had lived their entire life on Star Island. They were definitely on the odd end of the spectrum, but Lindsey had become rather fond of them and their quirks.

Now, if it just so happened that she had to use the local water taxi, operated by her ex-boyfriend Sully, well, what was a girl do? Borrowers needed books, and Lindsey was all about giving excellent customer service.

Luckily, Star Island wasn't too far out in the bay. She could be there and back within an hour. Easy peasy, or so she thought.

CHAPTER

2

BRIAR CREEK
PUBLIC LIBRARY

I t wasn't freezing. Lindsey supposed she should be grateful for that. Having a sunny day in the forties at the end of February in Connecticut was not something to complain about—not when there could be a blizzard dumping three feet of snow on the ground.

She left the library, crossing Main Street, and entered the small town park that sat right on the water's edge. She pulled her rolling plastic cart full of books behind her. She had contacted a few other islanders and now had three stops to make out in the archipelago to deliver and retrieve materials from the residents who lived year-round on their islands.

Thankfully, she was wearing her snow boots and her long wool coat, along with her hat, scarf and mittens. She had a feeling while it might be in the forties on land, on the water the temperature would plummet, taking her body heat with it.

She pulled her cart down the large wooden pier, listening to the wheels thump a rhythm against the uneven, weatherworn boards. The water taxi and tour boats were near the end, docked beside the small office that perched off to the side of the main pier. She glanced in the glass door to see Ronnie sitting behind the desk filing her nails.

If fifty was supposed to be the new thirty, Ronnie definitely was way ahead of the game. She was easily eighty going on thirty with her bright red cranberry hairdo, her big plastic jewelry circa nineteen seventy-seven, her skinny jeans, Ugg boots and Coach accessories.

"Afternoon, Ronnie," Lindsey said as she pulled open the door.

Ronnie lowered her cat's-eye reading glasses and looked at Lindsey over the top of the lenses.

"Lip gloss, honey," Ronnie said. "You're supposed to be spending time with an eligible man this afternoon. Let's not get sloppy with the details now."

Lindsey grinned and pulled off her gloves. "Silly me, and here I thought I was going out to the islands to deliver books to the stranded."

Ronnie just stared at her, and Lindsey huffed a breath. She reached into her coat pocket and pulled out her lip balm in the shape of an egg.

"What is that?" Ronnie asked.

"Lip balm," Lindsey replied, and she swept it over her lips.

"No wonder you're single," Ronnie said with a shake of her head.

"What?" Lindsey asked.

"You need to get yourself a nice bright red lip stain, sweetie, then you'll be irresistible," Ronnie said.

"Now, Ronnie, my dear, don't go giving my girl pointers, I don't need any more competition," Sully said as he entered the room. He winked at Lindsey, and she felt her insides cartwheel at the sight of him.

His cheeks were ruddy from being out in the cold. She always liked that look on a man. It made her want to press her palms against the rosy skin to warm it. She resisted the impulse. Sully was wearing a dark blue wool cap over his red brown curls, and his heavy jacket was unzipped as if he didn't need to fasten it against the winter's chill because he was so used to the frigid temperatures from years spent outside.

"Last time I checked she wasn't your girl yet," Ronnie said. She glanced between them. "Have I missed something?"

"Nope," Sully said. "Just wishful thinking on my part."

Uncomfortable with the direction of the conversation, Lindsey glanced out the window and asked, "Calm water out there today?"

As if in answer to her question, the front door banged open behind her and in swept a middle-aged woman, looking every inch the picture of old New England money in her tailored knee-length camel coat and fur-lined boots.

Her meticulously maintained blond bob framed her square face, which was wiped clear of wrinkles. Her darker eyebrows formed perfect arches over her pale blue eyes, her nose was a cute little upturned button, and her lips were wide even as they curved up in the corners in a toothless smile.

Lindsey couldn't place her age until the woman removed her leather driving gloves and Lindsey saw the age spots on the backs of her hands, which put the woman somewhere in her fifties. Lindsey tried to remember if the woman had ever come into the library, but she was quite sure she'd remember her if she had.

"Sully, there you are." The woman strode around Lindsey to approach Ronnie's desk. "Would you be a dear and reserve your taxi for me for first thing tomorrow morning?"

"*I'd* be happy to," Ronnie said. "As making reservations is really my *thang* around here."

She gave the woman a chastising look, and the woman shook her head.

"Oh, do forgive me, that was terribly thoughtless of me, wasn't it?" she said. She wrinkled her nose as if making a cute face would erase her faux pas.

Lindsey noted upon closer inspection that the woman was nowhere near as young as she first appeared. There was only so much a surgeon could do for jowls and a turkey neck, and this woman had both.

"No problem," Ronnie said. Lindsey noticed that her usual friendliness was missing, and she wondered at it.

"What time will you need the taxi, Mrs. Dewhurst?" Sully asked.

"Oh, call me Evelyn. After all, we're neighbors. Seven o'clock would be perfect," Evelyn said. She paused and then asked, "Unless you're available now?"

"Unfortunately, no," Sully said. He gestured to Lindsey. "I'm taking the librarian Lindsey Norris out to do her rounds."

"Librarian?" Evelyn spun around and looked at Lindsey. "Heavens, I didn't even see you there." She wagged her gloves at Lindsey and said, "Must be because you're a quiet little librarian." She clapped a hand over her mouth. "Am I being too loud? You're not going to shush me, are you?"

Evelyn laughed at her own joke while Lindsey forced one side of her mouth up. She had met Evelyn's type before. She was the sort who defined people by stereotypes and didn't see the individual beyond the classification.

"No, we're not in the library, so you're safe," she said. She glanced at Sully. "Are you ready to head out to Star Island and such?"

"Star Island?" Evelyn glanced between them. Her pale blue eyes glittered almost as brightly as the modest diamond studs in her earlobes. "You are allowed on the Rosens' island?"

"Sort of," Lindsey said. "Stewart usually meets me on the dock."

Evelyn opened her Chanel clutch and extracted an embossed business card. "Do me a favor? Give my card to Stewart. I have been trying to get on Star Island for months. I'm interested in preserving the islands, you know, and so far I've had no luck with the Rosens. Put in a good word for me, would you?"

"I'll be sure to give him your card," Lindsey said, feeling very diplomatic.

"Fabulous!" Evelyn cried. She pressed the card into Lindsey's hand and then looped her arm through Lindsey's, squeezing her close as if they were coconspirators. She turned back to Ronnie. "So, tomorrow morning, then?"

Ronnie tapped the keyboard on her computer. "It's available, so I've put you in."

"Terrific," Evelyn said. She still held Lindsey close, and Lindsey wasn't sure how to extricate herself from the woman without it being weird, which it already was.

"Well, it was nice to meet you," Lindsey said. She hoped Evelyn got the hint.

"You, too," Evelyn said. She wrinkled her nose again as if she just found the situation adorable. Then she let go of Lindsey to flip up the collar on her long coat. "Until tomorrow."

She hustled out the door, taking her manic energy with her. Lindsey blew out a breath and looked at the others.

"What was that?" she asked.

"Evelyn Dewhurst," Ronnie said with a curl of her lip. "Privileged princess from Fairfield County."

"Now don't hold back, Ronnie. Tell us how you really feel," Sully said.

"She's buying up all of the islands," Ronnie said. "She's bought ten in the past eighteen months!"

"Really?" Lindsey asked. "Why?"

"She says it's to preserve them," Ronnie said. "Pah!"

"You can't blame her if people keep choosing to sell to her," Sully said. "Besides, a lot of the properties she bought were falling into ruin, and she is refurbishing them. Her goal does seem to be to preserve the islands."

"But does she have to own them all? I mean, of course, people are going to sell. She offers them gobs of money," Ronnie said. "The last one went for ten million, and it was little more than a rock with a shack on it. It's madness."

Sully let out a small sigh, and Lindsey could tell that the situation worried him more than he was letting on.

Ronnie glanced at the clock and then at Sully. "You'd better get going or you and your girlfriend will be late to the Rosens."

Lindsey felt her face grow warm, and she saw Sully and Ronnie exchange an amused glance.

"She's cute when she's flustered," he said.

"I wouldn't know. She's not my type," Ronnie said. "Now get a move on, the two of you. You have to pick up Tim Kessler from Clover Island at four o'clock."

Sully saluted Ronnie and then came around the desk to take Lindsey's cart for her. With practiced hands, he lowered the handle until it formed a crate and then swung it up onto his shoulder.

"After you," he said and gestured for Lindsey to lead the way.

Lindsey pushed through the back door and out to the narrow stairs that led down to the dock that housed Sully's boats. He and his brother-in-law, Ian Murphy, owned the touring company together, but because winter was slow, Sully did most of the work in the cold months, bringing in Ian and Lindsey's downstairs neighbor Charlie Peyton to help with the summer high season.

"Has it been busy today?" Lindsey asked, feeling the need to talk over the sound of the water lapping against the boat's hull. She realized it was dreadful small talk, but being with him put her on edge, not in a bad way, and she couldn't seem to help it.

Sully was her ex-boyfriend. Lindsey didn't generally keep in touch with exes, mostly because her only other ex of any significance was one who made her long to back a car over him repeatedly. They had since worked through it and were now occasionally in touch, very occasionally, but it was more of a courtesy thing and not a true friendship.

Sully, however, was rapidly becoming one of Lindsey's closest friends. It sort of made the whole wanting to jump his bones thing dicey because, yeah, who wanted to mess up a perfectly good friendship?

It occurred to Lindsey that although the most recent backing off and taking time to reevaluate the relationship had been her idea, the slower they went, the more attached to him she became, which did not bode well if they didn't end up together.

During their first run at a relationship, Sully had hurt her very badly when he ended things between them to give her time she hadn't asked for to know her own feelings. When Sully had come back around, realizing that what they had was not like what either of them had experienced in the past, she had suggested a do-over, as in starting from scratch as friends. Her big, strong, silent boat captain needed to practice his communication skills. Sully was working on it, and it wasn't easy for him, which charmed Lindsey to no end.

She glanced at him out of the corner of her eye as she untied the ropes while he adjusted her box of materials in the storage bin to keep it dry.

It was like a brick to the temple to realize that if things kept going the way they were, he was going to have the ability to not just break her heart but to smash it to smithereens.

"Not busy, no," Sully answered her, bringing her attention back to the moment. "Other than a pesky tea-tippling British man, it's been fine."

"Robbie?" Lindsey asked.

She pushed the side of the boat clear of the dock, and Sully held out his hand to her. She grabbed his hand and jumped onto the boat. He steadied her before turning back to the controls.

"The same," he said. He started the engine, and they began to putter away from the shore.

"What did he want?" she asked.

"You mean other than to badger me and nag me and generally drive me crazy?" he asked.

Lindsey smiled. "Yes."

"I have no idea," he said. "But I ran into him having breakfast at the Anchor, and he was most definitely trying to find out where you and I stand with each other."

"Oh." Lindsey didn't know what to say to that, since she wasn't really sure where she and Sully stood either.

"I gave him nothing," he said. A grin spread across his face, and Lindsey knew he had enjoyed tormenting Robbie.

"That's not nice of you," she said. "He's a good guy. He really is."

Sully glowered. "Are you dating him?"

"No!" Lindsey said. "He's married."

"Apparently, it's more of a business arrangement," Sully said. "Or so he says."

He pushed the throttle until they were chugging out of the cove. Lindsey tightened the scarf about her throat.

"Married is married," she said.

"And if he wasn't?" he asked.

Lindsey couldn't even imagine a world where a famous actor like Robbie Vine was her boyfriend. A grin parted her lips, and she shook her head.

"I can't even imagine it," she said.

Sully studied her and then tipped his head to the side as he considered her words. "I'm pretty sure that's a good thing."

And there they were. It had been two months since they shared a smooch under the mistletoe in a misguided moment of affection. Lindsey's parents and her brother had been with her for the holidays, then the staff at the library had been hit with a nasty flu bug, keeping Lindsey chained to the building as she put in overtime covering the absences.

Other than the times Sully had surprised her by bringing her dinner to the library, she hadn't seen much of him. Weeks had passed, and they were almost exactly where they had left off, except the memory of that kiss burned brightly between them, giving Lindsey hope while at the same time making her nervous.

"So, what do you really think about Evelyn Dewhurst?" she asked. Nerves were trumping hope, and she was desperate to change the conversation before they ended up in an analysis of where they stood with each other. She wasn't sure she was ready for that just yet.

Besides, she suspected Sully had strong feelings on the issue of a wealthy woman buying up the islands in which he had spent his whole life and she wanted to know how he felt.

"Honestly? I'm not sure yet," he said. "She says she's buying them to preserve them, and the truth is some of them desperately need it and the people who owned them didn't have the finances to save them so I have to consider that a good thing."

"Has she approached your parents?" she asked.

"Yes," he said. He glanced at her and smiled. Lindsey knew his parents had lived on Bell Island for over forty years. She could just imagine how well Evelyn's offer had been received. "She wants to buy the island from them and then let them rent their house from her. Suffice to say, they passed."

Lindsey nodded. That was pretty much what she'd figured they'd do. Still, she was curious about Evelyn Dewhurst, and she made a mental note to research her as soon as she got back to the library.

They cleared the channel markers, and Sully opened up the throttle. Since Star Island was in a less treacherous area, Sully liked to go a bit faster and have a little more fun on the ride than he usually did navigating among the islands.

A seagull perched on a buoy watched as they sped by, churning up a frothy wake as they went. Lindsey sensed the bird didn't approve, but she found she didn't care.

The wind pulled at her long blond curls and tried its best to knock the hat off of her head. The salty spray of the sea danced up in the air, and the deep gray water looked bottomless when she glanced over the side.

It occurred to her that despite her fear of water over her head, she loved the feeling of speeding along the open water in a boat. It was liberating, being one with the elements, and she felt her spirits lift as Sully winked at her and sped up just a little bit more.

Lindsey was still savoring the intoxicating feeling of freedom when Star Island came into view and Sully began to slow down.

When Lindsey had started delivering books out to the islands, she had studied up on their histories. Star Island had been owned by the Rosen family for over one hundred years. It dated back to the heyday of the islands when the Thumb Islands were a summer playland for the wealthy, rivaling Newport, Rhode Island, in popularity. The archipelago had been a retreat for the prominent families of the time, including several U.S. presidents.

Originally, the islands had housed a wide variety of Victorian cottages, ornate in appearance and very exclusive. Sadly, the hurricane of nineteen thirty-eight had wiped out most of the original buildings. Only a few still remained, one of which was the Rosen house, primarily because it was fortunate enough to be blocked from a direct hit by the hurricane by several larger islands, which had sustained the worst of the storm.

As they approached the dock, Lindsey marveled at what a beauty the house must have been in its glory days. A multilevel house with ornate gingerbread wood trim decorating its eaves and wraparound porch, it boasted large arch-shaped windows on the upper story that looked out at the water like two expressive eyes. The building begged for fresh shingles and a snazzy paint job, but its inherent charm was still evident.

Since the Rosen brothers were decidedly elderly and one of them was in a wheelchair, Lindsey figured painting the house wasn't on the top of their priority list.

In truth, it wasn't just their age that kept them from working on their house. The Rosen brothers were known to be strange. With their hermit and hoarding tendencies run amok, Lindsey doubted they could handle any workmen on their residence, since they barely tolerated her. She suspected they only did because she brought them new books to read.

Sully cut the engine and gently banked the water taxi into the side of the dock while Lindsey scrambled out and tied up the boat. Sully retrieved her crate of books from the storage bin and joined her on the dock.

Lindsey straightened her back and glanced up at the deck where Stewart usually waited for her arrival. The wind was whipping across the water, and she supposed the cold had driven him inside. She knew he would be here in moments and that she should wait for him, as it had been made very clear to her when she had begun delivering books that she was never to leave the lower dock.

Sully stood beside her on the bobbing dock and glanced at the same spot on the deck above. There was still no sign of Stewart. He frowned.

"It doesn't seem like Stewart to not be waiting, does it?" he asked. "He always sees the taxi coming and is down here before we pull up."

"I was thinking the same thing," Lindsey admitted. "Maybe we caught him off guard. It's not like I can let him know I'm coming given that he doesn't have a phone or anything."

"Maybe he's busy taking care of Peter," Sully said. "I'm sure he'll be here as soon as he can."

They stood patiently leaning side to side with the rocking wood under their feet. Lindsey's crate sat between them on the boards.

"So, read any good books lately?" he asked.

Lindsey laughed. "Is that a librarian pickup line?"

"No, if it was a librarian pickup line, you would use it on me," he said. "So, I guess it's a sailor's line to pick up the hot librarian."

This time Lindsey laughed out loud. "I've heard worse."

"Oh, do share," he said. "I might need the material."

"Okay, I once had a guy say, 'Hey, beautiful, where can I get a card so I can check you out?'" Lindsey said, lowering her voice to sound more like a man.

Sully guffawed.

"Hey, it wasn't that funny." She punched him lightly on the arm.

"Please tell me the overactor did not use that on you," he said.

"No, that gem is from my library school days," she said. "Let's see now. What's a good line to pick up a sailor?"

"Oh, this should be duly awful," he said.

Lindsey scanned her brain for good puns and then snapped her fingers, although the sound was muffled by her gloves. She lowered her voice again and said, "Hey, there, sailor boy, how about you drop anchor in my port?"

"You did not just say that," he said, shaking his head, clearly trying not to laugh.

"Yep, yep, I did," she said.

"Then you just got yourself a hot date," he said.

The twinkle in his gaze made Lindsey's heartbeat kick up a notch. She knew they were taking things slow, like snail pace slow, but right now she was darned if she could remember why.

She forced herself to look away before she evaporated from the heat sizzling between them. Sully had always had that effect on her, but it appeared to be getting worse.

She glanced at the deck above them and realized Stewart had not made an appearance yet. Given how protective the brothers were of their privacy, it was very odd. Sully followed her gaze, and his smile vanished and he looked concerned.

"Is it just me or does this feel wrong?" he asked.

CHAPTER

3

BRIAR CREEK
PUBLIC LIBRARY

"It's not you," Lindsey said. "Stewart should have been here by now."

The small dock led up a winding staircase to a deck above. Stewart always waited on the upper deck.

"We could wait for him up there," she suggested. "Maybe he didn't see us coming."

"Maybe," Sully said. He hefted the books onto his shoulder and gestured for Lindsey to follow him.

With a sense of urgency that she couldn't fully explain, Lindsey hurried after him across the dock and up the stairs to the deck above. The sight that met Lindsey's eyes when she stepped onto the deck left her speechless. She had heard that the brothers collected all sorts of things, she'd gathered as much from the titles of the books they requested, but she'd had no idea it was this extreme. The deck was littered with odds and ends, and they had to pick their way to a space clear enough to stand.

Sully maneuvered around a rusted car engine, a shopping

carriage full of flowerpots, several bicycle frames and a hand truck before finding a spot to put the crate down.

Lindsey stood beside him and glanced from the deck to the house, which was set back about fifty feet on the center of the island. A brick path was the only visible patch of ground between the deck and the house, as the small rocky yard on both sides hosted several steel sculptures that looked like windmills, as well as piles of old tires, shovels, some pruning shears, an old water pump and a fire hydrant—and that was just what her eyes could register at a glance.

Lindsey turned to look at Sully to see if he was having the same overwhelmed reaction that she was. He didn't look surprised, so she guessed he had already known what they were stepping into.

"I had heard the Rosen brothers had a hoarding issue," she said.

"Oh, it's more than an issue," he said. "I think we're looking at a full-blown case of hoarder loco."

"I had no idea," she said. She glanced at the house. There was no sign of life in any of the windows. "Maybe they're not home."

Sully glanced back down at the dock. "Stewart's boat is tied up right where it always is. It's the only boat they own, so I don't know where he'd be without it."

"Should we go to the house?" she asked.

She knew she didn't sound very enthusiastic, but if the deck and the yard looked like this, what could the house look like on the inside? She squashed a shiver of alarm. Barely.

"I think we have to," he said. "Just to make sure they're okay."

"Agreed," she said. "Although, standing out here and yelling for them until they answer has some merit, too."

"Maybe I should go by myself," he said. He gave her a worried look.

"Why?" she asked. "What aren't you telling me?"

"Well," he drew out the word and Lindsey stared at him. "Yes?"

"The brothers really don't like visitors," he said.

"I got that when they very clearly told me to wait on the dock below and not to come up to the house," she said. "Now I can see why. The mess is unbelievable. How did they get all of this stuff up here?"

"Stewart has gathered most of it," Sully said. "You've heard he takes his boat into shore at night and wanders around town, searching through everyone's trash?"

"Yes, I'd heard, but I had no idea it meant . . ." Her voice trailed off. She had no words to describe what she was seeing with her own eyes. "I suppose I'd be afraid to let anyone see my home if it got into such a state."

"Oh, they're not embarrassed by it," he said. "More like protective of it."

Lindsey glanced around again, taking in a claw-foot bathtub, the cab of a pickup truck and a set of rusty golf clubs.

"Really?" she asked.

Sully nodded. "So much so that there are booby-traps all over the island."

"What?" she asked. She moved to stand closer to him. "Where? What do they do?"

"A variety of things," Sully said drily. "But from personal experience I can tell you that Stewart likes to have them explode sharp projectiles."

He shifted the collar of his jacket and pointed to a scar on his neck that Lindsey had just assumed had been from his days in the Navy.

"What happened?" she asked.

He gave her a chagrined look and hoisted up her box of books.

"Step wherever I step and no place else," he said.

He began to walk across the deck, and Lindsey followed, stepping exactly where he stepped just as he'd instructed.

"You're not going to tell me?" she asked. "Oh, come on. You have to tell me. I will die of curiosity. Seriously, die. You don't want that on your conscience, do you?"

He led the way down the stairs and paused at the bottom on the brick pathway to the house. He glanced back at her with an expression that could only be described as embarrassment.

"Fine, but you are now one of four people who know this story. Two of my buddies and I got curious, and we rowed out here to take a look at the place. We tied up our boat and climbed up the rocks on the other side. We had heard that visiting was discouraged, but we didn't know how seriously."

"What happened?"

"Stewart had a nail gun rigged to a pressure pad of sorts. I stepped right on it like a big dope and took a nail to the neck."

Lindsey gasped and covered her mouth with her hand. "You could have been killed."

"Nah, it just grazed me," Sully said. "My buddy took a nail in his arm, which hurt like a son of a—well, you get the idea."

"Was he okay?"

"After sterilization and stitches, he was good to go."

Lindsey glanced at the yard, marveling at the mess and wondering at anyone's ability to feel anything but revulsion for the clutter and chaos. Her inner librarian was having small bouts of silent hysterics. "Good grief," she muttered. "There's so much junk."

"True, but those steel windmills actually provide power to the house," Sully said. "So, it's not completely unutilized."

She glanced at him in disbelief, and he shrugged.

"But, yeah, it's pretty bad," he said. "Just stay close to me and do not wander off the path and you should be fine."

He started across the brick walkway, and Lindsey fell in behind him, trying to put her feet exactly where he put his. She didn't realize she was holding her breath until halfway across the yard when she started to feel her lungs burn. She sucked in a breath and kept going.

Sully paused in front of the porch stairs. Lindsey watched as he examined every bit of the handrails and the stairs. When he finally seemed satisfied, he cautiously put one foot on the first step and carefully stepped up. Lindsey waited until he got up the second step before she followed.

On the third step, Sully put his foot on the board and then took it away. He stepped on it again and it bowed under the weight of his foot. He stayed on the second step and turned to look at Lindsey.

"Don't step on that one," he said. "It's been tampered with so that it will break under your weight and you'll fall right through it. Who knows what you'd be falling into—a pit filled with snakes or a rusty spear, the possibilities are endless."

Lindsey's eyes went wide, and she watched, holding her breath again, as Sully stepped over the middle stair onto the step above. He didn't fall through and managed to get up onto the porch without incident. She released her breath before navigating over the faulty step and joining him on the cluttered porch.

Lindsey's gaze took in the waist-high piles of birdhouses, picture frames, vintage typewriters and a stack of suitcases. There were boxes on top of boxes of which she had no idea of the contents and really didn't want to know. At this point she wouldn't have been surprised to find a box of shrunken heads.

She watched Sully as he put down her crate of books and rubbed the back of his neck as if the sheer piles of stuff caused his back to hurt.

Lindsey glanced at the front door. Like the rest of the house, its paint was peeling. The glass window built into the door had aluminum foil over it, making it impossible to see in. She looked for a doorbell or a knocker, but there was nothing but a captain's bell hanging by the front door.

"Do you think that's a trap?" she asked, pointing to the bell.

Sully cautiously stepped closer to examine it. He gave it a test tap, not enough to ring it, just enough to move it. Nothing happened.

"I think it's okay, but just to be on the safe side, duck down, okay?"

"What about you?" she asked.

"No worries. I've got this," he said.

He picked up a broom handle that looked to have long since lost its broom part. He hunkered down beside Lindsey and threw his arm over her shoulders, covering her from any harm. Then he reached up and smacked the bell.

It clanged repeatedly as the clapper struck the sides and the bell swung back and forth. Lindsey tensed waiting for the door to open, for someone to call out, for something to happen. The bell slowly stopped clanging, but no one answered the door.

"At least an axe didn't swoop down to lop off our heads," he said.

"Yes, but now I'm even more worried," she said. "There is no way they didn't hear that."

"Me, too. Let's try the door."

Sully moved in front of the door. He lifted the mat and ran his fingers over the doorframe. He checked the doorknob. It was locked.

Lindsey glanced around the littered porch. If the brothers kept a key out here, it could be tucked into any of the hundreds of items crowding the porch for breathing room.

Lindsey joined Sully by the door. There had to be a way in. Her anxiety was spiking as the brothers didn't answer, and she couldn't shake the feeling that something was terribly wrong.

"I can try to bust down the door," Sully offered.

Lindsey glanced at the old-fashioned window made up of nine smaller panes of glass that sat in the middle of the door. Something was off. Usually when people put aluminum foil on a window to block light, it was on the inside of the glass, but on the lower left-hand pane, it was on the outside. She leaned in closer. She poked one of the panes with her finger. The aluminum foil tore beneath her finger.

"I don't think we need to break anything but some tinfoil," she said.

She stepped back and showed Sully. He raised his eyebrows.

"I'm impressed," he said.

"Don't be," she said. "I'm afraid to stick my hand in there."

He bent down and peered through the small hole she'd made.

"I think I'm afraid, too," he said.

He made a comically terrified face, and she smiled. Then, without hesitation, he reached in and unlocked the door from the inside. He pulled his hand out and shook it as if to make sure all of his fingers were still attached.

"See? Nothing to worry about," he said.

Lindsey went to turn the doorknob, and he grabbed her hand, stopping her.

"Wait!"

"What?"

"Just because we could unlock it doesn't mean it isn't booby-trapped," he said. "In fact, I'm pretty sure if you're the type who is going to rig up a trap, you're going to set it for when people open your door."

"Good point," she said.

"Let go on three," he said. "One, two, three."

Together they released the knob. There was no *kaboom* or *kablooey*, so that was a relief.

"So, now what?" she asked.

Sully stared at the door as if willing an idea to come to him. He paced in front of the threshold a few times, clearly mulling through the logistics.

"It's stepping inside that's the issue," he said. "I want you to stand back, out of sight of the door, while I push it open. If they've rigged a projectile, I should be able to duck out of the way in time."

"I really don't like this," she said.

"Me either, but I'm worried that we've heard nothing from inside," he said. "They could be sick or injured. We have to find out."

Lindsey nodded. She moved back to stand behind an old icebox that looked to be from the thirties.

"Okay, then," he said.

He turned the knob and shoved the door using the momentum to dive back into a pile of debris. A whoosh and then a snap sounded, and Lindsey peeked around the icebox to see what had happened.

"Sully, are you all right?" she cried.

He had thrown himself into a pile of old clothes and newspapers. His nose was wrinkled, as if he found the circumstances quite disgusting. Lindsey felt herself grinning partly in relief that he was okay and partly at his look of dismay.

"I'm fine," he answered, pulling himself out of the pile. "You?"

"I'm good," she said. They met in front of the door, and Lindsey felt her jaw drop. A large board full of nails had swung forward and would have hit whoever stepped into the house first right in the face. She looked at Sully to see him frowning.

"That could have been ugly," he said. He poked one of the nails with his finger. "Sharp and rusty."

Lindsey shuddered. If he hadn't stopped her from opening the door, her head would have been turned into a sieve. Eep!

Sully led the way into the house, carefully stepping around the board. Lindsey pressed up against his back, again trying to step exactly where he stepped.

It wasn't as if there were a lot of options. A path had been carved out of the stacks of stuff that filled the interior of the house. It led them straight through the foyer and into a sitting room.

"Shouldn't we call out and let them know we're here?" she asked.

"I suppose," he said. Lindsey got the feeling he really didn't expect anyone to answer.

"Hello!" she cried. "Stewart? Peter? It's Lindsey Norris from the library. Captain Sully and I have brought you some books. Hello?"

They stood still, listening for an answer. There was nothing.

Sully reached back and squeezed her hand, and Lindsey knew he was feeling the same sick-to-the-stomach dread that she was. Something had to be very, very wrong for the brothers not to have responded to people being in their house.

They wound their way through the sitting room. Piles and piles of books, floor to ceiling, filled most of the room. The neglect of so many volumes hurt her book-loving heart. In addition to the books, there were newspapers, magazines and old record albums stacked and crammed haphazardly into every available space.

Sully stopped walking and held up his hand for her to do the same.

"Do you hear that?" he asked.

Lindsey strained her ears for the sound of a voice, but no. Instead, she heard a ticking sound.

She looked at Sully in alarm. "Do you think it's a bomb?"

He shook his head. "No, but . . ."

He moved forward down the narrow passage and through the doorway into the next room, which Lindsey imagined was supposed to be a dining room. It was full of clocks. The walls were covered in clocks. The table, chairs and floor were littered with bits and pieces of clocks. There was a box full of batteries, some leaking acid, and a bag full of extension cords. Three upright pianos were wedged one on top of another against the rear wall, and Lindsey felt a heretofore unknown fear of closed-in spaces surge through her, causing her windpipe to shrink in mild panic.

"I don't think I can take in much more of this," she said.

Sully blew out a breath. "It is overwhelming. I think the kitchen is next. That should tell us if they've eaten recently, at least."

Lindsey didn't want to imagine what the kitchen looked like. In fact, she was pretty sure she was going to go home and throw out every single nonutilitarian thing she owned because she was so freaked-out.

Sully moved forward, however, giving her no choice but to follow. He stepped into the doorway of the kitchen and froze. Lindsey bumped into his back and kept herself from falling by grabbing his jacket. She could tell by the hard set of his shoulders that something was wrong.

"What is it?" she asked.

"I found Peter," he said. His voice was low and heavy as if weighed down by the worst sort of news. Lindsey knew without asking that Peter was dead.

CHAPTER

4

BRIAR CREEK
PUBLIC LIBRARY

Lindsey dodged to the side, before Sully could stop her, to peer into the kitchen. She gasped and clapped a hand over her mouth to keep it from becoming a scream. She had never seen Peter Rosen before, but his resemblance to his brother, Stewart, with his same thin build, prominent features and fringe of white hair just above his ears, which curved out on the top, was unmistakable.

Peter was sitting in his wheelchair at the rectangular Formica table in the corner of the kitchen. Dried blood was caked on his shirtfront, surrounding the gaping hole in his chest. A loaf of bread and a block of cheese sat on a plate in front of him, untouched.

Lindsey stepped forward with the hope that maybe he wasn't dead, maybe the eyes staring vacantly at the wall were just lost in thought and she could help. Sully looped an arm around her waist and pulled her close, stopping her.

"Don't. There might be another trap," he said.

"But we need to check if he's alive," she said.

Sully nodded, but Lindsey could tell he had already accepted the obvious. There was nothing they could do for Peter.

"I'll go in and check him," Sully said. "You stay right here."

He pushed her into the rubble that stood just outside the door.

"But I know first aid," she protested. He ignored her.

"Don't move unless something comes at you," he said.

He turned back to the kitchen and began to examine the doorframe, looking for trip wires or pressure pads or anything that indicated another trap.

Satisfied there were none, he stepped into the kitchen and moved closer to Peter. Lindsey was torn between hiding her eyes and forcing herself to watch. It seemed to her that the only way to support Sully was to give him her attention while he dealt with the mess before him, so she stayed focused on his examination of Peter even when her gag reflex kicked in.

It was quickly quite clear that there was no need for an ambulance or medical attention. Sully checked for a pulse at Peter's wrist, being careful not to step in the debris that surrounded his wheelchair, but it proved unnecessary. Even from where she stood, Lindsey could see from the stiffness and discoloration of Peter's limbs that rigor mortis and lividity had already set in.

Sully stepped back, wiping his hand on his jeans. He turned to look at Lindsey, and she saw the horrible truth in the set of his jaw.

"There's nothing we can do for him. It looks like he took a bullet right through the heart," he confirmed. He left the kitchen and met her in the doorway. "Let's get out of here and call Chief Plewicki."

Lindsey nodded. She let Sully take the lead, figuring his naval training made him better at guiding them out of the house; well, that and the fact that she was fighting off a case of the dizzies. So much blood. Sheesh, there had been so much blood.

They went outside the house and huddled on the porch. Sully pulled out his cell phone and called the Briar Creek police station. Lindsey watched as he tipped his head back and squinted up at the cloudless sky.

"Hi, yeah, it's Sully. I need to talk to Chief Plewicki," he said. "I can wait."

He lowered his head to gaze out at the horizon, then he reached for Lindsey's hand. He wrapped his fingers around hers and gave her a reassuring squeeze. It was almost as if he knew she was fighting to keep her lunch down.

"Hi, Emma." He paused, and Lindsey suspected he was trying to find the right words. "Listen, I'm out at Star Island. Lindsey and I were delivering books to the Rosens, but no one came down to the dock to meet us."

Lindsey heard Emma say something in response, but she couldn't make out the words.

"We did go up to the house," Sully said. Emma started to talk again, but Sully cut her off. "I know. I was careful. Look, that's not the point. The thing is . . . Peter Rosen is dead."

This time Lindsey could hear Emma Plewicki's high-pitched voice come out of the phone like a battering ram as she fired questions at Sully.

"Lindsey and I are both fine. It looks like a gunshot—"

He was cut off by more high-pitched chatter.

"Other than checking Peter's vitals, I didn't touch any-thing," Sully said. He looked at Lindsey and made a face like he was being chastised like a boy breaking curfew. "I have some training in these matters, you know."

There was more squawking and then the questions started again.

"Yes, I'm very sure," Sully sighed. "Rigor mortis and livid-ity have both set in. No, there's no sign of Stewart, but I didn't check over the house, because I figured calling you was priority one."

Lindsey heard Emma issuing orders.

"Yes, ma'am," Sully said. "We'll meet you on the dock."

He ended the call and put his phone back in his coat pocket.

"Not a fun call to make," Lindsey said. He was still holding her hand, and she squeezed his fingers with hers, returning his gesture of comfort.

"No," he agreed. "Come on. Let's go down and meet the chief."

"After you." When Lindsey would have let go of his hand, he held on tighter.

"Stay close. There could be triggers planted on the way out to get people who were smart enough to miss the booby traps on the way in," he said.

They both stepped over the middle stair and began to pick their way down the path toward the dock. Lindsey glanced back at the house, wondering if Stewart was still inside, and if so, where was he and why hadn't he come out?

She glanced at the arch-shaped window on the right. Was it her imagination or had the curtain moved? Could it be just a draft? She stared until Sully's insistent tug pulled her down the path.

Although the sky was a pristine pale blue and the sun shone eye-wateringly bright, the wind had picked up and carried the distinct nip of February on it. Maybe it had just been an air current from the open front door that had moved the curtain. Lindsey wished she could be sure.

She felt the tip of her nose get cold, and she moved her scarf up over her face. The weatherman on the news had said there was a chance of snow in the next few days, and she suspected by the moist feeling in the air that it was more than a chance.

Once they were on the lower dock, she was struck by how quiet it was on the island. Other than the lapping of the waves and the occasional cry of a seagull, the world was hushed, almost as if it knew of the tragedy that had happened in the house perched above them.

It occurred to Lindsey that living on an island must be very lonely. She wondered what daily life was like for Stewart and Peter with no neighbors, no means of communication, no one but each other.

She glanced at Sully, who brilliantly produced a thermos of coffee from a cupboard on the boat for them to share. He handed her the plastic cup, and she let the warmth seep into her fingers through her gloves before taking a sip.

"What do you think life was like for them?" she asked.

Sully shrugged. "I only know what I've heard, which is gossip and rumors."

"And?" she prodded him.

He nudged the cup toward her lips, and she dutifully took another sip.

"The Rosen house has been in the family for several generations," he said. "As far as I know, Peter and Stewart have the distinction of being the only ones actually born in the house, however."

Lindsey gasped. "No hospital? No doctor?"

"Their father, Benjamin Rosen, was a doctor, and he delivered them himself," Sully said. "Or so I heard."

"Wow, how do you keep a baby from falling off the island into the water. The constant vigilance required to raise toddlers out here is mind-boggling," Lindsey said. "Their poor mother."

"No, not poor at all," Sully said. "The Rosens were one of the wealthiest families in the islands. They had a full house staff. In fact, each boy had his own nanny."

"Oh, so they were a 'what's a weekend?' sort of family," Lindsey said.

"Precisely," Sully said. "Dr. Rosen didn't work because he had to but because he enjoyed it. By all accounts he was a brilliant man with a hideous bedside manner. He was a surgeon in New Haven, so he lived there during the week and came to the island on the weekends to be with his family."

Lindsey frowned. "His wife must have been terribly lonely."

Sully nodded. He glanced at the house as if trying to imagine it back in the day. "Isabel Rosen was a beautiful woman, a concert pianist who had traveled all over the world. She was in a car accident and damaged one of her hands. Dr. Rosen was her surgeon, and they fell in love. He moved her here to the island shortly after they were married, and she stayed here until the day she died."

"She never left the island? Ever?"

"Rarely. The staff maintained the house and grounds, so there was never any need," he said.

"What happened to Dr. Rosen?"

"He was killed in a boating accident in the early nineteen sixties," Sully said. "Peter was with him and tried to save him but tragically broke his own back from the effort. He lived but has been in a wheelchair ever since."

They both glanced up at the house this time, thinking of their grisly discovery in the kitchen.

"That must have been horrible," she said. "Trying to save his father and ending up with a broken back and still losing his dad."

"The broken back, for sure, but from what I've heard, their father was a miserable, mean old man who hated his sons because neither of them became a surgeon like him. Stewart was more of an engineer, and Peter was a musician like his mother. I'm not certain they felt his loss in the way sons normally do."

"Were they close to their mother, at least?"

"You would think so, because they never left her. But the people in town who knew her described her as a very cold woman, aloof and withdrawn," Sully said. "The brothers did take care of her until the day she passed, so maybe she was warmer to them than she was to the other island residents."

"I hope so," she said. Her chest felt tight at the thought

of the two brothers having two awful parents, never leaving their island and never having any sort of a life of their own.

"Here comes Emma," Sully said. He pointed to a small speedboat headed their way.

Lindsey turned to look toward town. Sure enough, she could see the heavy police coats that the officers in the boat wore. The long dark hair of Emma Plewicki, the current chief of police, streamed out from under her hat. Next to her, driving the boat, was Officer Kirkland, the newest member of the Briar Creek PD.

"How do you think she's going to take this?" Lindsey asked Sully.

"That it's you and me finding the body?" he asked. "At a guess, not well."

Lindsey sighed. She liked Emma. She was smart, efficient and dedicated to serving her community. Lindsey considered her a friend, but still, things had happened in the past where they had withheld information from each other, and their relationship was a bit strained at the moment. Lindsey didn't think the fact that she had found another body was going to help the situation.

Kirkland cut the engine and let the boat gently glide up beside the dock. Sully grabbed the boat to steady it. Emma leapt out with a messenger bag slung crosswise over her shoulder before the boat stopped moving.

"Kirkland, head back to the town dock and bring the ME out as soon as he arrives," she said.

"You sure you don't want backup?" Kirkland asked.

Emma gave him a closed-lip smile. "Don't worry. You can examine the scene with the ME when you come back out."

Kirkland nodded, but Lindsey could tell he was disappointed.

Sully gave the boat a shove, and Kirkland headed back to shore. Emma turned to face them. Her eyes narrowed as she studied them with concern in her warm brown gaze.

"Sully, Lindsey," she said. "How are you, all right?"

"We're fine," Lindsey said. She glanced at Sully, and he nodded.

"Can you tell me exactly what you found?" Emma asked.

"Wouldn't you rather I showed you?" Sully said.

"No, I want to keep the foot traffic up there to a minimum," Emma said. "Until we know what we're dealing with, exactly."

She didn't say that it could be murder. She didn't have to. A gaping hole, probably caused by a bullet to the chest, usually only meant one thing. Lindsey felt her anxiety spike.

Where was Stewart? Was he in the house somewhere? Had he been shot, too? Had it been a break-in? Should they have stayed to look for him? The whole thing had been so shocking she didn't know what to think or do or say.

She let Sully do the talking. He warned Emma about the middle step on the stairs and the traps they had already found. He then described the state of the house and how they had found Peter. Emma listened without interrupting. She then looked at Lindsey.

"Can you think of anything else?" she asked.

"No." Lindsey shook her head. "That covers it."

"Okay, then, look out for the middle step, and check all of the doorways and the flooring," Emma said. She shouldered her bag and began to walk away. At the stairs, she turned back around and said, "Sully, when Kirkland gets back, you two can leave, but I'd like you to stay for now and keep an eye on things here."

"No problem," Sully said. "Shout if you need me."

Emma waved and jogged up the stairs to the deck above. Lindsey wondered what the police chief would make of all the clutter. She turned to say as much to Sully but then paused. She couldn't believe she hadn't seen it before.

She grabbed Sully's arm, and he glanced from the deck where he was watching Emma's progress to Lindsey.

"Are you okay?" he asked. "You look like you've seen a ghost."

"I think I'd prefer it," she said. She pointed to the end of the dock. "Is it just me or was Stewart's boat tied up here when we arrived?"

Sully whipped his head around. "It's not you. His boat was here."

He walked over to examine the metal tie-downs. He squatted down and reached into the water. He pulled up a length of rope still knotted to the metal bracket on the dock. It was short and cleanly severed as if it had been cut. Whoever had left on Stewart's boat, they had been in too much of a hurry to untie the boat properly.

Sully dropped the rope and shook the water off of his fingers. He stuffed his hand in his pocket in an attempt to warm up.

"He must have been here," Lindsey said. "Why would he leave?"

"I don't know," Sully said. His voice was grim.

Neither of them voiced the obvious conclusion that Stewart had left because he shot his brother. Lindsey wouldn't say it because she just didn't believe it.

"I don't think Stewart has ever left the island in daylight before. As I mentioned, he generally only goes out at night," Sully said.

"How does he get all of that stuff up there by himself?"

"No idea," he said. "But I suspect there is a lot we do not know about the Rosen house."

"I know Emma told us to stay here, but if Stewart, or whoever, just left, there's a chance we could spot them somewhere in the islands if we take the taxi out," Lindsey said.

Sully stood and took his phone out of his pocket. "I'll call it in to Emma. I don't want to leave her here alone without letting her know why."

He scrolled through the contacts in his phone and then pressed the display before putting it up to his ear. He was staring at the house as if willing Emma to pick up. After several seconds, he ended the call with a frown.

"It went to her voice mail," he said.

"Maybe she's on another call," Lindsey said.

"Or she's in trou—"

BOOM!

The sound of an explosion cut off Sully's words and made them both jump. The dock rocked beneath their feet, and Lindsey flailed her arms in an effort to regain her balance. Sully reached out a hand to steady her, and she grabbed his arm.

"What the hell was that?" he asked.

"It came from the house," she said.

"Are you good?"

Lindsey nodded, and he let her go. He sprinted for the stairs, and she was right behind him. As they reached the upper deck, they saw smoke billowing out of one of the second-story windows.

"Emma!" Lindsey cried and she pushed around Sully to race into the house.

CHAPTER

5

BRIAR CREEK
PUBLIC LIBRARY

S ully caught her around the waist and held her back. Lindsey struggled, but it was useless.

"Lindsey, stop!" he ordered. "You can't go racing in there. Who knows what has been triggered. There could be more explosions."

"But Emma," Lindsey protested.

"I know, but we have to go in carefully," he said. "Just like we did before, step where I step. Ready?"

Lindsey nodded, and he let her go. He hurried up the walkway, scanning back and forth as he went. Lindsey felt numb as she stumbled along behind him. It was too much, first finding Peter and now knowing Emma was in trouble. She didn't think she could bear it if this went as badly as she feared.

They moved swiftly as they retraced their steps. Whatever had exploded, it seemed to be coming from upstairs. They entered the house, and Sully veered right to the staircase that led upstairs. He hurriedly checked that there were no traps on the stairs. Lindsey didn't see how there could be, since the stairs were jam-packed with more boxes, books and clothes, leaving a very narrow path against the wall to ascend.

"Emma!" Sully called out as they made their way up. "We're on our way!"

Lindsey thought she heard a moan, and she hoped with all that she had that it was their police chief and that she was okay. At the top of the steps, Sully paused. Lindsey glanced around his shoulders and felt her jaw drop. The small landing looked like it had been hit by an earthquake.

"Here! I'm over here!"

Sully moved cautiously forward, trying to pick his way through the mess without causing more damage or setting off any nasty surprises. Lindsey shadowed him.

Emma was on the floor in the doorway to one of the bedrooms. She was pinned facedown under a white wrought iron table. It looked as if she'd been trying to pull herself free. She glanced over her shoulder at them and pointed into the bedroom.

"Fire first!" she croaked.

Sully stripped off his jacket as he stepped over Emma and into the room. Several boxes were on fire, and he began to beat the flames out with his coat.

Lindsey knelt beside Emma. "If I lift the table, can you pull yourself out?"

"It's too heavy," Emma protested.

"Let's try anyway," Lindsey said.

She moved back to where the tabletop had Emma trapped. She tried to get a grip on the table, but the cascade of slippery magazines beneath her feet made it impossible to attain any leverage. She kicked the heap out of the way. Squatting down, she grabbed the table edge and said, "On three. One, two, three."

Lindsey heaved with all her strength. The table was a backbreaker, and she gritted her teeth as she lifted. Emma pulled herself out just as Lindsey was losing strength.

"I'm clear!" Emma cried, and Lindsey lowered the table.

She glanced at Emma's face and saw beads of sweat on her lip and brow. She glanced down at Emma's leg. Her pants looked tight, as if they were about to burst at the shin, and her foot dangled limply. It was clearly broken, and Lindsey could only imagine the amount of pain Emma was in.

The flames of the fire were reduced, but Sully was still fighting it. Lindsey knew she couldn't carry Emma down the stairs. Sully had to be the one to do it, but the fire had to be controlled, too.

She stepped carefully into the room in the tiny space available and noted that a window had been smashed wide open, probably by the explosion. She moved in beside Sully and took one of the old suitcases that was on fire and tossed it out the window. Sully looked at her in surprise, then he followed her lead. Together they threw out anything in the room that was on fire or smoking, and in minutes, the flames were gone and the smoke dissipated.

"Good thinking," he said. His chest was heaving, and he was covered in soot and ash. Lindsey knew she looked the same.

"Emma's leg is broken," she said, sucking in some of the clean air by the window. "Can you carry her down?"

"On it." Sully handed Lindsey his charred coat as he dashed back to Emma.

To her credit, Emma only cried out once when Sully lifted her into his arms. Lindsey knew that Emma had to be about to black out from the pain. Once outside, Sully put her down on the porch. Lindsey called the station requesting medical attention for Emma while Sully hustled out to the front yard and very carefully stamped out the fires from the items they had tossed through the window.

They were just settling in to wait when Officer Kirkland and the medical examiner, Dr. Griffiths, appeared on the upper deck above the dock.

"Chief!" Officer Kirkland broke into a run. "What happened?"

"Stupidity," Emma answered on a groan.

Before Kirkland could hit the steps, Sully grabbed him.

"Stop!" Sully said. "The middle step is rigged. You'll break your leg or worse."

"What?" Kirkland tried to shake him off.

"Listen to him," Emma said. "I should have."

Kirkland stopped struggling and looked questioningly at Sully.

"The Rosen brothers discouraged visitors by booby-trapping the property. Traps are everywhere." Sully pointed to the open front door, and they all glanced at the board with the nails still hanging low in the doorway.

"Whoa," Kirkland said.

Dr. Griffiths moved passed him, stepped over the rigged stair and knelt beside Emma. His long gray coat spread out about him, and he pulled off his leather gloves and shoved them into his pockets. Both his gray mustache and his gray fringe were ruffled, clearly signifying his agitation.

"Just the leg?" Griffiths asked as he opened his bag and pulled out some scissors.

"That's not enough?" Emma returned. "Aw, man, do you really have to cut the pants? They're new."

Lindsey glanced at Emma's face. It was pasty pale and coated with a sheen of sweat that dampened the hair at her temples despite the frigid air.

"Yes, I do, and be thankful that's all I'm cutting. If you were one of my cases, I'd be splitting your abdomen and weighing your intestines," Dr. Griffiths said.

"Comforting," Emma grunted. "Your bedside manner is top-notch, really."

"And now you know why I'm the medical examiner and not a general practitioner," Dr. Griffiths said. He put his scissors back in his bag and moved aside the cut fabric. He ran his fingers over the large knot on Emma's shin. "Looks like you have a closed fracture of the tibia. With any luck, it's also incomplete, meaning cracked and not snapped in two."

While he was talking, Emma took out her phone and started texting.

"Oh, I'm sorry, is my diagnosis interrupting you?" Dr. Griffiths asked.

Emma gave him a dark look, which he matched. "I'm texting for backup to help investigate the scene with you since clearly I'm out of commission."

Lindsey noted that she sounded completely put out by this.

"Did you hear what I said?" Dr. Griffiths asked.

"Fracture, tibia, blah, blah, blah," Emma said. She was in full-on pout now, which was pretty impressive given the amount of pain she had to be in.

"Here," Sully said. He had been carefully inspecting the porch while they talked, and he handed a short, flat board to Dr. Griffiths. "We'll need to brace her leg until we get her to the ambulance that's meeting us on the pier."

"This will do," Dr. Griffiths said. He opened his bag again and pulled out a pack of bandages. While he worked on her leg, Emma addressed Sully.

"Officer Kirkland can bring me to shore and pick up Detective Trimble on the way back. Will you stay with Griffiths until Kirkland returns?"

"Sure, no problem," Sully said.

"Griffiths, you don't go anywhere, not one step, unless Sully gives you the okay," she said. "Am I clear?"

"Careful, Chief Plewicki, or I'm going to think you care," he said.

"Don't get crazy," she said. He tightened the bandage that held her leg to the board, and she visibly paled. "It's just hard to find decent medical examiners these days."

"Piss and vinegar, that's what you're made of, Chief,"

Griffiths said with a chuckle. He looked at Sully and Kirkland. "I'm going to need you two to carry her down to the boat and get her settled."

Sully and Kirkland moved to stand on either side of Emma. She raised her arms, and they hauled her up, balancing her weight between them. Dr. Griffiths and Lindsey followed. It was slow moving to get Emma down the steps, and the rocking motion of the dock made it that much trickier for Sully and Kirkland to support her between them.

Lindsey hurried ahead to hold the boat steady while the men lowered Emma onto one of the seats. Once she was settled, Kirkland assumed the controls, and Sully gave the boat a shove in the right direction.

"Keep the leg up!" Griffiths yelled over the sound of the motor, and Emma gave him a thumbs-up.

"She's not going to listen to me," Griffiths muttered.

"Nope," Sully agreed.

"Which is why I prefer to work with the departed," Griffiths said. "They seldom talk back."

Once they were back up at the house, both Sully and Griffiths refused to let Lindsey enter the house with them. It was deemed too dangerous, so she reluctantly waited out in the cold on the porch. She took the opportunity to check in at the library. Given that she had been due back an hour ago, she knew Beth and the others had to be wondering what had kept her.

She took out her phone and discovered she'd missed two calls and three text messages. She always kept her cell phone volume off in the library because of the noise, but it meant she usually didn't catch her calls and texts until she went to use her phone. She glanced at the messages. They were all from Beth, and they got increasingly frantic. Lindsey felt badly about worrying her friend, but really, there had been no time to check in.

She opened her contacts and selected Beth, who answered on the first ring.

"Where have you been? What is going on? We just saw Emma Plewicki being loaded into an ambulance and then Detective Trimble arrived and took off in a boat with Officer Kirkland. Explain!"

In a town the size of Briar Creek, Lindsey knew keeping things quiet was a doomed objective from the start. But still, they didn't know exactly what had happened in the Rosen house, so she figured it was best if she just stuck to the facts, no details.

"When Sully and I arrived on the island, no one was there to meet us, so we went up to the house," she said.

"That's odd," Beth said. "Stewart is always waiting for you."

"I know. And it gets worse," Lindsey said. "When no one answered the door, we went in and discovered Peter Rosen in the kitchen, deceased."

"Oh no!" Beth wailed. "How is Stewart taking it? This has to be horrible for him. For as long as I've lived and worked here, the Rosen brothers have only had each other."

"Well, there's no sign of Stewart," Lindsey said. She thought about his boat being at the dock and then disappearing, but she didn't mention it.

"Oh well, he is a recluse. Maybe he is just processing all that has happened. Still, that doesn't explain Emma in the ambulance," Beth said. "What happened?"

"When Emma arrived, she went into the house on her own to investigate and set off one of the booby traps, which caused a small explosion and toppled a table onto her leg, which is now broken."

"How awful!" Beth hissed a breath through her teeth.

"It was pretty bad, but Dr. Griffiths thinks it might just be cracked and not broken all the way through," Lindsey said.

"That's so strange about Stewart," Beth said. "I mean, he's been taking care of his brother for fifty years. Oh dear, do you think the grief was too much for him? You don't think he did himself any harm, do you?"

"I don't know, but I don't think so," Lindsey said. Her shoulders sagged as she thought about it. The stress of the day was beginning to feel overwhelming. "Listen, don't say anything to anyone about Stewart. I don't know how much Emma wants everyone to know."

"Got it," Beth said. "Is it okay if I mention that Peter Rosen has passed on? I mean, that's going to be hard to keep quiet with the ME out there and all."

"Yeah, I think that's okay," Lindsey said. She realized she hadn't told Beth how Peter had died and thought that was probably best kept quiet as well.

"How are you?" Beth asked. "You weren't the one to find him, were you?"

"Sully actually spotted him first," Lindsey said.

"I'm glad he was with you," Beth said.

"Me, too," Lindsey said. She glanced at the house, realizing how much she meant it. She couldn't imagine being here and dealing with all of this without Sully.

"How long are you staying out there?"

"Emma asked us to wait for Detective Trimble to get here to assist Dr. Griffiths, and then we're free to go, so I'm hoping to be back within the hour," Lindsey said. "Is all well at the library?"

"The lemon is having a fabulous time, giving her shusher a workout while you're not here," Beth said. "I saw old man Krakauer give her the stink eye when she gave him a 'Shh' with the raised eyebrows and pointer finger to the lips combo."

"Oh brother," Lindsey said. "The lemon" was Beth's nickname for Ms. Cole, the library's old-school librarian who really enjoyed shushing and fines. Lindsey knew she should discourage the use of the name, but it fit so perfectly and it had been in use long before she became the director. It was a dilemma.

"In all fairness to the lemon, he deserved it," Beth said.

"He was watching a soccer match from Germany on one of the computers and was getting a bit boisterous."

"So long as she's not targeting the crying babies and toddlers then we're good," Lindsey said.

"That's what I figured," Beth said. "See you soon."

"I'll text you otherwise," Lindsey said.

"Be careful."

They ended the call, and Lindsey glanced across the water back at town. She could just see the old stone captain's house that was now the library; well, mostly she could see the flags on its flagpole flapping in the breeze, but still, she knew it was right there waiting for her. She wished she was in her office with a nice hot mug of coffee and some budget worksheets instead of freezing her tail off here in what was turning into a house of horrors.

She began to pace to keep her blood flowing and try to warm up. She was on her second pass back along the brick path from the deck to the house when she heard the sound of a motor. She turned around and saw Officer Kirkland with Detective Trimble from the state police pulling up to the dock below.

She waved, and Detective Trimble waved back. He was a good-looking guy, somewhere in his midthirties, always a snappy dresser in a full suit with a tie. He was on the state police force and had helped Emma as well as the previous chief of police work some homicide cases in Briar Creek. Lindsey was quite fond of the detective and had come to think of him as one of their own.

"Hi, Lindsey, I hear it's been a rough afternoon for visiting librarians," Trimble said as he and Kirkland joined her on the upper deck.

Lindsey shook his hand. Through their gloves, it was impossible to get a good read off of his handshake, but the strength was there, and Lindsey knew from past experience that Trimble was honest and diligent, two qualities that worked really well in a detective.

"Worse for police chiefs, but yeah, not a great visit," Lindsey said. "Come on. I'll show you where Sully and Dr. Griffiths are. You've been warned about the booby traps?"

"Yes," Trimble said. He frowned at the backyard and all of its junk.

"Try to step only where I step," Lindsey said. She turned and led the way to the dainty Victorian.

Trimble fell in behind her while Kirkland brought up the rear. She guided them over the middle step in the stairs and pointed out the board with the nails in the doorway. If Trimble hadn't appreciated the precariousness of the situation up until now, she knew this would cause him to reevaluate.

"Fifteen years on the force and I've never seen anything like this," he said.

"Brace yourself. It's about to get worse," Lindsey said.

CHAPTER

6

BRIAR CREEK
PUBLIC LIBRARY

Once Trimble and the other officers had control of the scene, Sully and Lindsey left. As they climbed back into the water taxi, Lindsey was sure she'd aged at least five years since they'd arrived at the dock.

"Are you all right?" Sully asked. He fired up the engine and turned the boat toward shore.

She thought about lying and pretending she was unaffected by the horror they had seen, but instead of giving him a nod, she shook her head. He lifted up his arm, and she scurried under it, hopefully giving as much comfort as she was receiving.

"It's all right," he said. He ran his hand up and down her arm. "I'm feeling a bit shaky myself."

Lindsey held on to him as if he were a life preserver in a choppy sea. He was solid and warm, and he smelled good, like linens drying on a spring breeze. She had thought she'd never get the smell of death out of her nose, but Sully was clearly an antidote.

When they pulled up to the dock, Lindsey realized the sun was already setting. She had missed the entire second half of her workday, and Sully had, too.

"I don't know about you," he said, "but I need a drink."

Lindsey nodded. "Sounds like a plan."

They checked in with Ronnie, who was closing up the office for the night. Sully's partner Ian had picked up Tim Kessler on Clover Island in their backup boat. Since there'd been no more pickups or drop-offs scheduled for the water taxi, Ronnie had forwarded the phone to send the calls to Charlie Peyton, Sully's part-time help, who would be on call for the rest of the evening.

Sully and Lindsey made their way down the big pier to the Blue Anchor, the local watering hole owned by Sully's sister, Mary, and her husband, Ian, also Sully's business partner. They joked that it gave Ian, who was a talker, a captive audience for all of his bad jokes and trivia knowledge about anything and everything.

Sully opened the door for Lindsey, and she was immediately engulfed in the familiar scents and sounds of the pub. At a glance, she could see that the bar was full and most of the tables were, too.

She took out her phone and sent Beth a text letting her know where she was. She didn't want to cause any more worry, but her nerves were shot and her feet were frozen. She needed a few minutes to decompress.

Residents called out greetings to Sully and Lindsey, and they smiled and waved, but by mutual unspoken agreement, they kept in motion and didn't engage anyone in conversation. Lindsey could see that several people looked like they wanted to ask about what had happened on Star Island, but Sully put his back to them all as he kept Lindsey in front of him, blocking her from the crowd.

Lindsey was relieved. She wasn't ready to discuss the day,

and she suspected from the firm set of his jaw that Sully wasn't either.

They found a tiny table for two in the far corner. It was shoved up against the wall tucked in behind the end of the bar as if it were an extra piece of furniture that Mary and Ian had put there just to get it out of the way. Perfect. They took turns cleaning up in the restroom so as not to lose their table. Lindsey went first.

Hot soapy water had never felt so good on her hands and face. Thankfully, her hat had protected her hair from the soot and ash of the fire, but the ends were covered in the gray ash, and she took a minute to brush it out with a comb from her purse and felt better for it. Knowing Sully was waiting for his turn, she didn't linger.

Mary must have been on the lookout for them, because as soon as Sully returned from the restroom, she arrived at their table with two shots of Jameson. She plopped them down in front of them and said, "Ian says to drink up."

Together Sully and Lindsey tossed back the Irish whiskey. Lindsey felt its ball of heat ignite in her chest, and she coughed against the burn in her throat; still, it soothed her frayed nerves, and she smiled at Mary.

"Thanks."

"Don't mention it," Mary said. She had the same magnetic blue eyes as her brother and the same reddish brown curls, except her hair was much longer and she wore it in a huge knot on top of her head. She scooped up the empty glasses and gave Sully and Lindsey each a quick hug. "I'll be back in a few minutes with your dinner."

"But we didn't tell you what we want," Sully protested as he hugged his sister in return.

"You'll eat what I put in front of you," Mary said. "I've got Terrence whipping up some soul food for the two of you, because you sure look like you need it."

With that, she left them, and Lindsey smiled in bemusement. "Was she always this bossy?"

"Yes," Sully said. "And she's only gotten worse since she married Ian and has to manage him as well."

"Manage me?" Ian barked as he approached the table, bearing two pints of ale. "I'll have you know, I wear the pants in the family."

"That's only because your legs are no match for hers," Sully said.

Ian gave Lindsey a lopsided smiled and said, "That's a fact. She has an amazing pair of legs. They go all the way up to her . . ."

"Ahem, brother," Sully said and pointed to himself as if to remind Ian that he was talking to his wife's sibling.

"Oh, right," Ian said. He turned to Lindsey and made a comical face. "Never marry your best friend's sister. It makes it all so complicated."

"My best friend doesn't have a sister," Lindsey teased. "So I think I'm safe."

"Lindsey, I've been looking for you. Are you all right?"

Lindsey glanced over Ian's shoulder to see Robbie Vine approaching.

"Oh goody," Sully said. "My day wouldn't be complete without a visit from the mincing mime."

"Can it, water boy," Robbie said.

Ian looked like he wanted to pull up a seat and watch the verbal sparring match between the two men, but Lindsey shooed him away as she rose to greet Robbie.

"Hi, Robbie," she said. She gave him a quick hug. "Would you care to join us?"

Sully made a sound like he was being strangled, and Robbie frowned at him.

"Thank you, love," Robbie said with a pointed look at Sully. "But I can't. I'm taking the train into New York for a meeting, but I wanted to see you before I left."

"Oh," Lindsey said.

She wasn't sure what to say, since she and Robbie were friends, good friends, but that was it, at least on her end. As she had told Sully, she didn't do the dating-a-married-man thing even if he was married in name only. She was firm with Robbie about this, and they had been awkward friends ever since.

"I heard about what happened today out on Star Island," Robbie said. "Are you all right?"

"It was rough, but I'm rallying," she said. "Thanks for checking on me."

"Of course," he said. "You know how important you are to me. I'll cancel my trip if you need a supportive shoulder to lean on."

Sully rolled his eyes and made a huffing sound.

Lindsey reached out and squeezed Robbie's arm. "That's very kind of you, but I'm all right. Please don't cancel anything on account of me."

Robbie ran a hand through his reddish blond hair, making it stand up in exasperated tufts. Lindsey got the feeling he was struggling with what to say, which was unusual for a man who was so fond of the sound of his own voice.

"The truth is, Lindsey, the meeting concerns you," he said.

"What do you mean?" she asked.

Robbie opened his mouth to speak and then glanced at Sully, who was now watching them with undisguised interest.

"Do you mind?" he asked Sully. "Could we have a minute in private here?"

Sully glanced at Lindsey, and she nodded that it was okay. He rose from his seat and glowered at Robbie.

"I'll be right at the bar if you need me," he said to Lindsey.

"*Need* him?" Robbie asked. He sounded outraged. "What exactly would you need him for if you're with me?"

Lindsey blew out a breath. "What did you need to tell me, Robbie?"

"I think it would be safe to say that things have been at a

standstill between us," he said. He took her hands in his and turned her away from the table so they were facing each other.

"There is no 'us,'" Lindsey said. She squeezed his hands in hers in what she hoped was a kind gesture. "We're just friends."

"Because I'm married," he said.

"Well, yes," she said.

He studied her face as if he was trying to decide something and then he nodded as if he had made a decision. "I have something to ask you, and it's very important."

CHAPTER
7

BRIAR CREEK
PUBLIC LIBRARY

"Oh, all right," she said. "What can I do for you?"

"I need you to make me a promise," he said.

"This sounds serious," she said. She tipped her head to study his earnest expression. For a man who made his living by wearing his emotions on the outside, she was having a tough time figuring out what was going on in his head. "I'll make the promise if I can."

"Excellent. Tell me you'll be here for me when I get back," he said hopefully.

"Well, of course, I'll be here. I live here. Was that it?" she said. She was relieved his request hadn't been for something more serious, something she wasn't prepared to give.

"That's all I ask," he said.

Before Lindsey had a second to register it, he pulled her close and planted a kiss on her that was as hot and steamy as one of his romantic liaisons from the silver screen, a real bone-wilter.

When he released her, Lindsey had to grab the back of her chair to steady herself. He grinned.

"See you in a few days, love," he said. He turned to leave and then turned back. "If you need me, for anything, call me. I'll come running."

Lindsey opened her mouth to speak, but nothing came out, so she nodded instead. This seemed to suit him, as he left the Anchor, whistling a sappy tune about true love.

"Please tell me that was an 'I've been deported' good-bye kiss," Sully said as he rejoined her at the table.

Lindsey noted the two spots of red on his cheeks, this time not from the cold, and the glitter in his eyes. She couldn't blame him for being irritated. If the situation were reversed and some woman had kissed Sully like that, she'd be thoroughly annoyed. Then again, she wasn't sure she'd be all that thrilled if Robbie kissed another woman like that either. *Ish*, what a mess!

"Well, he is leaving town for a few days," she said. She wasn't sure what stopped her, but she decided not to mention his request that she be here for him when he returned. She didn't want to vex Sully for no reason, and if Robbie was off to see Kitty, his manager/wife in name only, he might change his mind about wanting Lindsey to be waiting for him. "So, it was a sort of good-bye."

Sully's face cleared, and he looked almost chipper at that news. "How long will the canned ham be gone?"

Lindsey gave him a chastising look. "He didn't say, but I expect it may be a while."

"Well, I suppose I'll have to make the most of his absence," he said. He rubbed his hands together in anticipation.

"What do you—?" she began but was interrupted by Mary bearing two heaping plates of roast beef, mashed potatoes and green beans, accompanied by a basket of freshly baked sourdough rolls.

"Here you go," she said as she put the plates down on the table. "And I expect you to eat every bite."

Lindsey and Sully didn't have to be told twice. The hours spent in the cold had given them both an appetite, and they tucked into their plates as if they hadn't seen food in days instead of just hours.

Lindsey was swabbing the last of her gravy with a roll when Beth arrived. She grabbed an empty chair from a nearby table and sat down.

"Lindsey, we have to talk," she said.

"And hello to you, too," Sully said.

"Sorry." Beth cringed. "I'm on a mission. Let me have a do-over." She shook her head as if rewinding her brain. Then she forced a smile and said, "Hi, you guys, how are you?"

Sully and Lindsey exchanged a glance. He had one eyebrow up that clearly asked if Beth was kidding. She had to be, since she knew they'd been out on the island and had found Peter Rosen's body. Lindsey shrugged.

"It was a bit of a rough day," Sully said. "But we're doing better now."

He glanced at Lindsey as if to confirm, and she nodded. She noticed that Beth looked agitated, so she washed the bite of bread down with the last of her beer and asked, "Is everything all right with you?"

"No, it's a nightmare," Beth said. "An absolute nightmare."

"Did something happen at the library?" Lindsey asked. She was half out of her chair, ready to race back to her precious building, when Beth shook her head.

"No, it's me," she wailed. "I've been tallying my numbers for my story times and they're down."

Lindsey relaxed against the back of her seat. "Define *down*."

"Plummeting," Beth said. Her lower lip wobbled, and tears shone in her eyes.

Sully lurched back from the table as if launched by rocket fuel. He looked helpless against Beth's tears. "I'm just going to go settle up with Ian."

"Let me give you money," Lindsey said.

"No," he refused. "This is on me."

"But—" Lindsey started to protest, but he interrupted.

"No buts. If you need anything, call me."

His blue eyes were somber, and Lindsey knew that he meant if the vision of Peter Rosen hit her in the middle of the night, she was free to call him for support. She really hoped that didn't happen, but she appreciated the offer all the same. As he walked by her, she reached out and grabbed his hand, giving it a solid squeeze.

"Thanks," she said.

He kissed the top of her head before leaving them with a wave.

Beth was glancing between them. "Care to share?"

"Just bonding through adversity," Lindsey said. "Come on. Let's go get our bikes and you can tell me why you're freaking out on the way."

They left the Anchor, waving to Mary and Ian as they went. It was dark now, and the temperature had dropped. Lindsey burrowed into her coat, pulling her scarf up over her nose as they walked across the park back to the library.

"Okay, so I was compiling my data for my monthly report, and I noticed that my numbers dropped all month," Beth said.

"Isn't the flu going around?" Lindsey asked. "Couldn't it just be sickness keeping everyone away?"

Beth grabbed Lindsey's arm and turned her to face her. Her eyes were huge, and she said, "My numbers have never ever been this low. Never. Ever."

Lindsey raised her eyebrows. Beth always packed the house. She was the most popular children's librarian in the state of Connecticut, if not all of New England.

"The weather?" Lindsey asked.

"We've had the mildest January and February in decades," Beth said. "Lindsey . . . I . . . I think I'm losing my touch!"

Now the tears spilled over, making Beth's black eyelashes spiky while the tip of her nose turned bright red. Lindsey pulled her friend close and gave her a bracing hug.

"Now you listen to me," Lindsey said. "You are the best children's librarian on the planet."

"No, I'm not." Beth shook her head.

"Who was asked to present a workshop on story times at the American Library Association and the Public Library Association conferences and was given an award for her contribution in the field of library services to children?"

"Me," Beth said. "Still—"

"No," Lindsey interrupted. "No one is more committed to children's literacy than you. There is a logical reason why your numbers are down, like maybe the scheduled times and days need adjusting, and we're going to figure it out. Okay?"

Beth drew in a long, shuddering breath. Then she wiped the tears off her cheeks and nodded.

"You're right," she said. Her breath puffed out in a white cloud. "I just have to figure it out. There has to be a logical explanation."

"I'm sure there is," Lindsey said. "No more fretting."

They continued on their way to the library, and although Beth had stopped crying, Lindsey got the feeling the discussion was far from over. She knew her friend well enough to know that Beth wouldn't rest until she knew why her program attendance was down.

Lindsey arrived bright and early at the library to catch up on the work she had missed the day before. So it was no small wonder that by midafternoon she was dragging and needed a serious java booster shot to make it to the end of her shift.

Jessica Gallo, a part-time library assistant, had handed in her notice a month ago to take a full-time job in another town. Lindsey would have loved to have kept her in Briar Creek, but there just wasn't money in the budget for another full-time librarian, and Jessica had worked too hard to get her degree not to use it. Since her departure, the library had been short staffed, and Lindsey was pulling extra hours on the reference desk to maintain coverage.

Working the desk got Lindsey out of the weekly deadly dull department head meetings in town hall and gave her research skills a solid workout, so she really didn't mind. In fact, she had debated stalling on hiring Jessica's replacement but then figured if she didn't hire someone soon the town might rescind the position, thinking she didn't need it. As much as she liked working the desk, she couldn't do it all the time. Her inbox was backing up into a teetering pile of have-to-do's she had to address.

She made a cup of coffee in the break room and took her steaming mug out front. Ms. Cole gave her a beady-eyed stare for taking a beverage onto the public floor, but Lindsey ignored her. She had been up half the night fretting over the Rosen situation. Who had shot Peter? Where was Stewart? How could they live in that cluttered filth?

The last thought wasn't nice, she knew, but still, it made her head hurt just to think about the boxes and bags and piles of refuse. She found herself cleaning off the top of the reference desk, picking up stray paper clips and sticky notes and making sure all of the pencils and pens were capped and standing up in their holder. Anything extra was relegated to the appropriate desk drawer.

Lindsey sat and sipped her coffee, surveying the neat desk and feeling herself calm down. When the pages, the library's teen workers, came in this afternoon, she was going to have them tackle the storage room after they did their shelving. She knew it was probably a weird sort of posttraumatic stress reaction, but the need to clean and sort the library was like a worm in her brain. She would not feel at ease until there was no indication of any hoarding in the library.

"Lindsey, I'm sorry to be a bother, but . . ." Jean Garabowski paused in front of the reference desk and looked at Lindsey with big, sad eyes. "Help."

"Absolutely, Mrs. Garabowski," Lindsey said. She sat up straighter. "What can I do for you?"

Jean was an older patron with short gray hair that she wore in tight curls all over her head. Her reading glasses hung from a beaded rope around her neck, and she was partial to elastic waistband slacks and turtlenecks with a plaid flannel shirt over them.

"My friend—well, she was my friend, I don't know what she is now—she just unfriended me on Facebook," she said. "And I don't know what to do."

Mrs. Garabowski's voice wobbled with genuine distress, and Lindsey felt her heart pinch with sympathy.

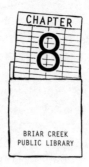

CHAPTER

8

BRIAR CREEK
PUBLIC LIBRARY

"Unfriend is such a harsh word, isn't it?" Lindsey asked.

"Yes," Jean said. "It's not nice at all."

"Do you know why the person unfriended you?" Lindsey asked.

"No idea," she said. "Can you help me?"

"I can certainly take a look," Lindsey said. She followed Mrs. Garabowski to a table where she had left her laptop open. The social media site was up, and Lindsey glanced at it. "I don't want to invade your privacy, but in order to assist you I need to look at your activity."

"Oh, I just put up pictures of my flowers," Mrs. Garabowski said. "There's nothing private. I don't put up any personal information. I heard people will take your information and clear out your bank account."

"Very wise." Lindsey began to scroll through Mrs. Garabowski's page. "You've won a lot of awards for your flowers."

Mrs. Garabowski preened. "I have a greenhouse, so I can

garden all year round, and I just won first place for my roses at the American Rose Society show in Boston."

"By any chance is the person who unfriended you also a gardener?" Lindsey asked.

"Why, yes, how did you know?" Jean asked.

"This is just a guess," Lindsey said, "but I'm seeing by your activity that you post a lot of pictures and write quite a bit about your roses, but I don't see you liking or commenting on other people's posts so much."

"Oh," Mrs. Garabowski said. Lindsey showed her how to read the activity log.

"A good rule of thumb for social media is one out of five," Lindsey said.

Jean looked at her in confusion, and Lindsey clarified. "At most, one in five posts should be about yourself, your flowers, your whatever. And you really need to make sure you like and comment on other people's posts so that it's more of a conversation and less of a monologue."

"You're saying I'm a rudesby," Mrs. Garabowski said.

"No, well, yes." Lindsey cringed. Sometimes the truth was ugly, but better Mrs. Garabowski hear it from her than lose all of her friends.

"How mortifying." Mrs. Garabowski put her hands on her cheeks as if to cool a heated blush. Lindsey patted her arm.

"It's all right. You're new at this," Lindsey said. "I think most people make the same mistake when they're new. There's nothing wrong with wanting to share what's important to you. You just have to acknowledge others as well. Here, let's like some other people's posts for practice."

She spent the next fifteen minutes giving Mrs. Garabowski a quick tutorial on social media etiquette.

"This is great," Jean beamed at her. "You should teach a class."

Lindsey nodded. The idea had some merit, since they were

already teaching other computer classes, and it didn't look like social media was going away anytime soon. Maybe if everyone had to take a class in online etiquette, the amount of cyberbullying would go down, but probably not. She hoped her solution worked for Mrs. Garabowski, but there was also the possibility that the person who unfriended her was a meanie who would strike again. Lindsey figured they'd deal with that if and when the time came.

She had just settled back into her chair when two men approached the reference desk. One was tall and thin with a thick thatch of straw-colored hair that made him look almost like a scarecrow. The other was short and stout with a neatly trimmed beard that was rapidly turning from black to gray. They both wore heavy coats, jeans and work boots and looked like the sort of men who knew how to fix things.

Lindsey tried to remember if she had called anyone to fix anything lately, but she was sure the last request she had put in was for the toilet in the children's bathroom, which Beth had told her had been fixed yesterday. Usually, the town maintenance men took care of all repairs, but occasionally they had to call in specialists. As far as Lindsey could recall, there had been no calls like that made for the library.

"May I help you?" she asked.

"I hope so," the tall one said. "I'm Kevin Perkins, and this is my partner, Calvin Hodges. We're looking for some information, and my mother, who is a librarian, taught me that whenever I find myself in a strange place, I should go straight to the library and ask the librarians."

"Smart woman," Lindsey said with a smile. "I will do my best. How can I help you?"

"We're collectors, and we've come to see the Rosen brothers out on Star Island. The only problem is, we don't know how to get there."

Lindsey went completely still. "I'm sorry, what did you say?"

"We're from the Chicago area," Kevin explained. He

reached into his coat and took out a business card, which he handed to Lindsey. It was plain white with embossed lettering and a picture of an antique shop.

"We travel all over the country buying antiques and collectibles for our shop. Currently, we're touring New England, and my partner got a line on the Rosen brothers' as a place to check out."

Lindsey blew out a breath. "Welcome to Briar Creek. I'm Lindsey Norris, the library director. Have you been in touch with the Rosens lately?"

"Not since we left Chicago," Calvin said. He looked up at his partner. "When was that, two weeks ago?"

"About that," Kevin agreed.

"You won't have heard, then," Lindsey said. She made an apologetic face as she studied the two men. "I'm sorry to report that there's been a tragedy at the Rosen home. Peter Rosen is dead."

Both men gave her startled looks.

"That's terrible!" Kevin said.

"When did this happen?" Calvin asked.

"He was discovered yesterday," she said.

"Peter was the brother I was in touch with," Calvin said. He looked stunned. "What happened?"

Lindsey sighed. How much could she say to complete strangers? The news of Peter's death had rocketed through the town, but Stewart being missing wasn't common knowledge just yet. Of course, in a town this size, it was only a matter of time before everyone knew, which would probably be when Stewart resurfaced to do his nightly foraging.

"I'm sorry," she said. "I can't tell you anything else. You may want to stop by the police station and talk to Chief Plewicki, as she can give you more information on the situation."

Kevin looked at her with a concerned expression. "Is there a reason we'd want to talk to the police?"

Lindsey hesitated.

"How did he die?" Calvin asked.

"I'm not sure what I should or shouldn't say about the situation," Lindsey said. "I apologize for sounding mysterious. The best I can do is tell you that his death is under investigation."

Both men were silent, studying her.

"Well, given the circumstances," Kevin said, "maybe we should move on to our next location."

"No!" Calvin argued. Both Kevin and Lindsey looked at him in surprise. He looked sheepish and put a hand on the back of his neck. "Peter and I share a love of old mechanical banks. We became friends online when we both posted to the same auction house on a vintage bank from nineteen ten. It was so cool, it . . ."

He glanced up and noticed both Kevin and Lindsey looking at him.

"Sorry. Nature of the business," he said. He looked at Kevin. "You know, I wouldn't feel right leaving until I know what happened to him, and I'd like to talk to his brother, Stewart. From some of the things Peter said, I gather there were some issues there. Given the situation, I'd feel horrible if I just left without finding out what happened."

Kevin nodded. "I get it, but we can't linger. We're on a tight schedule."

Lindsey studied Calvin. Issues between the brothers? Stewart had been taking care of Peter for over fifty years. Had he suddenly snapped? She couldn't imagine it, but what did she really know about the Rosens?

She certainly never would have guessed that they had online access to auctions, because they sure never used a computer to send her a message at the library, or search for books at the library, or anything as forward thinking as that. Their requests always showed up in the book drop in an envelope, containing a very polite handwritten note, requesting the specific item. If they had a computer, why not use it?

She thought back to the house on Star Island. She hadn't

seen a computer, but then again, she hadn't seen the whole house either. Maybe they had one off in a spare bedroom, or perhaps they both had the latest in cell phone technology.

"If you're looking for collectibles, you might want to pop in at the senior center and ask around," Lindsey suggested. "We have a large retired population."

"In a town like this we may get lucky. Who knows what else we'll be able to find. Can you recommend a place for us to stay?" Calvin asked Lindsey.

"There's only one place in Briar Creek, and that's the Beachfront Bed and Breakfast run by Jeanette Palmer," Lindsey said. "We're not a peak tourist spot in late February, so she should have availability. Follow Main Street to the end and then turn right. She has a sign out front, so you can't miss it."

"Great. Thanks," Kevin said.

"Thanks," Calvin added. "Just for my own curiosity, do you have any articles or any information on the Rosen brothers as well as the history of the surrounding area?"

"I have several books about the town's history, and I'm sure the Rosens are mentioned in them, as their family has been here for generations," Lindsey said. "But for more in-depth information, you probably want to talk to Milton Duffy."

Lindsey came around the desk and walked them over to the far side of the library. Sure enough, Milton was in his usual spot in the corner, doing one of his favorite yoga postures where he stood on one bent leg while the other was wrapped around it and his arms were twisted around each other as well. Lindsey knew if she tried it, she would have landed on her behind, but Milton was holding it without even wobbling; not bad for a guy cruising into his mideighties.

"He's the head of the historical society and can tell you anything you want to know about Briar Creek and the Thumb Islands."

As they approached, Milton opened his eyes and studied

them. Lindsey could see he was doing his breathing, and she hated to interrupt, so she stayed back until he began to unwind from the posture.

"Garudasana, also known as the Eagle Pose," he said as they approached. "Opens the shoulders and strengthens the back, hips, thighs, calves and ankles."

Calvin and Kevin looked at Milton, then at each other, and then at Lindsey.

She smiled. Milton was tall and thin with a neatly trimmed goatee, a shiny dome and sparkling blue eyes. He radiated good health and positive energy, and he was not only on the library board but was one of Lindsey's favorite patrons, even though he was keeping company with Ms. Cole, also known as the lemon, which no one seemed to understand except for the two of them. Lindsey supposed that was exactly as it should be.

"Milton, we have two visitors from Chicago looking to learn more about our town," she said. She gestured to the two men beside her. "Kevin Perkins and Calvin Hodges. They're collectors."

The two men exchanged handshakes with Milton. He was wearing his usual tracksuit and picked up a towel from the chair beside him and draped it around his neck.

"Is there anything in particular that you wanted to know?" Milton asked.

Lindsey smiled at them and gestured that she had to get back to the desk. They all nodded, and she hurried back to her coffee, hoping it was still hot.

What were the odds that there were two men here to see the Rosens just when tragedy struck? On the one hand, she'd seen life work like that before, but on the other hand, she didn't really believe in coincidence.

She glanced at the card Kevin had given her and then turned to her computer and typed the name of their company, Perkins and Hodges Antiques and Collectibles, into

Google. Their website popped up as the first option, and Lindsey went right into the About Us option.

The photo that came up was definitely them, so that was good. She read their history and discovered that the two of them had been in the collectibles business for years. They had three part-time employees and worked out of a large warehouse in the Chicago suburbs. They frequently traveled around the country, looking for antiques with which to stock their shop. Kevin had a love of classic car engines and old gas station memorabilia, while Calvin was partial more to odds and ends like antique lamps, vintage movie posters and mechanical banks.

Lindsey thought back to the house on Star Island. It had been crammed to bursting. She wondered if Stewart or Peter had collected anything of interest to Kevin or Calvin, and if so, would the brothers really be willing to part with it? Well, would Stewart be willing, if he was ever found?

Again, she wondered where Stewart was. As far as she knew, no one had seen him since before Peter was found dead. Lindsey didn't know Stewart well, but he was always polite when she brought their books, and he seemed devoted to taking care of his brother. She just couldn't imagine that he had harmed Peter, but if it wasn't Stewart who shot Peter, then who did?

She glanced out the window behind her desk. The gray sky blanketed the bay and the shoreline with the sort of gloom that begged to be split wide open by a sharp blade of sunlight rending through the cloud cover. Lindsey scanned the thick flannel sky. There was no sunbeam, not even a hint of one, anywhere to be seen.

She was worried about Stewart out in the damp cold. He wasn't a young man, and if he hadn't gone back to his house, where was he? Was he safe? Warm? Fed? She hated to think of him wandering aimlessly on his own.

She sipped her coffee and pondered the situation. Where would Stewart go? If he was foraging about town like he did at night, was there any way she could get him to come into the library and talk to her? Should she even try?

Feeling like she was spinning her wheels, she decided to call Emma, Chief Plewicki, and see how her leg was, and if Emma happened to mention something about the Rosen case, well, who was Lindsey to stop her friend from talking about what was on her mind?

"Chief Plewicki," Emma answered on the third ring. She sound cranky.

"Emma, it's Lindsey. How's the leg?"

"Broken," Emma said.

"Oh, I'm sorry," Lindsey said. She could hear voices and the distinct sound of a police radio in the background. "Wait, what are you doing at the office? Shouldn't you be home with your leg up while you eat copious amounts of ice cream and watch old romantic comedies until you are mended?"

There was a snort on the line, letting Lindsey know exactly what Emma thought of that idea.

"I have a dead body," Emma said. "I'll eat ice cream and watch movies when I figure out what happened and not one second before."

Lindsey heard a male voice rumble in the background.

"What's that?" she asked. "I can't hear."

"Detective Trimble, choking on coffee cake at the thought of me taking a day off during an investigation," Emma said.

Lindsey smiled. She wondered at the relationship between Emma and the detective. Trimble had been in town several times to assist with investigations. Word from all the matchmakers in town was that he was single. She figured it would be perfectly natural for them to form an out-of-the-office situation.

She shook her head. Clearly, she was spending too much time with the crafternooners if she was pondering the status of other people's relationships like the crafternooners debated hers.

"So, there's been no sign of Stewart?" Lindsey asked.

"No," Emma said. "In fact, I was thinking that your library might be one of the places he feels safe. If he shows up—"

"You will be my first call," Lindsey said. "Listen, there are two guys here who were supposed to meet with Peter about buying some of his things for their collectibles shop. I'm thinking you might want to talk to them on the off chance Peter said something to them that would be helpful."

"Explain," Emma said.

Lindsey told her their names, where they were from and that their website appeared legit.

"But it's weird, right?" she asked. "I mean the fact that they're here right when there just happens to be a tragedy."

"Right," Emma said. "Very coincidental."

"I mentioned that they might want to talk to you about Peter," Lindsey said. "So they may stop in to see you."

"And if they don't, at least I know where to find them," Emma said. "You gave them Jeanette's info?"

"Yes, I think they plan to stay with her for a couple of days. Calvin said he would feel odd not connecting with Stewart after they've come all this way."

"Nice work, Lindsey. I may have to deputize you yet," Emma said.

Lindsey opened her mouth to answer when Beth came roaring up to the reference desk. Instead of her usual story time outfit, Beth was dressed in a professional-looking skirt and blouse with high heels on her feet and makeup on her face. It looked like she'd even styled her spiky black hair. In other words, she looked like a grown-up.

It took Lindsey a moment to remember that Beth had been at a professional development meeting for children's librarians in southern Connecticut that morning and had just arrived at work.

"I'll be right—" Lindsey began, but Beth cut her off.

"I figured it out!" she cried.

CHAPTER

9

BRIAR CREEK
PUBLIC LIBRARY

"E mma, I'm going to have to call you back," Lindsey said. "I have a library situation here."

"No problem," Emma said. "I think we're done for now unless you have the new Dana Stabenow book in? I'm having a hard time sleeping with this leg and all, and I could use a good read."

"I'll fast-track a copy through processing for you and have one of our pages walk it over to the station this afternoon," Lindsey said.

"Thanks," Emma said. "You know you're my favorite library director, right?"

"Ha! I'm also the only library director you know," Lindsey said.

"That doesn't make it any less true," Emma said.

Lindsey laughed and hung up. Then she sighed. Her hold on the Stabenow book had just come in, but since Emma was injured and all, she supposed it was only right to let her have it. Emma's broken leg earned her a pass to the front of the line.

Lindsey glanced up at Beth, who was looking like she might explode if she didn't get to share her news soon.

"Sorry." Beth cringed. "That was unforgivably rude."

"Not completely unforgivable," Lindsey said. "The conversation was done. What's up?"

"I figured out why my numbers are down," Beth said.

"Oh, well, that's good, right?" Lindsey asked. "So you can fix it."

"No!" Beth cried. "It's even worse than I feared. I've lost my people to the competition!"

Lindsey looked at Beth's distraught face. Beth had a flair for the dramatic, so Lindsey paused before rushing in and offering any suggestions. Well, that and her supervisory training had taught her to listen to her staff and see if they could problem-solve their own issues before she offered any advice.

"Do not give me supervisor face," Beth said, obviously calling Lindsey out on her strategy.

"What?" Lindsey shrugged.

"You know what," Beth said.

She grabbed a chair from an empty table and dragged it over to Lindsey's desk. She sat down and propped her elbow on the edge of the desk and set her chin in her hand.

"I'm not some card catalog–hugging old-school librarian who is resistant to new technology who you have to guide into solving her own problems," Beth said.

Lindsey raised her eyebrows. "That obvious?"

"Yes," Beth sighed. "Now this is serious. I have seen the competition, and he is . . . oh man."

Lindsey reached for her coffee and took a sip. It was getting cold, so she chugged it. She had a feeling this story was a doozy. She leaned back in her chair.

"Tell all and leave nothing out," she said.

"At the youth services meeting this morning, there was a new librarian from Branford," Beth said. "Oh, what does it matter? I'm doomed."

"How can that be?" Lindsey asked. "You're the best children's librarian ever. How can this new guy be better than you?"

"I don't think his knowledge of children's literature or his ability with felt boards, puppets and finger plays is really factoring into the equation," Beth said.

Lindsey frowned. "Well, unless he's handing out free hot chocolate with marshmallows, I don't see why he's all that."

Beth heaved a sigh. "Let me break it down for you. Who goes to story times?"

"Babies to preschoolers," Lindsey said.

"And how do they get there?" Beth gave her a pointed look.

"Their moms?" Lindsey asked. Truly, she was lost.

"Exactly!" Beth cried. "Have you seen my story times? Have you seen who has been bringing their kids?"

"Lately? No."

"It's been all dads," Beth said. She slapped her hand on the desktop as if she were banging a judge's gavel.

"Call me crazy, but isn't that a good—no—great thing?" Lindsey asked. "To have dads engaged in the critical first five years is terrific, right?"

"Yes, but where are the moms?" Beth asked.

Lindsey shrugged. Clearly, Beth was working up to something, and Lindsey was just going to have to be patient.

"They're at *his* story time," Beth said. "And why?"

"I don't know. Why?"

"Because he is freaking gorgeous," Beth said. Then she thunked her head down on Lindsey's desk as if she had expended the very last bit of energy in her soul. "He's like the Ryan Gosling of youth services. I want to die."

Lindsey bit her lip to keep from laughing. Her friend was obviously distraught. She would not laugh. She would not chuckle. She would not guffaw. She bit her lip harder.

"Maybe he's just a novelty," she said. "If he's not a good storyteller, the kids will get restless and the moms will let go of the eye candy and come back for a really good story time with you."

"But what if he's good?" Beth moaned. "Then I'm ruined. My career is over. No one will come to story times anymore. I'll just die clutching my finger puppets to my chest and singing an endless loop of 'Head, Shoulders, Knees and Toes.'"

Now a snort did escape out of Lindsey's nose. When Beth glanced up at her, she held up her empty coffee cup and pretended to be choking.

She thumped her chest with her other fist and said, "Sorry, wrong pipe."

"I should just hand in my resignation now," Beth said.

"Okay, stop the crazy talk," Lindsey said. It was all fun and games until her staff was ready to quit. Now she was in full-on director mode. "Think. How can we find out if his story time is any good?"

"We could ask one of the traitors who has left my story time for his," Beth said. She raised her head back up, and with a fiery glint in her eye, she scanned the library for one of her people.

"Yeah, no, I don't see that going well," Lindsey said. "I could call his director. She likes me. I could just ask her casually how her new hire is working out."

"Like she's going to tell you the truth," Beth said. "With the numbers they're rocking, she now has bragging rights for best programs in the area. She'll be afraid you're poaching, especially since we have a part-time vacancy."

"You're right," Lindsey said. "Damn competitive librarians."

She was joking, mostly, but Beth was not appreciating her humor.

"Covert op," Beth said. She snapped her fingers. "That's what we have to do."

"Excuse me?" Lindsey asked.

Beth opened her purse and pulled out a folded-up piece of paper. "Today. Lunch. Me and you are doing story time recon."

Lindsey opened her mouth to protest, but Beth was out of her seat and striding toward the children's area.

"Don't worry, I have disguises for us to wear," Beth called over her shoulder.

"Yeah, that was my big worry," Lindsey said after her, but Beth was too far away to hear.

"No one is going to believe I'm a grandmother," Lindsey said. "For that matter, no one is going to believe that Curious George there is a baby."

"Don't be such a doubter," Beth said. "This will totally work. Besides we only need a solid fifteen minutes of observation to know whether he's got any skills or not."

"If anyone recognizes us, what are we supposed to say?" Lindsey asked.

"Simple," Beth said. "We're auditioning for the next community theater play and we wanted to get into our characters."

Lindsey rolled her eyes. She looked like a drunken Mother Goose with a bad gray wig, granny glasses and a pair of sensible lace-up shoes. How did Beth talk her into these things?

"You owe me," Lindsey said. "Big time."

"Noted," Beth agreed. She adjusted her blond wig and smoothed her flouncy skirt.

They were standing in the parking lot beside the minivan they had borrowed from Ann Marie, their part-time library clerk. Ann Marie had been more than willing to loan the vehicle to them with the understanding that they would return the van with a box of goodies from Cheri's Bakery on Main Street.

Lindsey waited while Beth strapped on a baby sling that contained her large Curious George doll. She had dressed it in baby clothes, and Lindsey had to concede that he looked like a baby bundle in there, but if anyone caught a gander of his face, it was going to be game over for sure.

"Come on," Beth said. "Story time just started. We can slide in a little late, which is even better for us."

"Yeah, because we want people to notice us," Lindsey grumbled as she let Beth pull her up the steps of the Blackstone Library.

Lindsey loved her small stone library building all the way down to her squishy middle. But the Branford Public Library, also known as the Blackstone Memorial Library, was a show-stopper. The exterior was built of Tennessee white marble in the neoclassical revival style and sported columns modeled after the Athenian Acropolis. The building even had a dome, a freaking dome, the inside of which housed enormous paintings that illustrated the history of bookmaking.

Lindsey assured herself that it was perfectly normal to feel the green-eyed monster rear its spiky head when she walked through the big bronze front doors and paused to marvel at the beautiful building around her. Perfectly normal.

"Come on," Beth said. She had her arms wrapped around George in a protective way as she marched toward the children's department.

Lindsey followed, trying not to feel self-conscious, but her wig itched and the toes of her right foot were pinched. She began to hobble, which she figured only added to her image as an elderly lady.

They slid into the story time room and had to shuffle through the mass of people just to find standing-room-only spots in the far back corner along the wall. The good-sized space was packed with moms, toddlers and babies. There were even a few women who had children who were clearly school-age, sitting right up in the front row.

Lindsey glanced at Beth, who pointed to several of her regulars sitting in the crowd and mouthed the words *I told you so.*

Music was playing from an iPod set in a little speaker stand. The room was restless, as if everyone was waiting. The music started to get louder, and the toddlers wiggled in their seats. A baby fussed, but a mother quickly stuffed a pacifier in its mouth. The music gave way to the sound of sirens, and all of a sudden a fireman burst into the room.

For a moment, Lindsey wondered if there was a fire in the building, but, no, it was the librarian they had come to see. Lindsey could tell because Beth's jaw had thumped onto the ground and stayed there.

Wearing a full-on fireman costume, the male story time librarian strode into the room, singing all about fire trucks. In no time, the toddlers were up and dancing and pantomiming all of the moves that the librarian made. They drove the fire truck and felt the door for heat. They dropped to the floor and rolled. Then they opened up the hose and put the fire out. The moms helped their babies make the same moves with their chubby little fists. It was ridiculously adorable.

Lindsey glanced at Beth out of the corner of her eye. Her friend was singing the song along with the group, but instead of smiling, she looked distraught, as if it was taking all of her inner strength to keep from wailing. Oh dear.

The song finished to much applause, and Lindsey heard one of the moms let out a loud "whoop whoop" as if she were at a strip club and she now expected the fireman to take off his clothes. Lindsey glanced at the male librarian. Chiseled good looks? Check. Engaging grin? Check. Warm brown eyes? Check. Good physique? Check.

Yeah, it was easy to see why the mom got confused. To his credit, the librarian just grinned at her as if he thought she was carried away by the song and not him. Humility? Check.

Lindsey blew out a breath. She did not want to be the one to break it to Beth, but, yeah, her story times were screwed. There was no way she could compete with this guy, not in the man-starved world of baby and toddler moms, who usually left their houses just happy to not have spit-up on themselves.

This guy was charisma to the tenth power. Lindsey didn't even have kids and she wanted to go to his story times. The man took off his fireman's helmet and sat down on the floor. Several kids made a beeline for his lap, and he laughed and let them pile on top of him until he had a lapful.

He picked up *Curious George and the Firefighters* and began to read. He had a deep voice that he modulated as the story needed, making comical faces as he went, which caused the children to laugh.

"We can go now," Beth whispered to Lindsey as he finished the story. "Just watching him with these kids is making my uterus hurt."

Lindsey nodded. She could see where he would have that effect on a woman. She turned to head to the door only to discover that more people had arrived after them and there was no way they were getting past them to leave.

"We're stuck," she said over her shoulder to Beth.

"Aw, what?" Beth asked. She glanced past Lindsey and then sighed. "This is going to be torture."

She was right. Not because the story time was bad; rather it was because the guy librarian was just that good. In fact, as Lindsey watched his music time with the kids, she realized that he reminded her of Beth with his over-the-top enthusiasm and his sunny disposition. It was like he was channeling her.

Finally, the story time ended to a huge round of applause. The good-looking librarian parked himself at the door handing out high fives, hand stamps and hugs as people left. Lindsey noted that a lot of the moms wanted hugs.

As they got closer to the door, Beth seemed to be stalling, letting people get ahead of her.

"Is something wrong?" Lindsey asked. She glanced at her cell phone. They were pushing their lunch hour to the max. As it was they would probably be at least ten minutes late back to work.

"I can't talk to him," Beth whispered. "He might recognize me from the meeting this morning."

"This is only occurring to you now?" Lindsey asked.

"I was on a mission before," Beth said. "I thought we'd be out of here by now. Quick, see if there is an exit door in the back and check if it is alarmed. If we run, I bet they can't catch us."

"I am not going through an alarmed door," Lindsey said. "You're just going to have to brazen it out."

When they turned around, they were the last two people in the room. The male librarian was peering at them as if he thought he knew them. Then he broke into a grin.

"Beth?" he asked. "Beth Stanley?"

"Uh-oh," Beth muttered.

CHAPTER

10

BRIAR CREEK
PUBLIC LIBRARY

"Let's go with plan B," Lindsey muttered.

"Okay, what was that again?" Beth asked.

"Community theater production," Lindsey said as the man walked toward them.

"Right, got it," Beth said. She gave a bright if somewhat forced smile to the story teller. "Hi."

He narrowed his eyes. "It *is* you."

"Guilty, ha!" Her voice was loud in the empty room, and Lindsey cringed.

"Hi, I'm Lindsey, Lindsey Norris," she said and extended her hand.

The man took her hand in his and said, "Aidan. Aidan Barker."

"A pleasure," Lindsey said. She glanced at Beth, who was studying the toes of her shoes.

"I didn't realize you were a mom," Aidan said to Beth.

He sounded disappointed, and Lindsey noticed he was staring at Beth's left hand as if it had deceived him.

"Oh, she's not," Lindsey said. "Not married and no kids, right, Beth?"

Aidan's eyebrows rose as he looked at the baby sling, as if he thought Lindsey was missing something.

"I'm sorry, what?" Beth glanced up from her shoes, and Lindsey noted that her cheeks were bright pink with embarrassment.

"You don't have any children," Lindsey said.

Beth gave Aidan a sour look. "Well, not anymore, I don't."

"No, not your story time kids," Lindsey said. "You don't have any children of your own."

"Oh, right, no kids," Beth said.

Aidan looked at both of them and then at the bundle strapped to Beth's chest. "So, this one belongs to . . ."

"The library," Beth said.

Aidan looked alarmed, and Beth finally caught on that he didn't realize it was a doll. She started to laugh and reached into her sling and wrestled Curious George out. She turned him so that Aidan could see his face.

"See? He's a library baby," she said.

Aidan sagged with relief. "For a minute there, I didn't know what to think."

"I'll bet," Lindsey said. She started to walk toward the door, figuring now was as good a time as any to make their escape. "Well, we'd better get back. Ready, Beth?"

Beth started to follow, but Aidan said, "Wait! If you weren't here as a mom with a baby, why were you at my story time? And while I'm at it, isn't your hair usually short and black?"

"Oh yeah," Beth said and clapped a hand on her blond wig. She pulled it off and twirled it on her hand. She swallowed and then said, "We're just working on our parts for the Briar Creek Community Theater. You know, trying to get into character while being out in public."

Lindsey closed her eyes. She was pretty sure Beth was the worst liar ever, but to his credit, Aidan didn't call her on it.

"Really?" he asked. He was looking at Beth as if he thought she was the greatest thing since the story time bubble machine. "That's so clever. Leave it to you to come up with something so creative. You know I'm your biggest fan, don't you?"

"Huh?" Beth looked bewildered.

"It's true. I think you're amazing, and here you are at my story time. I did okay, didn't I?" he asked. "I mean, I modeled my whole program after yours."

"You did?" Beth asked. Her voice was high-pitched and squeaky.

"Yes, you did a three-day presentation in my children's literature class in library school last year about creating story times. It was amazing and easily the best class I took in the entire master's program. I thought you were awesome."

Beth looked completely dazzled and turned to Lindsey and said, "He said I'm awesome."

"He's right," Lindsey said, trying not to smile. "Do you two need a few minutes to talk shop?"

"That would be great," Aidan said. "I have a ton of questions."

"Fifteen minutes?" Beth asked, glancing at the clock on the wall. "We can buy extra pastries so our staff will forgive our tardiness."

Lindsey knew a losing battle when she saw one.

"All right, sure, I'll just go catch up with your director," Lindsey said. "It'll be nice to have a director-to-director chat. Meet me out front when you're ready."

Beth nodded, but Lindsey wondered if she'd even heard her. No matter. Lindsey would just text her when it was time to go. She was curious whether Beth would come clean about their real purpose for being there. She had a feeling she would. Beth was not one for secrets.

Aidan Barker seemed like a nice guy. Hopefully, if Beth was honest with him, he'd find it amusing and not be put off. Maybe he'd even ask Beth out on a date. Lindsey hadn't seen a ring on his finger either, but then again, he was a guy, and they could be cagey about that sort of thing. She shook her head. What was wrong with her? She wasn't a matchmaker, really, she wasn't.

Lindsey stopped by the front desk and asked to speak with Ellen Clancy. The staff person took her name and disappeared, returning in a few moments with Ellen right behind her.

"Lindsey? Um, er . . ." Ellen's smile faltered as she took in her appearance.

"Oh, sorry," Lindsey said. She snatched off the wig and glasses and stuffed them in her purse. "I forgot I was in costume."

Ellen raised one eyebrow and gave her a sidelong look. "Costume?"

"Long story," Lindsey said. "Really long story."

Ellen's lips curved up in a small smile. "Come have a cup of coffee with me and you can give me the abbreviated version."

Lindsey followed Ellen back to her office, where she enjoyed a quick cup of coffee and commiserated on the intricacies of dealing with library boards and managing wayward children's librarians, before she left to meet Beth at the front of the library. She didn't have to text her, as Beth was standing in the rotunda, still chatting with Aidan.

Beth was talking animatedly, her hands waving wildly in the air as if she were conjuring up a magical spell. One look at Aidan, and Lindsey was pretty sure it was working. He was tall and lean, with close-cropped light brown hair and a matching goatee. He leaned in toward Beth, which caused him to lean a bit over her in a charmingly protective way.

He said something in response to Beth's gesture, and they both laughed. They looked natural together, like two halves that made a whole. Lindsey supposed she might be jumping the gun a bit, but Beth's last relationship had been a catastrophe, and she had been single for a long time. Lindsey figured she was way overdue for a nice guy.

"It's all about the presentation," Beth said as Lindsey approached.

"I couldn't agree more," Aidan said. "Kids are the best audience in the world, but they are also the most perceptive. If you don't believe what you're telling them, they won't either."

Beth grinned up at him, and he looked momentarily blinded.

"Sorry to interrupt the shoptalk, but we have to go," Lindsey said regretfully.

"All right." Beth nodded and held out her hand to Aidan. "It was a pleasure to see you again."

"You, too," he said. He turned and shook hands with Lindsey as well.

"Bye," Lindsey said. She and Beth began walking toward the door.

"Good luck on your audition," Aidan called after them. "Break a leg."

Beth stopped walking and then turned around to face him. She was holding Curious George in her hands and looked like she was strangling him as she twisted him by the neck. Realizing what she was doing, she quickly hugged the stuffed monkey.

"I can't do this," she said.

Lindsey opened her mouth to stop her, but Beth forged on before she could warn her off.

"There is no audition," Beth confessed to Aidan. "I just came to check you out because all of my story time people have left me to come to your story time." She hung her head. "I'm sorry."

Aidan's eyebrows lifted, as he was clearly taken aback by her confession, then he stroked his goatee, looking thoughtful. He dropped his hand and walked forward until he was right in front of Beth. Lindsey held her breath, wondering what he would say.

"Well, that changes everything," he said.

Beth glanced up at him, looking like she was bracing for him to rip into her.

"I suppose it does," she said. She looked so forlorn that Lindsey wanted to hug her and drag her away from Aidan and his stern look.

"We're just going to have to get together and adjust our schedules so they don't compete with each other," he said. "I'm a novelty act, but you're the real deal. I don't want the kiddos missing out on you because I'm the new kid in town. Hey, maybe we can do a cooperative thing where we do our story times together."

"I . . . that . . . yeah," Beth stammered. "That'd be cool."

"Great." Aidan grinned at her, and Lindsey was pretty sure Beth was going to melt into a puddle of goo. "I'll call you. Wait, forget that. Is dinner tonight too soon?"

"Um . . . no," Beth said, then she giggled.

It was so adorable, Lindsey almost giggled herself. She choked it back and figured she'd better get them out of there before she ruined their moment completely.

"That sounds great," she said. "Why don't you pick Beth up in front of our library at seven?"

"It's a date." Aidan grinned.

"Excellent." Lindsey hooked her arm through Beth's and dragged her toward the door. "Come on. We still have to stop at Cheri's Bakery or Ann Marie will never let us borrow her van again, and we're already late as it is."

"Bye." Beth waved at Aidan right before Lindsey pushed her out the door. He waved back as the door shut behind them.

They climbed into the van, and Lindsey took a left onto Main Street toward the bakery. She had a feeling Beth would want to dissect their encounter with Aidan, so she said nothing, waiting for Beth to start.

"Do you . . . Did he . . . What does . . ." Beth turned in her seat to look at Lindsey.

"Do I think Aidan noticed you?" Lindsey guessed. "Yes.

Did he mean it when he asked to work together? Yes. What does it mean? He's clearly warm for your form."

Beth gasped. "Do you really think so?"

"Yes, otherwise why would he have looked so down in the mouth when he thought you might be married and have a baby?" Lindsey asked.

"Oh wow," Beth said. "Oh no, what do I do if he asks me out?"

"Call me crazy, but I think he already did, and you said yes," Lindsey said.

"I did?"

"Well, I did for you, but same thing. Seven o'clock tonight at the library, and he's picking you up."

"But I haven't dated in forever," Beth said. "I won't even know what to do."

"It's like riding a bike," Lindsey said. "It'll come back to you."

"What should I wear?"

Lindsey glanced at Beth's flouncy skirt and the blond wig she had plopped back on her head. "Anything but that, and I think you're good."

And so continued their discussion during their stop at the bakery and all along their drive back to Briar Creek. By the time Lindsey pulled into the library parking lot, they had thoroughly scrutinized Aidan's every look, every word, and every gesture. She hoped she was right and that Aidan thought tonight was a date, too, because she didn't think she could stand to watch Beth be disappointed.

Beth must have been thinking the same thing, because she looked at Lindsey as they let themselves in the back door of the library and said, "What if he doesn't show up? What if he cancels? What if this is just a work thing for him and not a date?"

"He'll show up," Lindsey said. "And the rest of it will figure itself out. Relax."

"But—"

"No buts," Lindsey said. "It's clear he is in awe of your mad story time skills, and he definitely noticed you in the boy-meets-girl sense, if you get my drift."

Beth put a hand over her heart. "Oh, I hope you're right. I—"

"Well, how good of you to join us," Ms. Cole said as Lindsey and Beth entered the workroom. "I was beginning to think we needed to send out a search party."

"Really?" Lindsey asked. She was not at all intimidated by the lemon's bluster. "I called and spoke to Ann Marie, and she assured me that everything was running perfectly in your capable hands."

Ms. Cole looked both pleased and puckered at the compliment.

Beth held up the bakery box. "Cupcake?"

Ms. Cole peered into the box and carefully lifted out a carrot cake cupcake and then turned away and strode back toward the circulation desk. "Mr. Tupper never left the library in the middle of the day and brought back cupcakes. Pity."

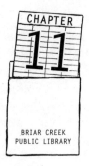

CHAPTER

11

BRIAR CREEK
PUBLIC LIBRARY

Lindsey and Beth exchanged a wide-eyed look.

"Did she just . . ." Beth began, but Lindsey interrupted.

"Disparage Mr. Tupper," Lindsey said. "Yes, but let's not say anything for fear of jinxing it."

"Agreed," Beth said. "I'm going to let Ann Marie know we're back and put these in the break room."

Lindsey nodded and went straight to her office. She had already eaten two cupcakes and was feeling the sugar rocket through her system like jet fuel. She knew when it wore off she was going to want to nap long and hard.

She had just stored her purse, removed her wig and kicked off her orthopedic shoes in favor of her comfy loafers when the door to her office opened. Milton Duffy stuck his head in and gave her a concerned look.

"You're back," he said.

"Just walked in," Lindsey said. "We brought back treats

from Cheri's Bakery. They're in the staff room. Make sure you get one."

"I'm not staff," Milton said.

"No, but you're on the library board, you hold a chess club here every week and you're dating a staff person, so I think you qualify for a treat," Lindsey argued her point.

Milton's bald head flashed a bright shade of red, and he cleared his throat. "Yes, well, thank you."

Lindsey changed the subject to ease his embarrassment. "Has there been any news about Stewart Rosen?"

"Nothing official," Milton said.

"But . . ."

"Sally Renault told me that Kari Lassiter told her that Tom Hardaway said he saw someone who looked like Stewart walking through town at two in the morning last night."

"Why didn't he call the police?" Lindsey asked.

"Tom said it was because Stewart vanished before he could make the call, but Kari suspects he didn't want his wife, Linda, to know he was just leaving his poker buddy's house at two in the morning," Milton said. "Other than that, there's been no sign of him. It's as if he vanished."

Lindsey felt a chill creep over her skin, and she shivered. She tried to shrug it off. People didn't vanish.

"Do you think whoever killed Peter got Stewart, too?" she asked. It was the nagging worry that had been dogging her ever since they'd left the island.

"I don't know," Milton said. "I saw Sully this morning at the coffee shop. He said when you got to the island Stewart's boat was tied up but when you left it was gone."

"It could have been Stewart," she said. "Unless the killer was on the island at the same time we were and took the boat while we were occupied."

The shivery feeling returned, but Lindsey staunchly ignored it.

"That's a terrifying thought," Milton said. "I'm thinking

you and Sully were lucky not to have arrived any earlier than you did. We can't discount that the killer and Stewart are one in the same, however."

"Do you think Stewart killed Peter and fled?" Lindsey asked. She knew that she didn't see Stewart as a killer, but she was curious about what Milton thought.

"Anything is possible, I suppose," he said. He sounded as reluctant as she was to believe the worst of Stewart.

"I was just going to make some tea. Would you care for some?" she asked.

Robbie usually popped in a couple of times a week to have afternoon tea with her. And right now she found that she missed his lighthearted companionship.

"That would be nice," Milton said. "We should discuss what to do about Sandra Lippins and her many issues. Also, I can tell you about my time with the collectors Perkins and Hodges."

Sandra Lippins was a new library board member, and as far as Lindsey could tell, she was only on the library board because she wanted to create a hullabaloo over their current hours to make herself feel important—that and Sandra clearly enjoyed the sound of her own voice as she droned on and on and on. Lindsey did want to hear Milton's take on the collectors, however.

"We might need something stronger than tea. Come on. You can pick out a cupcake while I get the water ready," Lindsey said.

Together they entered the break room. Lindsey left Milton to pick out his pastry while she filled the kettle and went back to her office to plug it in.

She glanced out the window and noted that it was still gray and cold out there and it felt as if the sky were a giant gloved hand pressing down on their little town. Maybe it was just her own projected anxiety about the Rosen brothers, but still, her heart felt heavy.

The kettle whistled, bringing her attention back to the task at hand. She was just putting the cozy on top of the ceramic teapot where the loose-leaf brew was steeping when Milton returned.

He took the seat across from Lindsey's desk, and they debated how they could structure the board meeting so that Sandra would have her say without holding the rest of the board hostage as she proselytized about library hours and policies and how she wanted it all changed.

Lindsey poured the tea while Milton polished off his cupcake. They agreed that they would implement a timekeeper at the next meeting so that things could keep moving forward instead of spending an inordinate amount of time on one nonissue and not getting to the rest.

"We have the minutes from the last meeting," Lindsey said. "We can start documenting the discussions should we need to point out the problem to Sandra more directly."

"Let's try keeping time first," Milton said. "If she doesn't take the hint, then we can approach her more straight on."

"Excellent," Lindsey said. "I think this will work well. I hope it will. I don't want to embarrass anyone."

Milton sipped his tea with a thoughtful look on his face.

"Is something else bothering you, Milton?" she asked. "Do you have another idea on how to curb Sandra's enthusiasm?"

Milton glanced up from his teacup with a grin "I like the diplomatic way you put that. But no, I'm afraid my thoughts circled back to Stewart. I just can't get his disappearance out of my head."

"I know," Lindsey said. "I don't know what happened at the house, but I'm worried that he's out there somewhere, lost and confused."

"Or on the run. As you said, we don't know what happened," Milton said. "Stewart's never been out of Briar Creek. If he is off-island, I suspect he won't have gone far."

"I'm sure Chief Plewicki and Detective Trimble are searching everywhere," Lindsey said. She finished her tea and put her cup aside.

"Not that it will do them much good. Stewart has been roaming the town at night for years. He probably knows all of its nooks and crannies," Milton said. "If he doesn't want to be found, he won't be. There's really no way to lure him in."

"Unless he feels safe," Lindsey said. "Unless he trusts someone."

"Such as?" Milton asked.

"I was thinking about the collectors," she said. "I know they were in touch with Peter, but he must have told Stewart about them, don't you think? And clearly they share a love of . . . stuff."

"Maybe, but he's never met them face-to-face," Milton said. "From what they told me, I don't think they'd recognize Stewart if they ran into him, and it's doubtful he'd recognize them either."

"So, who does that leave for Stewart to trust?"

"You." Milton gave her a keen look.

"Me?" Lindsey blinked. "I mean, I've gone out to their island every other week for over a year. Stewart and I have gotten to the point where we're pretty good at talking about the weather, favorite authors, the weather."

Milton smiled. "If there is one thing a New Englander knows how to talk about, it's the weather."

They were both silent for a moment. Milton finished his tea and put the cup in the saucer on the edge of Lindsey's desk.

"You know, our board meeting runs right up to closing tonight," Lindsey said. "We may have to clean up afterward, leaving the lights on and the door open on the off chance that someone may wander by."

Milton scratched at his goatee as he considered her words. "I could stay out front in the reading area, keeping an eye on things, while you sit at the front desk where you are visibly cleaning up."

"We can play it by ear if anyone comes into the library," Lindsey said.

She wasn't sure why she didn't want to say out loud what they were clearly planning to do, but she gathered from Milton's nod that he felt the same way.

"I think that's an excellent idea, and it's perfectly reasonable that we'd be tidying up after a meeting," he said. He rose from his seat and took Lindsey's empty cup and saucer along with his own. "I'll take care of these."

"Oh, thank you, Milton," she said. "I'll see you at the meeting tonight."

"Seven o'clock," he confirmed and left her office.

Lindsey leaned back in her seat and blew out a breath. She wondered if she should call Emma. She didn't want to bother her if their crazy scheme came to nothing. Just because Stewart hadn't ever left Briar Creek before didn't mean he hadn't left now, and that was assuming he was off on his own and not the victim of a murderer like his brother.

Lindsey shook her head. She rejected the idea that Stewart had been killed, partly because she liked him and really hated the idea but also because there was nothing to indicate that he had been harmed. Of course, there was the issue that if he hadn't been harmed, he might have been the one to kill his brother, but until they knew for sure, she chose to operate on the assumption that he was on the run from the killer and not a killer himself.

Lindsey thought back to the books Stewart had requested for Peter over the past year and how when he spoke of his brother, it was with obvious concern and affection. She couldn't reconcile that with Peter's murder. She just didn't see Stewart committing fratricide.

Her cell phone chimed from its spot on her desk. She picked it up and glanced at the display. A small smile tipped her lips when she answered.

"Hi, Robbie," she said. "How's New York?"

"Dreary," he said. "I'm sitting in a café on Broadway, and they have a wall full of books but no adorable librarian to tease, and their tea is abysmal."

"That does sound dreary," she commiserated. "However will you survive?"

"It's a mystery," he said. "I was hoping to have a nice long-distance tea with you. Are you available?"

"Sadly, I just finished afternoon tea," she said.

"What? With whom?" he demanded. His crisp British accent sounded perturbed, and Lindsey felt badly for teasing him. "It wasn't the son of a sea dog, was it?"

"No, it was Milton Duffy," she said. "We were planning for tonight's board meeting and catching up on the local gossip."

"Ah yes, speaking of which, what is the news on the incident back there? Have they figured out exactly what happened to the poor chap on the island yet?"

"No," she said. "The medical examiner is performing an autopsy, and Chief Plewicki is doing her best."

"She is remarkably capable," he said.

"You only say that because the two of you were in cahoots not so long ago," she said. She leaned back in her chair and stared at the ceiling while they talked. She was surprised to find she had really missed Robbie's company, and it was comforting to talk to him now.

"Now, now, all was forgiven," he said. "Extenuating circumstances and all that. Tell me what else is happening at home."

"Home?" Lindsey asked. "I didn't realize you thought of Briar Creek as home. Don't you have houses all over the world?"

"Houses, not homes," he said. "There is a difference. And yes, I do think of Briar Creek as home. My son is there, as well as two of my oldest friends and you. That makes it more of a home to me than anywhere else on Mother Earth."

Lindsey felt her insides get all warm and fuzzy. She knew Briar Creek was mostly home to Robbie because it was where he'd discovered his teenage son, but it felt nice to be included in his list of important people.

"I haven't lived here for very long either, and I feel the same way," Lindsey said. "There must be something about this place that makes a person not want to leave."

Her voice trailed off as her words brought her back to the Rosen brothers.

"Uh-oh," Robbie said.

"What is it?"

"I know that tone in your voice," he said. "You swerved over into thinking about the incident, and I'll bet you're butting into the investigation, aren't you?"

"No!" she cried. It came out more defensively than she would have liked, and Robbie took it to mean he was right.

"Aha! I knew it!"

"You know nothing," she said. "Oh, look at the time. I have to go.

"No, you don't," he said. "You're just avoiding my questions. What are you planning, Lindsey Norris?"

"Nothing," she said.

"If you don't tell me, I'll call Emma," he said.

"On what grounds?" she asked. "Your suspicious nature?"

"No, on my excellent sense of people and my intuition when someone is planning something brainless."

"Ah!" she gasped. "Brainless? I'll have you know Milton and I put a lot of thought . . . Damn it."

"I knew it! Milton, eh?" he asked. "That does up the ante, doesn't it? Spill, darling, or I'll call Sully."

"You wouldn't," she said.

"Try me," he said.

"All right, fine, but I'll have your word that you won't interfere," she said.

"How can I give you my word when I don't know what you're up to?" he asked.

"You have to trust me," she said.

Robbie was silent, and Lindsey could hear the ticking of her wall clock while she waited for his answer. She would not waver on this; either he gave his word or the conversation was over.

CHAPTER

12

BRIAR CREEK
PUBLIC LIBRARY

"**B**ollocks!" he cursed. He was silent for a moment, wrestling with his decision. "Fine, you have my word."

Lindsey told him everything. To his credit, Robbie didn't interrupt her but listened with careful consideration.

"What's your plan if he does show up?" he asked.

"I'll call Emma," she said.

"Right away?" he persisted.

"Yes," she said.

"You hesitated," he accused. "Love, what are you hoping to accomplish if he does come into the library? Are you looking to get a confession out of him?"

"I did not hesitate," she said. "I'm just being thoughtful about my answers. Mostly, I'm just worried about him. He's elderly. He's out there alone."

"And he could be a bloody nutter who just committed a homicide," Robbie added.

"He's not," Lindsey insisted.

"You don't know that," he said.

Lindsey tipped forward in her chair. She knew she was right about Stewart. No, she didn't know it for a fact, but she felt as if she did.

"As an actor, you trust your intuition, right?" she asked.

"Have to."

"Well, as a librarian, I have to trust my instincts, too," she said.

"Wouldn't they be more geared toward judging the literary merits of a book?"

Lindsey smiled. "Maybe, but as a public servant, I have to trust my gut when it comes to my patrons. I have to have a sense of who they are, what they need and how I can help them."

"You're worried the old duffer is going to freeze to death out there or worse," he said.

"Yes," she said. "If I can get him to come to the library, I can make sure he gets the care that he needs."

"Why?" Robbie asked. "I mean, why is he so important to you?"

Lindsey thought about all of the times she'd stopped out at the island to bring the Rosens their books. Stewart had been so shy at first. He hadn't made eye contact. He'd spoken with a mumble. The very first time she'd arrived, he'd hidden behind a piling at the dock and peered out at her like a little boy instead of a grown man. She had grown fond of him, and it had felt a lot like taming a wild bird to get him to trust her.

Eventually, he had spoken to her and even joked with her. The last few times she'd been out to the island, it had been to find him pacing the dock, waiting for her. Yes, she was fond of him, but also she felt sorry for him. From what she'd learned, he seemed to be a prisoner in his own life, and his only escape had been books.

"Because I could be him," she said. The words surprised her. She wasn't quite sure where they'd come from, but their truth made her squirm a bit in her seat.

"Meaning that if your life had played out differently, you could be a hermit, living alone with limited human contact whilst hiding in books," Robbie said. His voice was full of understanding.

"Yes," she said. "When I was younger, I used books as a shield to keep separate from others. If it hadn't been for my brother, Jack, forcing me out of my shell, I don't know what would have become of me."

"I don't think you give yourself enough credit," Robbie said. "I think you're more sociable than you realize, and maybe it is all of those books and all of those characters that you became while reading that have given you your social skills."

"Maybe," she said. She'd never thought of it that way before.

"Either way, it's a very lucky thing that you ended up in such a demanding community as Briar Creek, where it's impossible to hide," he said.

"That's for sure," she said.

"Stewart is going to be all right," he said. "From what you've told me, I'd wager he's a survivor."

"I hope so."

"Text me tonight and let me know what happens," he said.

"But you'll keep your promise not to tell anyone beforehand," she said.

"Only if you text me and let me know you're all right," he said. "Otherwise, I will call everyone, the crafternooners, Emma, even that blasted buoy boy."

Lindsey laughed. Robbie could splutter all he wanted, but she knew she could trust him to keep his word.

"Thank you," she said. "I promise to let you know what happens right away."

"Now we have one more very important thing to discuss," Robbie said.

"What's that?" she asked. She felt herself get nervous. She

never knew what he was going to say next and she found it just a little nerve-wracking.

"How much do you miss me?" he asked.

"Quite a bit, actually," she said, smiling at his flirtatious tone. "But that's not surprising. I always miss my friends when they're away."

"Oh! The word *friends* is like a dagger to the heart," he cried. "Shakespeare wrote about this sort of thing, you know."

"'Friendship is constant in all other things / Save in the office and affairs of love,'" she said.

"*Much Ado About Nothing*," Robbie identified the play.

"Precisely," she said, and he laughed.

"Well played," he said. "All right, I will try not to make much ado about this situation, but I don't like it, and I will worry."

"Don't. Milton will be with me, and I'll keep you informed," she said. "I promise."

They ended the call shortly after that, and Lindsey found herself smiling when she thought of Robbie and his silly chatter. He hadn't told her what exactly he was doing in New York and she found she was curious. She shook her head as if to rid herself of the thought. Even though he was her friend and there was something unspoken between them, what he did during his time away really wasn't any of her business.

At seven o'clock, the board members began to file into the library. Lindsey waited by the front desk, not to greet them but to see Beth off.

Aidan had arrived at ten minutes to seven, which sent Beth into a tizzy, because even though she'd been ready for over an hour, she was convinced she wasn't wearing the right clothes, her hair was a mess and her red lipstick was too loud.

"I can't do this," she wailed, looking like she was going to bolt into the back room.

Lindsey was about to talk her down when Ms. Cole glanced up from the computer where she was checking in a stack of books and snapped, "Get ahold of yourself!"

Beth turned to give her what for, but the lemon held up her hand in a stop gesture.

"You are creative, funny, clever, smart and cute. If the man doesn't see all of that, he is not worth a second of your time. Now get out there and stop being such a ninny."

Beth opened her mouth and then closed it. She smoothed her pencil skirt with her hands and took a deep calming breath.

"Thank you," she said to Ms. Cole. She strode out from behind the desk with her head held high and an engaging smile on her lips.

Ms. Cole nodded in approval as she and Lindsey watched Beth walk to the door to greet Aidan, who stepped into the building looking quite dashing in a dark wool coat with a Black Watch plaid scarf draped about his neck.

"That was . . . well done, Ms. Cole," Lindsey said.

"Eh, we'll see if this one lasts. Goodness knows that girl always picks the lame duck," Ms. Cole said, and she turned back to her books.

Lindsey pressed her lips together to keep from smiling. Glancing around the room, she could see the library was doing just fine, so she set out for the stairs that led to the small room above, where the board would convene for the meeting.

Milton greeted her at the door, and they exchanged a look. No one else knew about their new strategy, and Lindsey could only hope, for the sake of the board, that it worked.

The library board meeting was the most successful one they'd had since Sandra Lippins had joined. For the first time in months, everyone got a chance to speak, and while it was difficult for Sandra, she seemed to catch on pretty quickly that the meetings were no longer just about her. She didn't look happy about it, and when she left she gave Lindsey a sour look.

"Did you know that I am next-door neighbors with Mayor Hensen?" she asked.

"I believe you've mentioned it, yes," Lindsey said.

"I'll be sure to visit him this weekend," Sandra said. She gave Lindsey a pointed look.

"Do give him my best," Lindsey said.

Sandra turned on her heel and flounced from the room. This was most impressive, because Sandra was a thickset middle-aged woman with chin-length blond hair that she wore in fat curls around her head while she favored vibrantly colored sweaters with lots of dazzling rhinestones on them, neither of which worked with a huffy, flouncy exit.

Lindsey exchanged a look with Milton, and he grinned and shrugged.

"That was the most productive meeting we've had in a long while," Jim Truman said as he passed Lindsey. "Don't you worry about Sandra talking to the mayor. He's a golf buddy of mine and he can't stand her long-winded rants either."

"Good to know," Lindsey said.

The rest of the board members said good night and hurried out of the room before the library closed for the night. Lindsey and Milton joined the rest of the staff for closing and then made excuses about how they had to clean up after the board meeting.

Once Lindsey had shut and locked the door behind her staff, she turned to Milton and said, "Okay, now what?"

"Now we clean the meeting room so we aren't actually lying, and then we stake out our spots."

"Sounds like a plan," Lindsey said.

Cleaning the room took no more than fifteen minutes. Afterward, Lindsey unlocked the front door and made sure the lights were on so that if Stewart was out there, he would think the library was open.

Milton stationed himself in a seat near the front door so

he could discourage anyone that wasn't Stewart from coming in and keep an eye on Lindsey, who perched at the circulation desk, thumbing through a stack of copies of *Publishers Weekly* and *Library Journal*. She supposed it was a good thing she was so behind on reading book reviews.

She had texted her landlord, Nancy Peyton, and asked her to keep her dog, Heathcliff, for a while longer. Nancy had texted back that she was happy to, so Lindsey didn't feel like a completely neglectful doggy mama.

An hour passed. Only two regulars had to be shooed away. Lindsey felt the long day taking its toll, and she rested her head in her hand while she flipped through another trade periodical.

She glanced over to see Milton's head bobbing a bit as he read, and she felt guilty for keeping him out when he could be home, drinking his herbal tea and doing his evening yoga or canoodling with Ms. Cole. She was just about to call the whole thing off when the front doors whooshed open and in wandered Stewart Rosen, blinking against the bright light.

He looked pinched from the cold, as if his weathered skin had become hard and brittle in the February air. His face was pale, making the dark gouges under his eyes stand out even more in the library's harsh fluorescent light. Lindsey wasn't sure whether she should offer him a sandwich or a hug or both.

Milton had bolted up in his chair, but Lindsey held up her hand, gesturing for him to be still since they didn't want to scare Stewart away.

"Good evening, Mr. Rosen," she said. She tried to keep her tone even, as if it was no big deal to have him here in the library where she was quite sure he had never set foot before.

Stewart's pale eyes looked at her, but Lindsey got the feeling he was looking through her at something else. She wondered if exhaustion was making it difficult for him to concentrate.

"Is there something I can do for you?" she asked.

She rose to stand and then moved around the counter, approaching him cautiously, as if he were a stray cat who had entered the building and needed care, which she supposed he was, in a sense.

Although Stewart was wearing a coat, it was unzipped and his teeth were chattering. He had no hat and no gloves. Lindsey figured she'd better get something hot inside of him and quick.

"Here, I think we have some soup in the staff break room," she said. "How about we heat it up for you?"

Gently, she took Stewart's arm and started to lead him to the back. She could hear he was humming something to himself, but she couldn't make out any words or a melody. She signaled to Milton to lock the door so that no one else wandered in.

To her surprise, Stewart allowed her to lead him without balking. She motioned for him to sit at the small table and went to the cupboard to find some of the soup she always kept on hand for those days when grabbing lunch or dinner was near impossible because of meetings or schedule issues.

She went with chicken noodle, figuring even non–soup eaters were good with that one. While it warmed in the microwave, she got him a big glass of water in case he was dehydrated, and a spoon. Stewart said nothing but rocked back and forth in his seat, still humming the same short tune over and over.

Lindsey patted her pocket for her cell phone. She needed to call Emma. Her pocket was empty. Damn it. She'd left her phone out on the front desk.

She wondered if she should go get it, but she was afraid to let Stewart out of her sight. He didn't seem well. He looked frailer than she'd ever seen him, and clearly he wasn't processing well, since he had yet to say a single word.

"Drink some water, Stewart. It'll make you feel better," she said.

His skin looked papery thin and fragile. She could see the blue veins on the back of his hands, which she noticed shook when he reached for the glass. He drank it all, and she refilled it. Given the state he was in, she figured it would be all right if she fed him before she called the chief. Surely, Emma would understand.

The microwave oven chimed, and she took out the soup and put it on a plate, removing the plastic lid. It was steaming hot, so she added an ice cube from the freezer to help cool it more quickly so he could eat.

"We've all been very worried about you, Stewart," she said. "I'm glad you came into the library."

She put the bowl down in front of him and put the spoon in his hand. He looked confused until she pointed to the soup. A small smile lifted the corners of his mouth, and he tucked into the small bowl. Lindsey foraged in the cupboard until she found some crackers to go with it.

She opened the wax wrapper and put the crackers beside the plate. Again she thought about going to get her phone, but she didn't want him to panic if she left. She knew Milton was keeping an eye out front, because with the lights on, anyone might wander up to the doors and try to get in. Milton was to wave them away while keeping an eye out for Lindsey in case, well, in case Stewart was dangerous.

Looking at him now, Lindsey couldn't imagine it. She didn't see a killer. Instead, she saw a cold, hungry, befuddled elderly man. It broke her heart to think that he'd been out there wandering the streets with no one to help him.

He took a break from the soup and ate some crackers. Then he drank another full glass of water. Lindsey noticed that his hands were less shaky and some color was coming back into his face.

"Stewart, can you tell me what happened to Peter?" she asked.

She supposed it was a bit blunt, but if Stewart saw something, if he knew who had killed his brother, then she wanted to help keep him safe, and she could only do that if she knew what had happened.

He glanced up at her and then down at his soup. He fiddled with his spoon. He stopped humming and looked as if he wanted to say something.

"It's all right," she said. "You're safe here."

She met his gaze, and his pale eyes searched her face, as if he was trying to decide if he could trust her or not. Lindsey didn't move, didn't even flutter an eyelash as she was so afraid of scaring him off.

Stewart opened his mouth to speak when a loud bang and a shout sounded from the front of the library and they both started. Stewart looked as if he was going to get up and run. Lindsey put a hand on his shoulder as she stood.

"It's all right," she said. "Milton is out there keeping watch. Stay here while I go see that all is well."

She hurried from the room and down the hall toward the front of the building. A draft was sweeping in through the open front doors. *Open doors?* Lindsey doubled her speed.

She stepped onto the automatic mat and gasped. Lying facedown on the sidewalk at the bottom of the stone steps was Milton.

CHAPTER

13

BRIAR CREEK
PUBLIC LIBRARY

"Milton!" she cried as she raced down the steps. "Are you all right? What happened?"

Milton pushed himself up onto his hands and knees. A trickle of blood was running down the side of his head from a nasty gash over his left eye.

He rose to his feet and swayed a bit. "I'm all right."

"No, you're not," Lindsey cried. "You're bleeding!"

"Am I?" He blinked at her and then gingerly felt the wound on his head. He looked at the blood on his fingers in wonder.

"What happened?" Lindsey cried.

"I think I got jumped," he said. He stared at Lindsey as if he couldn't quite believe the words he was saying.

"Don't move," she said. "Are you dizzy, nauseous, losing your eyesight? Oh my God, if you're hurt I'll never forgive myself!"

Milton took Lindsey's hands in his. Suddenly, he was the one calming her down.

"It's okay," he said. "I scraped my head on the step when I was knocked down."

"Knocked down?" Lindsey asked. "Here, let's get you inside."

Lindsey took Milton's arm and led him up the stairs and into the library. She ushered him to one of the armchairs by the window and then dashed for the first aid kit that Ms. Cole kept behind the desk.

Lindsey brought the metal kit over to Milton. Her fingers were shaking as she tried to pop open the latches. It was a first aid kit—why was it made sturdy enough to survive a zombie apocalypse? Milton reached over her and unhooked the lid for her. Lindsey gave him a rueful smile.

She took out an antiseptic wipe and swabbed the blood off of his head. Under the blood, it turned out to be a gash, but not too deep, and she felt herself relax a bit.

"What happened?" she asked as she applied pressure to the cut to stop the bleeding.

"I was monitoring the front doors," Milton said. "And keeping an ear on your conversation with Stewart just in case he, well, you know."

"Uh-huh," Lindsey prompted him.

"I was pacing by the doors, and then I looked out and there was a person lying facedown on the ground," he said. "It looked like they fell, so I manually opened the door and hurried down the steps. I thought they'd slipped on a patch of ice or on the dusting of snow we're getting."

Lindsey glanced out the window. Milton was right. It had begun to snow. She'd been so frantic when she saw him she hadn't even realized.

"Who was it?" she asked. "Were they hurt?"

"I don't know," Milton said. "When I got near them, someone snuck up from behind and whacked me in the back of my knees and knocked me down. I conked my head on the steps and was just getting my bearings when you came out of the building."

"But that sounds almost as if they lured you out . . . Oh my God, Stewart!"

Lindsey turned and ran to the break room at the back of the library. She darted into the room only to find it empty. She quickly checked the staff bathrooms around the corner from the staff room, but they were empty, too. She raced through the library, checking every dark corner and in between every shelving unit.

She hurried back to Milton. "Stewart is gone."

"Oh no!" he said. He got to his feet, dropping the gauze he'd been holding to his head. "But how?"

"I think whoever was outside was trying to lure you out so they could get inside and get to Stewart," she said.

"And I fell for it," he said. He gave Lindsey a stricken look. "They probably ran in when you ran out to get to me. He's likely been kidnapped by whoever murdered his brother."

"He also might have left when I came out to check on you," she said. "It could be that Stewart heard the commotion outside and was frightened away."

"But we didn't see anyone leave," Milton said.

"Maybe he used the staff entrance," Lindsey said. "I'll go check."

"I'm coming with you," Milton said.

"Let's lock up first," she said.

Lindsey stopped by the front doors, manually pulling them closed and locking them before she led the way to the staff entrance. Together Lindsey and Milton pushed open the heavy metal door.

The snow was falling faster now, and it pelted their faces while they peered into the small area illuminated by an overhead security light. Lindsey saw a fresh set of footprints in the snow. Someone had definitely been here very recently.

"I think Stewart bolted," she said.

The footprints led away from the building and out into the parking lot. She was willing to bet they belonged to

Stewart. She glanced at Milton. Despite assuring her that he was fine, he looked pale and shaky, and a knot was forming beneath the cut. She was taking him to an urgent care facility. Period. But she needed someone to look for Stewart.

"Come on," she said. "We're going to get your head examined."

"Not the first time it's been suggested," he said. His tone was wry. "But it's not necessary. I'm fine."

"Sorry, but it's not negotiable." Lindsey shook her head. "Wait here while I get my things."

She hurriedly shut down the library and grabbed her jacket and purse. She knew Milton had left his car parked in the back of the library. She would use it to drive him to the doctor, whether he liked it or not, and she would call Sully on her way and ask him to do a sweep for Stewart. It was the best she could do under the circumstances.

Yes, she would have to call Emma, too, but after she had Sully already looking. She knew Stewart felt okay with Sully, whereas the sight of the police would probably cause him to run.

She and Milton exited out the staff door, making sure they didn't walk over Stewart's footprints on the off chance they led to his whereabouts. Lindsey took Milton's keys and handed him her phone as she assisted him into the passenger's seat.

"This is a manual," Milton said. "Do you know how to drive a stick shift?"

"It's been a while," Lindsey said. "But I'll manage. Call Sully and tell him what happened."

Milton looked from the phone to Lindsey as if she'd just handed him a live snake. Scratch that—she had a feeling he would have preferred a live snake.

He turned it around in his hand as if looking for the on switch. Lindsey took it back and tapped the button that lit up the screen, then she opened her contacts and called Sully's number.

"It's ringing," she said. She stepped on the brake and the clutch, stabbed the key into the ignition and cranked on the engine. She then released the brake and eased her foot off the clutch at the same time that she stepped on the gas.

Since she had taken a pact to be more ecofriendly when she moved to the small town and got around primarily by bicycle or pedestrian power, Lindsey's driving skills were the teensiest bit rusty, especially when it came to a manual transmission. Her stick shift skills had atrophied like an unused limb.

The car bucked and bounced, and she quickly moved the stick into second, but she didn't press the clutch in fast enough and it made a horrible grinding noise.

"Oh dear God, my baby!" Milton cried. Milton, who never lost it, looked like he was about to have a meltdown.

"No worries," Lindsey said. "I've got it now."

Sure enough, as they picked up speed she managed to shift into third without grinding the gears, and she turned onto the main road.

"What?" Milton said into the phone. "Oh, hi, Sully, it's me, Milton, not your darling."

Lindsey gave him a sidelong glance, and he gestured for her to keep her eyes on the road.

"She's fine. She's right here, but she can't talk because she's driving my car. Well, driving might be an overstatement," Milton said.

"Tell him what happened," Lindsey said. "And ask him to go and look for Stewart."

Milton proceeded to recite the events of the evening to Sully with Lindsey shouting tidbits that he forgot into the phone. Finally, Milton lowered the phone from his ear.

"He said he'll head right out and sweep the area for Stewart," Milton said.

Lindsey blew out a relieved breath.

"He also said that as soon as you get me to the medical

center, you need to call Chief Plewicki and tell her everything, and after that he wants to talk to you."

Lindsey felt her shoulders ratchet up to her ears again.

Milton must have sensed her stress, because he added
gently, "Maybe Sully will find him."

"Maybe," she said. She didn't want to admit it, but she
had a very bad feeling about the whole situation.

While Milton was taken into an exam room, Lindsey waited
in the lobby. She paced back and forth a few times, trying
to figure out what she was going to say to Emma. There was
just no good way to say, *I had your missing person and I lost him.*

With a heavy sigh, she took out her phone and called the
chief's direct number.

The snow had tapered off, and a light breeze was blowing
what had fallen across the walkway outside. Lindsey watched
it twist and swirl in the lamplight while the phone rang.

Emma picked up on the third ring. "Chief Plewicki."

"Hi, Emma, it's Lindsey," she said.

"Lindsey?" Emma sounded surprised. "What can I do
for you?"

"Forgive me," Lindsey said.

There was a beat of silence.

"No conversation ever goes well that starts with those two
words," Emma said.

"That would include this one," Lindsey agreed.

"What happened?"

"Milton and I were in the library cleaning up after the
board meeting," Lindsey said. "We had the thought that if
we lingered it might invite someone who was out in the cold,
who has a good relationship with the library, to come in."

"Stewart," Emma said. "You stayed late, hoping Stewart
would show up. Did he?"

"Yes," Lindsey said. "And I was going to call you right away, I swear."

There was a smacking noise, and Lindsey got the distinct impression that Emma had just done a face palm, slapping her hand to her forehead in an expression of complete exasperation, for which she could hardly blame her.

"I'm seriously considering locking you up, you know that?" Emma asked.

CHAPTER

14

BRIAR CREEK
PUBLIC LIBRARY

Lindsey opened her mouth to answer, but Emma kept right on going.

"I could hit you for obstructing an investigation, for hindering the apprehension of a suspect and for being a terminal busybody," Emma raged. "Do you have a Miss Marple complex or something?"

"Maybe, although I'm partial to Hercule Poirot, you know, because I share the same love of hot chocolate," Lindsey admitted.

"But you're not a former detective, or Belgian, nor do you have a mustache—at least, not that I'm aware," Emma said. She still sounded mad, and Lindsey noted her emphasis had been on her *not* being a former detective.

"Are you ready to listen now?" Lindsey asked.

She heard Emma take a deep breath and blow it out. "Go ahead."

Lindsey told her everything from the end of the board

meeting to taking Milton to the medical center. Emma didn't ask any questions until the end.

"Stewart said nothing the entire time he was with you?" she clarified.

"Not a single word," Lindsey confirmed. "He just sat there humming. He did eat, though, and drink water. He looked cold, hungry and dehydrated."

"What did you say to him?" Emma demanded. "Did you tell him anything about the investigation?"

"Not a word," Lindsey said. "I asked him if he knew what happened to Peter, but he didn't answer. I got the feeling he was in shock."

"I should still arrest you," Emma muttered.

Lindsey felt a frisson of alarm course through her. Would Emma really do that?

"But you've given us the first confirmation that Stewart is at large and not murdered and missing, so I'll let it slide *this time*."

"I am sorry that I didn't call you right away," Lindsey said. "But when I saw him looking so frail, my first thought was to take care of him. I don't think he murdered his brother."

Lindsey expected Emma to mock her for making such a bold statement on nothing more than speculation, but she didn't.

"You're a good reader of people," Emma said. "I'll take your description of his condition into consideration."

"Thanks," Lindsey said.

"How's Milton?" Emma asked.

"He seems okay, but I wanted to get him checked out just to be sure."

"Have him call me as soon as he's able," Emma said. "I'd like to hear his description of everything that happened. If he was jumped so that someone could get into the library to get to Stewart . . ."

Her voice trailed off, and Lindsey knew she was mentally

sifting through all of the possibilities just as Lindsey had. Probably, she was coming to the same conclusion as Lindsey: that Stewart's situation was even more precarious than she'd realized.

"I'll have him get in touch with you," Lindsey promised.

They ended the call, and Lindsey felt relieved that Emma hadn't been more annoyed with her. Being hampered by a broken leg was likely making Emma more amenable than usual since she wasn't able to pound the pavement herself, she was more dependent on help from others. Still, Lindsey felt terrible that Stewart had fled or—worse—had been taken. She tried not to dwell on it, but the clawing fear that she might have unwittingly helped a murderer catch Stewart made her stomach clench.

She paced the empty waiting room and pondered the events of the past couple of days. The question she couldn't shake loose was why. Why had someone murdered Peter Rosen? The brothers kept to themselves on their island; they weren't quarreling with anyone locally. Their island was a booby-trapped disaster, so even if someone had thought to rob them, they would be putting their life at risk to do it. Why would someone do that?

None of this helped Stewart Rosen. In fact, all of it made him seem to be the most likely candidate for murdering his brother. But why would he? Lindsey wondered if taking care of his brother for all these years had suddenly become too much. Maybe he snapped and just couldn't take it anymore.

The idea just didn't sit right. Lindsey shook it off. She couldn't believe it of Stewart. She had seen the look of devastation in his eyes when she'd asked about Peter. It wasn't the look of a man who had killed his brother. It was the look of someone who'd had his best friend taken from him.

"Lindsey, are you all right?" Milton asked as he approached her.

Lindsey turned away from the window to see Milton coming over with a nice neat bandage on his head.

"That's not the question," she said. "The question is, how are you?"

"Perfectly fine," he said. "No damage done."

Lindsey narrowed her eyes at him. "Are you sure?"

"Do I need a doctor's note?" he asked.

"Maybe," she said. Then she smiled. She was very relieved that her friend was okay. "I spoke to Emma."

"How much trouble are we in?" he asked.

Lindsey walked beside him out into the cold.

"Scale of one to ten, with ten being big trouble and one being not so much, I'd say we're a solid seven," she said. "Maybe an eight."

Milton nodded. "Generous of her."

"Agreed," Lindsey said. "She does want to talk to you as soon as you're able."

"I'll call her when I get home," Milton said.

Lindsey's phone chimed while they walked out to the car. She checked the display. It was a text from Sully telling her that he hadn't found Stewart and to call him when she had the chance. Lindsey texted back that she was taking Milton home and would call him afterward. In seconds, another text from Sully arrived saying he would meet her at Milton's.

Lindsey couldn't tell from the texts whether Sully had any other news in regards to Stewart. She hoped not, since he didn't write anything else, but then again, Sully was the sort to give bad news in person.

When they got to the car, Milton held out his hand for his keys.

"But your head," Lindsey argued.

"Will be safer if I'm driving," he said.

Lindsey slapped the keys into his palm. "I'm not that bad of a driver."

"Scale of one to ten with one being terrible and ten being great," Milton said, "you're hovering between a one and a two."

Lindsey let him open the passenger door for her, and she

climbed in without huffing, mostly. They made good time to Milton's house. When they got there, it was to find Sully's beat-up pickup truck parked in front.

"I bet you're going to get a talking-to," Milton said. He had a teasing twinkle in his eye.

"Laugh all you want. When Ms. Cole sees the bandage on your head, you're going to get one, too," Lindsey said. Milton quickly sobered. "Not so funny now, huh?"

"Not even a little," he agreed.

They got out of the car and joined Sully next to his truck.

"You all right, Milton?" he asked.

"Fine, just fine," Milton said. "Lindsey took excellent care of me."

"But I'm never allowed to drive your car again, am I?" Lindsey asked.

"In a dire emergency, I might let you. Otherwise, no," Milton said. "Do you two want to come in? I could make some green tea."

"That sounds nice, but you have a call to make," Lindsey said.

"Oh yeah," Milton said. "Why do I think I'd rather be back in the urgent care getting poked and prodded?"

"Chief Plewicki," Lindsey explained to Sully.

"Ah," he said. "Good luck."

Lindsey and Sully gave Milton sympathetic glances as he said good night and turned and headed up the walkway to his old stone house.

"Is she very mad at you two?" Sully asked. He led Lindsey around to the passenger side of his truck and opened the door for her.

"I think she was so relieved to have it confirmed that Stewart is still alive that she's cutting us some slack—this time."

"Well, you're not going to get that lucky with me," he said. He shut the door and circled around the truck to get in on the driver's side.

He sounded a bit miffed. Uh-oh.

"Before you rip into me," she said as he shut his door and fired up the truck, "let me just say that I fully intended to call Emma right away if Stewart showed up, but I was half asleep when he did show up and then I forgot my phone. I was afraid he'd get spooked if I left him alone, so I fed him some soup and crackers. You should have seen how weak he looked. I figured I'd call Emma as soon as I could."

Sully put the truck into drive and left Milton's house behind, driving toward Lindsey's apartment on the other side of town. He reached across the middle and took her hand in his. Lindsey wasn't sure if it was a gesture of understanding or forgiveness, but she accepted the contact, grateful for the warmth of his hand around hers.

"I'm glad you gave him soup," he said.

He turned and gazed at her, and Lindsey had the feeling that her taking care of Stewart had changed Sully's mind about the situation.

"Me, too," she said. "He looked so cold and tired and sad. Oh, I wish he hadn't disappeared."

"Do you think he ran off, or do you think someone knocked down Milton to get to him?" Sully asked.

"There was only one set of footprints leaving through the staff door of the library," Lindsey said. "I think, I hope, he bolted."

"I hope so, too, but I found something that makes me think maybe not. We need to make a short detour. I have to show you something." Sully turned the truck into the library parking lot. He parked beneath one of the overhead lights and let go of her hand to take a flashlight out from under his seat. "Come on."

Lindsey hopped out of the truck and followed him. The snow had started falling again, adding to the thin coating already on the ground. Her breath steamed out of her nose, and she felt the bite of the wintery air pinch her cheeks while it made her nose run and her eyes water.

Sully strode to the far corner of the parking lot and paused by a bare patch on the ground. It was rectangular in shape, roughly the size of a car. Someone had been parked here while it was snowing. He switched on the flashlight and followed some prints on the ground.

Lindsey looked where he shone the beam of light. The details were as clear as a child's imprinted snow angel. There was one set of footprints going toward the building, but there were two sets coming back. Unfortunately, one of them had drag marks on the heels, as if they were being forced toward the rectangular bare patch. The prints met up in the parking lot in an area that was blurred and the snow was tamped down as if there was a scuffle. When she and Milton had looked out the back door, they had seen only one set of prints.

"Oh no," Lindsey said. She crouched closer to the prints. "Someone got Stewart, didn't they?"

66 I can't say for sure," Sully said. "But it doesn't look good."
Lindsey closed her eyes and pressed her temples with
the tips of her fingers. She could feel the mother of all head-
aches brewing in her skull just waiting to punch its way out.

"It might not be him," Sully said. He put his hand on her
shoulder in a gesture of reassurance, but Lindsey didn't
believe him, and she didn't think he did either. "I took pictures of the footprints and sent them over to Emma. She's
going to have one of her officers investigate it further after
they finish sweeping the area for Stewart."

"If he gets hurt or worse, I'll never forgive myself," Lindsey said.

Sully opened his arms, and Lindsey stepped into them.
She could feel a sob bubble up in her throat, but she swallowed it. It went down hard like a rock, lodging somewhere
in her gut.

"It's not your fault that he vanished off of the island or
showed up at the library or disappeared again," Sully said.

Lindsey pressed her forehead into his chest. "Yes, it is."

Sully drew back, trying to see her face. "What do you mean?"

"Milton and I stayed late at the library on purpose," Lindsey said. "We were hoping to draw him out."

"Oh," Sully said.

"See?" Lindsey asked. "If he was kidnapped by whoever murdered his brother, then it's my fault."

"That seems—" Sully began, but Lindsey interrupted him.

"Highly likely given the footprints," she said.

Sully opened his mouth to speak, but Lindsey's phone chimed. Thinking it might be Emma or Milton, she wrestled her phone out of her purse and checked the display. It was Robbie. Her chin dropped to her chest. In all of the excitement, she had forgotten to text him.

Before she could answer, the chiming ended. She figured he'd leave a voice mail, and in the meantime, she could send him a text letting him know all was well, which was a total lie. As she looked at her phone, she saw that she'd missed several calls and just as many texts. Uh-oh. Sully's phone started to ring.

He pulled it out of his pocket and glared at the display. Lindsey remembered Robbie's threat and tried to wave him away from the call.

"Don't answer—"

"Hello," Sully said into his phone, giving her a funny look. Then he lowered one eyebrow and pursed his lips. "Oh, it's you, Vine."

Lindsey closed one eye as if witnessing a train wreck and not being able to look away completely.

"She's right here," he said. "Yes, with me. She's fine."

Sully glared at Lindsey and mouthed the words *He knew?* She gave him a sheepish shrug.

"Here, talk to her yourself," Sully said. He handed the phone to Lindsey and said, "Come on. You can talk to him while I drive you home."

"Hi, Robbie," she said.

"You didn't text me, or call me, or send me a messenger pigeon, or anything," he said. He sounded grumpy.

"I know. I'm sorry," she said. Then she lowered her voice and muttered into the phone, "You really couldn't have picked someone else to call first?"

"Oh, I did," he said. "I ran through all of the crafternoon girls first."

Lindsey glanced at her phone. Sure enough, many of the messages and missed calls were from the girls.

"Oh boy," she said.

"Yes, they're all quite put out with you," he said. "So tell me what happened."

Sully had retrieved Lindsey's bike from the bike rack and put it in the back of his truck. She wondered what it meant that he knew the combination to her bike lock. With a grim look in her direction, he yanked open the passenger door for her, and Lindsey gave Robbie a rapid-fire account of the events as Sully walked around the car.

"I'm sorry, love, this all sounds very worrisome," he said. "Are you holding up okay? You know this isn't your fault, right? How are you?"

As soon as he asked her if she was okay, Lindsey cracked. All of the tears she'd been storing up since finding Milton laid out on the ground burst through her defenses, and she began to sob.

"No, I'm not. I'm a mess." The last part came out in a wail, and she sobbed, "I'll call you later."

She thrust the phone at Sully. He put it up to his ear and said, "Good grief, man, what did you say to her?"

Lindsey dug through her purse until she found a tissue and then blew her nose very loudly.

"Sorry, pal, I'd love to chat, but I have to comfort a crying lady," Sully said. "Of course, I won't take advantage of the situation! But feel free not to call her again, really."

Sully ended the call and dropped the phone into his coat pocket. As the truck's heater kicked warmth out over their cold feet, Sully lifted an arm and pulled Lindsey close.

"Are you all right?" he asked.

"No, I'm scared for Stewart," she said. "I'm worried and I feel guilty and stupid."

She blew her nose again. Sully ran a hand up and down her back. "He's going to be all right. Stewart Rosen is made of tough stuff if he's managed to live on that island as long as he has with no help."

"I hope so," she said.

"What did the overactor say that switched on the water-works?"

"He asked if I was all right," she said. Sully gave her a look, and she explained, "You know how you can bluff your way through grief and upset until someone asks you if you're okay and then *WHAM* you fall apart."

"Yeah, I remember a few episodes like that," he said. He looked at the windshield, watching the snow with a far-off expression that Lindsey knew meant he was revisiting some painful times of his own.

Lindsey hugged him close. He had suffered a significant loss in his youth that had caused him to feel guilty for his role in the bad outcome. She suspected this situation reminded him of those dark days, and she added that to the pile of things she currently felt bad about.

Sully shook his head and planted a kiss on her hair and said, "We'd better go. Heathcliff will be beside himself if he doesn't see you soon."

Lindsey could think of nothing better than hugging her dog.

"Step on it," she said.

Sully grinned and did just that. The small town was quiet at this time of night, and once he got through the center of town, he picked up the pace until they were pulling up to

Nancy Peyton's house, where Lindsey rented the third-floor apartment.

Sully got out with her and walked her up the front steps and into the foyer of the large captain's house. She turned to thank him when the door to Nancy's apartment on the first floor was yanked open and Beth popped her head out.

"Where have you been?" she asked. Nancy and Violet joined her in the doorway, all three of them frowning at her.

"Do you know what time it is?" Nancy asked. Her words were drowned out by the black ball of fur that darted through her legs to grab Lindsey around the knee as if he was hugging her. Lindsey knelt down and hefted her thirty-pound puppy into her arms while he licked her face.

"There's nothing that a little dog slobber can't make better," Sully whispered in her ear. Lindsey chuckled and squeezed Heathcliff tight. He wriggled in her hold, and she put him down, at which point he immediately greeted Sully with the same enthusiasm.

"Do you know that Robbie is looking for you?" Violet asked. "He's worried sick. Oh, hi, Sully."

To Violet's credit, she looked a little guilty mentioning Robbie in front of Sully. Lindsey knew that Violet and Charlene were hoping for her to give Robbie a reason to stay in Briar Creek, but they were also very fond of Sully.

"What are you two doing here?" Lindsey asked Beth and Violet.

"We came over when Robbie called and said that you were setting a trap for Stewart Rosen, but that you hadn't texted him and he was worried," Beth said. The foyer was chilly, and she shivered.

"Why are we standing in the cold? Come in, come in," Nancy said. "I have warm milk and molasses cookies."

The three women backed into her apartment, and Lindsey and Sully were ushered inside into the comforting warmth.

Nancy had her fireplace on, and Lindsey went right to it. It was lovely to stand beside it and thaw out.

Sully took her coat and hung it on the coatrack beside his, then he took a seat on the hearth beside her while Nancy fussed over them, pouring them mugs of milk and giving them each a plate of cookies.

To Lindsey's surprise, she was starving. She supposed she could be emotional eating, but all of a sudden the greatest thing she had ever tasted was Nancy's chewy molasses cookies washed down with the mug of warm milk. It was like a hug of comfort, and she felt her anxiety turn down a notch for the first time all night.

Sully took the lead while Lindsey guzzled her milk, wiping off her mustache with the back of her hand.

"Don't worry about Vine," he said. "We just spoke to him, so he knows everything that has happened."

"Which would be what?" Nancy asked.

She brought more cookies and left them on the coffee table in front of the couch she and Violet sat on. Beth leaned forward in her armchair and grabbed one.

"Milton and Lindsey thought they could draw Stewart out if they stayed in the library after closing and left the front door open."

"What?" Beth squawked. "And you didn't tell me?"

"You had a date. I didn't want to worry you. How'd that go, by the way?"

Beth beamed like a one-hundred-watt bulb but waved her off. "Your story first."

"Milton heard someone in town say that Stewart had been seen wandering around at night like he always does. We thought he might consider the library a safe place to go, so after our board meeting we lingered," Lindsey said. "We figured it was a long shot that Stewart would show up, but we wanted to try."

"Did he show up?" Violet asked.

Lindsey nodded.

"So, he's alive," Nancy said and put her hand over her heart. "Oh, thank goodness."

"Maybe," Lindsey said. She then told them the rest of the story. They were shocked about Milton being accosted and worried about Stewart, reaffirming Lindsey's own upset about the whole situation.

"But why would someone harm the Rosens?" Nancy asked. "They've lived here all their lives, and everyone knows they're a bit batty with the booby-trapped house and hoarding issues. Why harm them?"

"Did they have anything of value in their home?" Violet asked. "Maybe in their piles of junk, they collected gold bars or perfect diamonds, or something else of value that someone wanted enough to kill for it."

"You mean someone like those two collectors who came to the library?" Beth said. "Maybe they know what the Rosens had that would be worth killing for."

Lindsey felt a chill sweep across her back, and it wasn't from the cold. Rather, it was from the realization that there was evil in their midst, and it was stalking the Rosen brothers, and it had no problem taking out anyone in its way, like Milton.

"I don't know that Hodges and Perkins were planning on staying in town for very long," Lindsey said. "Unless Emma informed them otherwise, but I don't know that she'd have any reason to do so."

"Except that they'd been in contact with Peter, which might give her a reason," Beth said. "I heard they're staying at Jeanette's bed-and-breakfast."

"So they have to go elsewhere to eat lunch and dinner," Sully said. He turned and looked at Lindsey. "Dinner tomorrow at the Anchor?"

"It's a date," she said.

The room went still, and she glanced at her friends' faces

and sighed. She knew better than to lob around the *d* word in front of them—really, she did—but she was emotionally and physically exhausted. She most definitely did not have the stamina to deal with their input on her love life.

Still, the damage had been done. Nancy looked pleased and said, "I'll give you a lift into work, so you don't have to take your bike. Sully can bring you home. Right, Sully?"

"Sure," he said.

Lindsey glanced at the others. Violet looked reproachful and Beth excited. She knew there was no pleasing everyone, but at least Beth looked happy.

"I have a date, too," Beth said.

"Another one with Aidan?" Lindsey asked.

"Yup," Beth said. Then she blushed and giggled.

Both Nancy and Violet grinned at her, and Lindsey had the feeling that they'd spent a good portion of the time they'd waited for Lindsey listening to Beth talk about Aidan.

Lindsey was happy for her friend, but she also felt a tiny spurt of envy that Beth was in the salad days of her relationship. There were no issues with her and Aidan; everything was new and lovely. Lindsey missed those days.

She didn't know if it was the warm milk or the fire or the ebb of the adrenaline she'd been cruising on for the past few hours, but she realized she was weary all the way down to the marrow in her bones. A big yawn loosened her jaw, and she rose to her feet.

"I'm sorry, but I have to call it a night," she said. She reached over and squeezed Beth's hand in hers. "Details tomorrow?"

"Definitely," Beth said.

"I'm out, too," Sully said.

They said good night to everyone, and Sully followed Lindsey and Heathcliff to the door. They grabbed their coats on the way, and Lindsey stood by the front door, holding her coat over her arm while Sully shrugged his on.

A part of her didn't want him to leave, and it was on the tip of her tongue to invite him upstairs, but she knew it was for the wrong reasons. Tonight she wanted to have someone at hand to tell her that Stewart was going to be fine every time her anxiety spiked, which was likely to be every fifteen minutes, but that wasn't fair to Sully.

"So, I'll pick you up after work tomorrow?" he asked.

"I'm off at five," she said.

Sully stepped forward and cupped her face with his right hand. His eyes locked onto hers, and he said, "I know how you're feeling. But I want you to be clear that what happened tonight wasn't your fault."

"Yes, it was," she disagreed. "But thanks for saying it wasn't. I should have called Emma as soon as Stewart walked into the library, but I was stupid—"

"No, stop," he said. "There was no way for you to know that someone would attack Milton to try and get to Stewart, and we don't know for sure if they got him or not."

"But the footprints in the parking lot indicate that they did," Lindsey said. "I get sick to my stomach just thinking about it."

Sully pulled her close and gave her a strong hug.

"Remember, Stewart is a tough old coot. I don't think he'd be taken that easily."

Lindsey nodded. It was true. "I really hope you're right."

"I am," he said. He kissed her forehead and pushed her toward the stairs. "Go get some sleep. Everything is better after a good night's rest."

Lindsey put her foot on the first step, then she turned back, thinking again that she would ask him to stay with her just for tonight.

"Sully—"

The door to Nancy's apartment opened, and Violet and Beth appeared.

"Yes?" Sully asked. His gaze was intent upon her face, as if he knew what she'd been about to say.

Violet and Beth looked between them as they shrugged on their own coats.

"Thanks again for your help," she said. She figured the appearance of her friends was the universe's way of telling her that now was not the time to be having a sleepover with her ex-boyfriend.

"Anytime," he said.

Sully held the door open for Beth and Violet. They waved as they headed out into the night. Sully paused before stepping through the open door. He looked at her, and his ocean blue eyes twinkled at her.

"What?" she asked.

"Just so you know, the answer would have been yes," he said. Then he winked at her and slipped out into the night.

CHAPTER

16

BRIAR CREEK
PUBLIC LIBRARY

The door shut behind him, and Lindsey stood half on the bottom step, staring after him. She glanced down at Heathcliff, who looked up at her and wagged with his tongue hanging out of his mouth as if he was in on the teasing.

Lindsey reached down to scratch his head and felt a small smile lift the corners of her mouth. Heathcliff could always make her smile even in the darkest hours. She crossed the foyer and locked the door after her friends.

The metal knob felt icy cold to the touch, and Lindsey shivered. She hated the thought that Stewart was out there, but then she supposed it was a better alternative to his being kidnapped.

With any luck, Sully was right and Stewart had managed to get away. And maybe, just maybe, they could find him again before he came to any harm.

Preoccupied with Stewart's whereabouts, Lindsey had arrived early at the library and spent her morning studying up on the Rosen family. The town of Briar Creek had published a small weekly newspaper that had come out every Thursday afternoon since the town had been established as a resort town in the late eighteen hundreds.

The library had copies of every single *Briar Creek Gazette* on microfilm thanks to an archival project by the town's historical society back in the nineteen sixties. Currently, they were working on digitizing the film, but the progress was slow, as it was being done by volunteers.

Lindsey hunched over the microfilm reader, scanning the old issues of the *Gazette*, looking for any mention of the Rosen family. Engrossed in her project, she barely registered the arrival of Ms. Cole until the lemon began to unload the cart from the book drop with a relentless chorus of bangs, thumps and slams that was impossible to ignore.

Lindsey pulled her eyes away from the lit-up window of the film reader and glanced at the desk. Ms. Cole was looking positively green today. From her heather green sweater to her olive green skirt over her thick Kelly green tights, it was an off-putting outfit to say the least.

As if sensing her stare, Ms. Cole glanced up and met Lindsey's gaze. Her lips tightened into a severe line, and she thumped a thick hardbound Stephen King novel down on the counter. It made Lindsey jump, and she glanced around the library and noted that many of the patrons had stopped what they were doing to watch Ms. Cole as well.

Thump! Thump! Thump! James Patterson, Jayne Ann Krentz and Nora Roberts titles were slammed on top of King. Lindsey hopped up from her seat and hurried to the check-in counter before Ms. Cole could add to the pile.

"Is everything all right, Ms. Cole?" she asked.

"It most certainly is not," Ms. Cole snapped. "Of all the selfish, thoughtless, reckless, asinine things to do . . ."

Lindsey looked at the pile of books. She couldn't imagine what someone had done that had Ms. Cole worked up into such a mighty froth. Had they spilled a beverage on the books, marked their place by dog-earring the corners of the pages, what?

"Who are you talking about?" Lindsey asked.

Ms. Cole snapped up to her full height. "You!"

"Me?" Lindsey gaped. "What did I do?"

"You put my Milton at risk!" Ms. Cole cried. "What if he had been concussed or even worse, killed? How could you be so . . . so . . . so stupid?"

Lindsey felt the eyes of every single person in the library upon them. She felt her face grow warm, not from embarrassment because of the stares but because what Ms. Cole was saying was true. She had put Milton at risk. It had been inexcusable.

She glanced at Ms. Cole. She felt her chest get tight as she noted the glisten of unshed tears in the lemon's eyes. She reached across the desk and took Ms. Cole's hands in hers.

"You're right, Ms. Cole. Milton is one of my most favorite people in the world, and I . . . I can't even imagine . . ." She paused to take a breath. Ms. Cole's hands felt cold in hers, and there was a part of Lindsey that was shocked that Ms. Cole was even allowing her to touch her, so she clung harder, trying to give Ms. Cole some warmth. "I'm sorry. It was unforgivable of me to put him in harm's way."

Ms. Cole stared at her for a moment and then removed her hands from beneath Lindsey's. She didn't speak. She simply nodded in acknowledgment of Lindsey's apology and then turned back to her cart full of books.

If an anvil of guilt had fallen out of the sky and smashed Lindsey flat, she couldn't feel any more squashed with shame than she did. Knowing there was nothing more to be said, she turned and left the desk and went back to the microfilm machine.

The patrons who had been watching their conversation turned back to what they were doing, but Lindsey still felt horrible. She had finally been making some progress in her relationship with Ms. Cole, but now instead of just being disliked because she was new, she was reviled, and rightly so, for putting a beloved member of the community in danger.

Lindsey stared at the microfilm without seeing it. Maybe she should just pack it up and forget the whole thing. None of this was her business. Finding Stewart and figuring out who had shot Peter was a job for the police. She put her fingers on the crank to manually wind the film back onto its spool. The name Rosen hit her right between the eyes, and she stopped.

Lindsey glanced up at the date. It was the summer of nineteen sixty-one. The headline read *Dr. Rosen Drowns at Sea*. Lindsey read the short piece. It talked about Peter's heroism in trying to save his father's life and breaking his own back in the process. It gave the details of Dr. Rosen's memorial service even though his body hadn't been recovered.

Lindsey knew that the Rosen brothers were in their early eighties, so she figured Peter must have been in his mid to late twenties at the time of the accident. He had been in a wheelchair, virtually stuck on his family's island, ever since. She wondered what the house had looked like back then with a full staff and their mother still alive.

From what Sully had told her about Dr. and Mrs. Rosen, it seemed neither of them were ideal parents. Stewart and Peter had only had each other. No wonder Stewart had looked so shattered when she saw him. For the first time in his life, he was utterly alone.

Lindsey scrolled to the next week's paper. She wondered if there would be a report about the service. There was. It was held in the small Congregational church just down the street from the library. The reporter described the service as small but respectful and waxed on about Mrs. Rosen's first time off of her island in over twenty years. Despite being a virtual shut-in, the reporter described Mrs. Rosen's clothing as the height of fashion with her "little nothing" dress and her bouffant hairdo. There was a grainy picture of Mrs. Rosen and Stewart. Peter was not in attendance, as he was in New Haven at Yale–New Haven Hospital for his back. Lindsey wondered if that was the only time he'd ever been out of Briar Creek. She suspected it was.

She wished she could have known the Rosen brothers before their lives had been defined by tragedy. There were a few people in town, like Milton, who knew the brothers back when they were all young, but because the Rosens rarely left their island, there were no close friendships made and there was no one to say what they had really been like.

The only people who might know more about the brothers were the staff who had lived on the island with them. Lindsey glanced at the bottom of the article. There was a list of names of the people who had attended the service. She wondered if any of them had stayed in touch with the family and would be someone Stewart would turn to in a crisis. Without overthinking it, she printed the page.

She finished rewinding the film and put it away in its small box. She thought about showing the names to Milton, but the image of a teary Ms. Cole stopped her. She couldn't— she wouldn't—do anything to put Milton in harm's way or upset Ms. Cole again. She would have to find someone else.

She pulled out the metal drawer that housed the film and refiled the box. She was tempted to take another and continue her research, but she thought better of it. She would show the names to Sully tonight at dinner. Given that he'd spent his childhood on the islands, maybe he could give her some insight into the families of the people who had attended Dr. Rosen's funeral all those years ago.

She resumed her seat at the reference desk and willed a patron to come and ask her a question, any question. She'd even be happy to do in-depth research on the Connecticut state statutes if it meant she could stay busy and ignore the constriction in her chest that seemed to get tighter every time her gaze inadvertently landed on Ms. Cole.

The early afternoon dragged, but later, a crowd of students filled the small library to bursting, for which Lindsey was profoundly grateful. Midterm papers were under way, and she spent her afternoon helping fifty kids choose their science fair projects. They had it all going on with everything from manufacturing a manmade cloud to hair-raising projects with static electricity.

Milton arrived, and Lindsey noted that Ms. Cole gave him a frosty glare and then turned her back on him. Milton looked crestfallen, and Lindsey felt her chest get tight again.

This was her fault. She crossed the library and joined Milton in the room where he was setting up for his chess club. She knocked on the doorframe, and he glanced up from the board he was laying out with a hopeful expression. When he recognized Lindsey, he was clearly disappointed but quickly tried to hide it.

"Sorry," she said. "You were hoping for someone else?"

"Eugenia is a bit put out with me," he said. "She'll come around . . . eventually."

"I'm sorry," Lindsey said again. Truly, she felt as if all she'd done was apologize today.

"Not your fault," he said. He gave her a stern look. "It was my idea to linger after the meeting and my bad judgment to go outside without letting you know what I was doing."

"That's not—" she protested, but he waved her off.

"Yes, it was foolish. There'd been a murder, a cold-blooded murder, and I waltzed out into the night without even considering that it could be dangerous."

"Why would you?" Lindsey entered the room and picked a pawn up from the game board. She turned it over in her fingers. "We aren't criminals. We don't think like they do. Why would you have suspected danger when by all accounts it was a person in need of aid? It's not your fault any more than it's mine."

Milton gave her a closed-lip smile. "We'll shoulder the blame together then?"

"The burden will be lighter that way," Lindsey said. She gave Milton a half hug. "I am so glad you're all right. I couldn't bear it if you'd been more seriously injured."

"Me either," he said and then laughed.

The door banged open, and members of Milton's chess club began to stream in. Lindsey waved at him as she walked back out into the library. She could feel someone watching her as she crossed the room, and she didn't have to look to know it was Ms. Cole.

Time, she assured herself, refusing to look and see the hurt or accusation in the lemon's eyes. *It was just going to take time.*

Lindsey hurried out of the library at five o'clock on the dot. Sully's truck was parked at the curb, and he hopped out to open the door for her as soon as she appeared.

Sully gave her work outfit, a skirt and heels, an appreciative look as he helped her into the truck.

"I am pretty sure librarians didn't look like you back in the day," he said. "I would have noticed."

"Mr. Tupper was your town librarian for thirty years," Lindsey said. "I'm pretty sure he never showed this much leg."

"Thank heavens," Sully said, and Lindsey chuckled.

He shut the door after her and circled around the front. It was a very short drive to the Blue Anchor, but since they had no idea if the two collectors would show up or when, they were planning to be there for the long haul, and this way Sully could take Lindsey home afterward.

They parked in the lot next to the restaurant. As the cold chased them toward the building, Lindsey could hear the sounds of voices raised in chatter and laughter. The distinct smell of the restaurant, a savory combination of fried fish, malt vinegar and lemons, greeted them on a puff of warm air as Sully hauled the door open.

He gestured for Lindsey to go first, and she led the way into the dimly lit, lively restaurant. The bar was full, save for two seats on the far end. Sully made for them, gesturing for Lindsey to follow. Lindsey scanned the tables, which were mostly full, just to be sure that Hodges and Perkins weren't already seated.

As her gaze swept the crowd, she saw Carrie Rushton enjoying dinner with Dale Wilcox. Carrie was the president of the Friends of the Library, and Dale was an ex-con. They were an unlikely pair, but since Dale was a very well-read ex-con—he had even named his boat *Pilar* after Hemingway's—they did have common ground in the bibliophile sense.

Carrie saw Lindsey and waved, and Dale gave her a nod. Lindsey waved back and returned the nod, but Sully had her hand in his and was moving toward the two seats as if they were a checkered finish line, so there was no time to chat.

Lindsey shrugged off her coat and dropped it on the back of her stool while Sully did the same.

"Sorry, I didn't mean to rush you," he said, "but I didn't want to lose prime seating."

"No, I'm with you there," she said. She slid onto her seat. The view of the front door was spot-on. "These are perfect."

"Well, now my bar is the prettiest in the state," Ian Murphy said as he swabbed down the wood in front of Lindsey and Sully.

"I try," Sully said. He ran his fingers through his dark curls and fluttered his eyelashes.

"Oh please," Ian said. "A face like that is only good for making babies cry. I was talking about Lindsey."

"Making babies cry?" Sully gave him a look of mock outrage. "That may be, but it's better than that glass shatterer you call a mug. Honestly, how my sister wakes up to that every day, I'll never know."

"All right, you two," Mary said as she joined her husband behind the bar. "We all know that once you boys get started with the insults, the pair of you can go on all night, so I'm stopping it right now."

"He's just jealous of my rugged good looks," Ian said.

"Stop," Mary said. She threw a bar rag at her husband. "Go be useful and get these two their usual."

She glanced at Lindsey and Sully to confirm, and they both nodded.

"Ian is awfully chipper today," Sully said. "Anything happening that a big brother should know about?"

"What do you mean?" Mary asked. "The man only has two emotions: happy and giddy."

"It's true," Lindsey said. "I don't think I've ever seen him in a foul mood."

"It's not in his nature," Mary said. "Which is one of the many reasons why I love him."

Sully was studying his sister with a narrowed gaze.

"What?" she asked.

Lindsey watched the two of them face off. They had the same profile, same reddish brown curls, although Mary's was much longer, and the same blue eyes that missed nothing. But the clincher was the similarity in their expressions.

They shared a way of tilting their head, of smiling more on one side than the other in a charmingly lopsided way, and of forming a vee out of their eyebrows when they frowned, sort of like they were doing now.

"What aren't you telling me?" Sully asked. He leaned forward into his sister's personal space.

"Nothing." She leaned in as well, meeting him halfway across the bar.

Lindsey was so taken with the sibling stare-off that she forgot to watch the front door. Sully and his sister reminded Lindsey a lot of her relationship with her brother Jack. He had been in town for the holidays but had gone back to Boston to finish working on a project that had gone sour in South America.

He had promised to come back to Briar Creek before jetting off to another distant spot on the globe. Since he hadn't gone anywhere, Lindsey wondered if his newfound inertia had something to do with his coworker Stella, whom she was pretty sure had been upgraded to girlfriend status.

She hoped so. She liked Stella. She had a feeling the woman knew exactly how to manage Jack and, boy, did he ever need it.

The front door swung open, and Lindsey immediately remembered why they were there. She tugged on Sully's sleeve.

"Sorry to break up the staring contest, but we need to focus," she said.

"You're right," Sully said. He dropped his gaze from Mary, who looked triumphant right up until he added, "We'll talk later, sis."

"It won't do you any good," she said. "Chef is working on his new recipe for baked stuffed scallops. I'll order it for you two if you're interested?"

"Yes, please," Sully and Lindsey said together.

Lindsey glanced back at the front of the restaurant.

"I don't think we missed anyone coming in," she said. She scanned the bar and the tables, but it looked to be the same crowd as before.

Ian returned with a glass of wine for Lindsey and a pint of beer for Sully. He opened his mouth to say something but was hailed by a customer at the other end of the bar. He hurried off, and Sully watched him with a narrowed gaze as he went.

"The two of them are up to something," Sully said.

"Such as?" Lindsey asked.

"I don't know, but I'm going to find out," he said.

CHAPTER

17

BRIAR CREEK
PUBLIC LIBRARY

Lindsey shook her head at him, and he frowned.

"Are you waving me off?" he asked.

"Yes," she said.

"But—" he began to protest, but Lindsey interrupted him.

"She's your sister, and he's your best friend," she said.

"So?" he asked.

"So, they're married and you don't get to be in the middle of it."

Sully pursed his lips. Then he gave her a pointed look and said, "You're right. I suppose it would be a lot easier to mind my own business if I had some business of my own to mind."

"What's that supposed to—" she began, but this time he interrupted.

"They're here," he said.

Lindsey glanced at the door. Sure enough, Hodges and Perkins had just walked into the restaurant and stood stomping their feet on the rubber mat while glancing around the room for an empty table.

Ian noticed Lindsey and Sully watching the two men, and he waved them over to the empty table right behind them. Ian exchanged a look with Sully, who nodded.

"Do you two even need to speak to each other to know what the other one is thinking?" she asked.

"Only to insult each other," he said.

He grinned at her, and Lindsey shook her head. With his dimples fully engaged, the handsome boat captain was pretty irresistible.

As the two collectors took their seats at the table behind them, Lindsey spun around on her stool and feigned surprise at seeing them.

"Oh, hello," she said. "Mr. Perkins and Mr. Hodges, we met at the library the other day. I'm Lindsey Norris, the director. I didn't realize you were still in town."

The men exchanged a glance, and Kevin Perkins said, "Chief Plewicki asked us to stay for a couple of days on the off chance we could help locate Stewart Rosen."

"She did?" Lindsey asked.

"Asked, ordered, six of one," Mr. Hodges began.

"Half a dozen of another," Mr. Perkins finished. He glanced at Lindsey and said, "Please, call me Kevin, and this is Calvin."

"Lindsey," she said. "And this is Sully."

The men exchanged handshakes. There was an awkward moment, and then Lindsey decided the best strategy was to go on the offensive.

"I'd like to talk to you about your work," she said. "Do you mind if we join you?"

"Please do." Kevin gestured to the available seats, and Lindsey and Sully grabbed their glasses and moved to the small square table.

"Smooth," Sully whispered in her ear as he pulled out a chair for her.

Lindsey knew he was teasing her, but she didn't care, since she'd gotten what she hoped for, which was the opportunity to find out more about the collectors' connection to the Rosen brothers.

Mary stopped by their table and took the food and drink order for the two men. She looked puzzled that Lindsey and Sully were sitting with them, but Lindsey met her gaze and shook her head to indicate that she would explain later. Mary gave her a tiny nod and headed back to the kitchen.

"So, have you managed to do any collecting while you've been here?" Lindsey asked.

"Some," Kevin said. "There's a huge barn over in Madison that was loaded with stuff."

"Including rats," Calvin said.

Lindsey shuddered. "You must meet some fascinating people in your line of work."

"A fair few," Calvin agreed. "Some are more hoarder than collector, but it's amazing what you can find when you start digging."

"What sort of things are you looking for?" Sully asked.

"I'm partial to anything manufactured in the U.S., you know, back when the U.S. was a manufacturer," Kevin said. "Mostly, I like vehicle-related items, but really anything from old pottery to tin toys. Of course, I especially love its resale value."

"And how about you, Calvin?" Lindsey asked.

"The same," he said.

He seemed reluctant to say any more, and Lindsey wasn't sure how to keep asking questions without sounding like she was interrogating him. Then she thought of Stewart possibly kidnapped or out wandering in the cold, and she realized she didn't care if she sounded belligerent.

She opened her mouth to speak, but Sully stepped on her foot. She turned to look at him, and he gave her a cautious look. She wanted to huff out an impatient breath, but she respected him enough to listen to his advice even when it squashed her toes.

"I imagine you'll find items of value here. The heyday for

the Thumb Islands was the turn of the century," Sully said. "Most of the islands had small Victorian houses on them until the hurricane of nineteen thirty-eight hit and wiped most of them clean."

Both men studied Sully closely, and Kevin asked, "Are you a native?"

"Yep, I'm a Creeker," Sully said with a small smile. He then went on to tell the men a shortened version of the same spiel he gave when he took people out on his Thumb Island boat tour. Lindsey watched him talking and realized he was building a rapport with the two men, getting them to trust him so they would be more open to answering their questions.

"Did you grow up in the town or on the islands?" Calvin asked.

"I grew up on Bell Island."

"The one with three houses on it?" Calvin asked.

"That's it," he said. "My parents still live there."

"Our parents," Mary said. She hefted her tray onto a nearby stand and dished out their dinners.

"My sister, Mary," Sully said by way of introduction. Both men nodded at her in greeting.

"Have they lived there long?" Kevin asked. "I mean, it must get a bit claustrophobic living on an island."

Sully and Mary exchanged a look, and then they both shook their heads.

"You get used to it," Mary said. "Well, in our case we were raised there, so we didn't know anything else. I think so long as you have a boat, you're good. With Briar Creek right here, it's not much different than driving your car into town."

"Back in the day, way before our time, there was a grocery store, a movie theater and even a bowling alley on Watson's Island," Sully said.

"I would have loved to have seen that," Lindsey said.

"Watson's is the large, flat one in the center of the archipelago, isn't it?" Kevin asked.

"Yes," Mary said. "That woman Evelyn Dewhurst has been trying to buy it, but the Travers family won't sell it. Their grandfather ran the grocery store, so even though the buildings are long gone, they are sentimentally attached to it."

Lindsey could tell by Mary's sympathetic tone that she was on the family's side. She glanced at the others to see if they noticed. Sully and Kevin looked at Mary in understanding, but Calvin looked . . . odd. Lindsey studied him a bit longer than was polite, because she couldn't quite get a read on his expression.

As if he sensed her stare, he turned to look at her, and when his gaze met hers, she gave him a small smile and looked away. As she did, she realized that he looked anxious. Now why would that be?

"We've heard about Mrs. Dewhurst," Kevin said. He paused to put his napkin in his lap and pick up his fork. "The officer who took our statement mentioned her. He seemed to think her contribution to the islands is exceptionally generous."

"Well, she is preserving the islands that have fallen into disrepair," Sully said. "She's given new life to several of them."

"But at what cost?" Mary asked. "Islands that have been in the same families for generations are losing their history."

"I don't know," Kevin said. "I buy up the old and worn out, refurbish it and sell it to people who value it. I sort of see where she's coming from."

"Except she's not selling any of them," Mary said. "She's collecting them like they're dishes or cars or jewels."

"That is different," Kevin said. He glanced at his partner. "Can you imagine if we kept everything we bought?"

"We'd be buried alive," Calvin grunted. "Like a pair of crusty old hoarders."

Kevin laughed. Lindsey had a feeling it was the sort of joke only a collector could appreciate.

"How do the remaining islanders feel about her buying the islands and fixing them up?" Kevin asked.

"Mixed," Sully said. "Most won't sell, but some are happy to unload the tax burden."

"I've heard the taxes are outrageous," Kevin said.

"And how," Mary agreed. "Living on the shoreline in Connecticut doesn't come cheap."

Kevin nodded while Calvin studied his plate.

"If you need anything else give a holler," Mary said, and she shifted her tray under her arm and headed back to the kitchen.

They all tucked into their food, and it was a few minutes before anyone spoke.

"What will happen to the Rosen property if the missing brother doesn't turn up?" Calvin asked. "Would they declare him dead?"

Lindsey took a sip of her wine to brace herself. She didn't want to think about the possibility that Stewart might be dead. It was completely unacceptable to her that he might never be seen again.

"There have been some rumors that he was seen," Sully said. "So I don't think they'll be declaring him dead anytime soon, but the police are keeping it pretty quiet, so it's hard to know what to think."

Lindsey looked from Sully to the others and nodded, as if she was agreeing when actually she was just avoiding answering.

"Speak of the devil," Sully said.

She saw Kevin glance past her, and she turned to follow his gaze.

In the doorway stood Evelyn Dewhurst. She glanced around the restaurant until her eyes fell on their table, and then she strode forward, looking cheerfully determined.

CHAPTER

18

BRIAR CREEK
PUBLIC LIBRARY

Her blond bob was as sleek as water, and a diamond-encrusted bracelet sparkled on her wrist. Other than that she was all in black. High-heeled black boots, a luxurious black wool coat and a black cashmere scarf. She looked as if she'd be more at home striding down Fifth Avenue in Manhattan than here.

Evelyn crossed the room as if she owned it. Not a big surprise, as she could probably afford to buy the Blue Anchor one hundred times over. Lindsey felt a burst of thanks that Evelyn didn't seem to be interested in acquiring restaurants.

"Hello!" Evelyn waved her black leather gloves at them.

Lindsey glanced at Sully. Undoubtedly, Evelyn was looking to book his taxi again. She wondered how he felt about that and if Evelyn was as touchy-feely with Sully as she had been when Lindsey met her.

As Evelyn drew closer, her light blue gaze fastened on Lindsey. Evelyn wrinkled her nose at her as if Lindsey were a cute little puppy, and Lindsey felt the hair on the back of her neck prickle. She knew with her librarian's intuition that Evelyn was coming for her.

She set down her fork and put on her best people-pleasing smile.

"Ms. Norris, Lindsey, just the woman I wanted to see," Evelyn said.

"Good to see you again, Mrs. Dewhurst," Lindsey said. She put her napkin beside her plate and stood. "Allow me to introduce my dinner companions."

"Of course," Evelyn said. She looped her arm through Lindsey's and pressed herself against Lindsey's side. It was clear that she couldn't care less who Lindsey was dining with and was just being polite, sort of.

"Sully, you already know," Lindsey said. "And this is Kevin Perkins and Calvin Hodges. They own a collectibles business in the Chicago area."

The men all rose at the mention of their names and nodded at Evelyn, but Sully was the only one to remain standing after the introductions.

"A pleasure," Evelyn said. She didn't spare so much as a glance at the collectors but kept her grip on Lindsey.

"Would you care to join us?" Lindsey asked. She thought it might be the only way to get Evelyn to let go of her; then again, Evelyn might sit in her lap.

"Thank you, no," Evelyn said. "My driver is waiting. I just popped in, hoping that I'd find you here."

"What can I do for you?" Lindsey asked.

She noted that Kevin and Calvin weren't eating but were watching them as if it were a dinner theater production and they had front-row seats.

"I want to know where Stewart Rosen is," Evelyn said.

"I believe we all do," Lindsey said.

"But *you* know where he is," Evelyn said.

Lindsey didn't like the tone the woman was using. It was conspiratorial, as if she thought Lindsey knew something and was keeping it a secret. Maybe it was her guilty conscience because she had seen Stewart, but Lindsey felt her temper kicking in.

Sully was watching her from behind Evelyn. He moved his head from side to side, indicating that she should not say anything, or maybe it was to warn her against losing her temper. She knew both were excellent suggestions, and still, she desperately wanted to shake him off.

"Why do you say that?" Lindsey asked. She was pleased that her voice sounded even and not snarky. Evelyn still held her in a tight grip, and Lindsey couldn't figure out how to extricate herself from the woman's hold.

"Because you are the only person he allowed onto the island," Evelyn said. "Clearly, you know more than you're saying, and since the police seem reluctant to demand the information from you, I will."

Evelyn gave her arm a rallying squeeze, and she wrinkled her nose again, as though if she packaged her demand in cuteness, Lindsey would be unable to refuse.

Manners and fury had a duke-out in Lindsey's gut. Fury won.

"Are you accusing me of something?" Lindsey snapped. She pulled her arm out of Evelyn's hold and crossed her arms over her chest.

Evelyn drew herself up to her full height, which topped out at Lindsey's nose. One of her eyebrows ticked higher on her forehead in a look that said she did not approve of Lindsey's attitude.

"I want to buy the Rosen house," Evelyn said. "It is one of the last original buildings from the turn of the century. I must have it. I must. And I need Stewart Rosen in order to get it."

Lindsey noticed the entire restaurant had grown quiet as everyone was blatantly eavesdropping on their conversation. She decided she didn't like Evelyn. The woman could try to hide behind cuteness all she liked, but Lindsey had her number. She saw the glint in Evelyn's eyes. Owning the islands, all of the islands, had become a thing for her. She was collecting them like the Rosens had collected toasters or *National Geographic* magazines or whatever else caught their interest. It occurred to Lindsey that Evelyn's avarice for the islands was not unlike the Rosens' hoarding.

"Well then you'd better hope nothing bad has happened to Stewart," Lindsey said. "Or you'll never own that house. Never."

Evelyn looked as if Lindsey had slapped her. It was a mean thing to say. Lindsey knew that. She wasn't proud of herself. She had seen exactly where to stab the word knife into Evelyn's avaricious heart, and she had done it and twisted it without any remorse.

"What are you saying? Is he dead? What do you know?" Evelyn demanded. She looked panicked.

"I don't know anything," Lindsey said, "but it's a fact that estate paperwork can really jam up a property sale. It's all so much easier if the seller and buyer come to an agreement, don't you think?"

Evelyn pulled her coat more closely about her rail-thin body. "Of course, it is my fondest wish that Stewart be found so that I can offer him top dollar for his home."

No one at the table spoke, and Lindsey knew she wasn't the only one thinking that Evelyn Dewhurst could care less about paying top dollar. She wanted the island, and Lindsey suspected she would do anything to get it, perhaps even murder.

"I'm sure it is," Lindsey said. Her voice was thick with sarcasm, but if Evelyn heard it, she didn't show it.

She stared at Lindsey. Her face was impassive, and Lindsey realized she had no idea what Evelyn was thinking. Being a librarian, Lindsey did her share of studying people as she tried to help them find what they needed. All too often people attempted to make her job easy for her by keeping the information vague, like the time a man asked for a book about angel dust and came back to her after she sent him into the illegal drug section. Then he told her that he was sure it was about an Irish immigrant, at which point Lindsey handed him a copy of *Angela's Ashes*, which was what he had wanted all along.

She could usually tell when a patron withheld information or was operating on sketchy facts, and she'd gotten pretty good at gently prying details out of them. Looking at Evelyn now, however, she couldn't even hazard a guess as to what the woman was thinking. Evelyn blinked.

"Well, if you see Mr. Rosen, please tell him I'm looking for him," Evelyn said. She didn't grab Lindsey's arm or wrinkle her nose or anything. Instead, she simply turned on her heel and left.

"She's . . . interesting," Kevin said as Lindsey and Sully resumed their seats. It was obvious he was trying to be diplomatic.

"I suspect she's the sort who's never heard the word *no*," Calvin said. "Do you think Stewart will sell to her?"

"Assuming that he turns up," Lindsey began but then paused. She thought about the shell of a man she had fed soup to the night before. She had no idea what Stewart would do. "I honestly don't know."

They finished their meal with limited conversation that revolved around weather, sports and local politics. She didn't get the feeling that either of the collectors knew where Stewart was. In fact, Calvin seemed particularly concerned about the older man.

"I hope he's all right," he said. "I really enjoyed corresponding with his brother, Peter, about their different collections."

"How were you in touch?" Lindsey asked. "I mean, how did you find each other?"

"After we met in an online auction, he wrote an email to our shop," Calvin said.

Lindsey and Sully exchanged a glance. Lindsey knew he was thinking the same thing she was: that they hadn't seen any computers or high-tech gadgets in the Rosen house when they were in it, so how was it Peter had been using email?

"We get a lot of that," Kevin said. He glanced between Lindsey and Sully, clearly misinterpreting their look as one of confusion. He explained, "People contact us looking for rare and specialty items or looking to sell them to us. We do a ton of business online."

"Was Peter interested in buying or selling?" Sully asked.

"Peter inquired about the value of mechanical banks, which is one of my interests," Calvin said. "So, I answered him. We've been writing back and forth for several months now."

"Do you have the emails with you?" Lindsey asked.

"I have them saved on my laptop, and I printed the one where he invited me for a visit," Calvin said. "So Peter would know it was really me when I showed up."

"Did you show them to the chief of police?" Sully asked.

"I forwarded them to the chief," Calvin said. He looked uncomfortable. "I'm still surprised they didn't clear us to leave town after that. There really wasn't anything other than shoptalk in the emails."

"He's right, and I'm worried about the shop," Kevin said. "Our employees are great, but they're only part-time, so our hours have been dicey since we've been gone. We need to get back. Maybe we should stop by the station tomorrow and ask more specifically when we'll be able to leave."

"I should think you'd be cleared soon," Sully said. "I have part-time workers, too, for the summer's busy season. I can't manage without them but can't afford full-time, especially in winter."

They went on to compare small business operations in each of their towns. Kevin was boggled by the taxes Connecticut residents pay.

"If they hit us that hard, we'd have to shut down," he said.

"Location, location, location," Sully said.

Mary came by and asked if anyone wanted dessert. They

all declined. Lindsey had tried to do justice to her meal, but she was still sick with worry about Stewart and she knew she'd get no peace until he was found alive and well.

Sully drove Lindsey home. As soon as Sully climbed into the truck, she started analyzing what they'd learned.

"Email? Why does it seem weird to me that Peter Rosen was sending email?" she asked.

"Because the brothers were hermits, because they didn't socialize with anyone in town never mind out of town, because there was no evidence of any computers or cell phones or tablets or whatnot in their house," Sully said. "Frankly, it just never occurred to me that the Rosens might be surfing the Internet."

"I know," Lindsey said. She thought about Mrs. Garabowski and her issues with social media. "It just doesn't feel right, does it?"

"No, but then that seems judgmental," Sully said.

"Do you realize what this means?" Lindsey asked.

"Yes, that we have no idea who Peter Rosen was in touch with, making the list of suspects who ventured to the island to murder him longer than we imagined," Sully said. He sounded discouraged.

"Especially since we have no idea how he was on the Internet," Lindsey said. "Do you think Emma has found a computer or cell phone or anything?"

"She hasn't mentioned it to me, but she must be thinking like we are," he said. "Of course, there's always the possibility that it wasn't Peter."

"What do you mean?"

"What if it was just someone posing as Peter?" Sully asked. "What if someone was conning the collectors?"

"You mean like catfishing them?" she asked. "Using the Internet to pretend they're someone they're not?"

"Makes more sense to me than Peter using the Internet," Sully said.

"But who would do that and why?" Lindsey asked.

"I don't know, but I think it's safe to say that it cost Peter Rosen his life," Sully said. He blew out a breath as if he really didn't want to say what came next. "It could have been Stewart."

"Stewart?" Lindsey asked. "I don't see that just like I don't see him as Peter's killer."

"Me neither," Sully agreed. "But his disappearance when Peter was murdered looks terribly suspicious, plus he's wandered the town at night for years. Who knows what he's been exposed to or learned in all that time."

"Maybe," Lindsey said. "But it could be that he disappeared to escape the killer."

"Or he's out looking for Peter's murderer himself."

Lindsey gave Sully a worried look.

"What sort of vibe did Stewart give off when you saw him?" he asked.

"Mostly cold, tired and a little crazy," she said.

"So, the usual," Sully said.

"No, a little more crazy than usual with the humming and the no speaking," Lindsey said. "It hurt to see him like that when I have worked so hard to get him to trust me."

Sully reached across the truck and took her hand in his. She hadn't put her gloves on, and it felt good to have his warm hand wrap around her chilled fingers.

"He's going to be all right," he said.

She wanted to believe him. She really did. He didn't let go of her hand for the rest of the drive. His thumb ran across hers in a soothing way, and Lindsey tried to take comfort in the gesture.

"Do you know what I can't figure out?" she asked.

"What?"

"Why Hodges and Perkins? Why did Peter, or whoever was pretending to be Peter, pick a company that was so far away?" she asked.

"That makes me think it was someone posing as Peter,"

he said. "If it was Peter or Stewart, wouldn't they go with someone local for sheer convenience if nothing else?"

"You would think," Lindsey agreed.

Sully let go of her hand to navigate the turn into her driveway, and Lindsey felt the loss of his warmth immediately. The heater in the pickup truck was blowing a nice hot breath across her feet, so it wasn't his physical warmth that she missed but rather the warmth of human contact when the world seemed a chilling place.

Sully parked and then turned to face her. "But if it was Peter, why would he reach out now? Was he out of money? Was he suddenly tired of just having his brother for company? And again, why choose two collectors who are so far away and not local? None of this makes sense."

"Maybe he wanted them to be far away so that they wouldn't know about him or his brother or the fact that he lived on an island," Lindsey said.

"Again, why?"

"No idea," she sighed.

Lindsey pondered the question while Sully exited the cab of the truck. It was too cold out to have him open the door for her, so she opened it herself and hopped down from the truck, meeting him halfway so they could get into the warm house faster.

Sully took her elbow and led her up onto the porch. The door didn't bang open, and no Heathcliff appeared, wagging his tail off. Lindsey didn't know what to make of that, and she felt horribly guilty for being out late again. She made a mental promise to take the boy on a big walk the next morning.

"Thanks for dinner and the ride and being my wingman in the unofficial interrogation," she said.

"My pleasure," Sully said. "I wish we could have found out something a little more concrete."

"We will," Lindsey said. She hoped she sounded more confident than she felt.

Lindsey glanced at the door again. Whenever Heathcliff stayed with Nancy, he would burst through the front door the minute Lindsey stepped onto the porch to greet her as if she'd been away for weeks instead of hours. Nancy said he had a sixth sense and usually started getting excited a few minutes before Lindsey arrived.

"Where is our buddy?" Sully asked. He was frowning at the door as well.

"He should have come out by now," Lindsey said. "You don't think anything happened to him and Nancy, do you?"

Sully looked grim. He studied the door. "There's no sign of a break-in."

"Maybe it's unlocked."

Sully crossed the porch and turned the knob. It didn't budge. Lindsey dug her keys out of her purse. Her fingers were shaking, so she handed the keys to Sully. He unlocked the door and pushed it open. Lindsey led the way, feeling her anxiety spike as she was swamped by the feeling that something was terribly wrong.

"Maybe it was a gas leak and they're unconscious," she said. She sniffed the air by the door, but she didn't detect anything.

"Or maybe Nancy took him for a walk," Sully countered, more reasonably.

"This late?" Lindsey asked, a note of hysteria in her voice.

Sully handed her keys back as they stepped into the foyer and approached Nancy's door. It was unlocked, and he rapped on it twice before turning the knob and pushing it open. The entry was quiet. Nancy's apartment was dark except for one lamp by the gas fireplace, which was lit.

"Nancy!" Sully called out, They waited but there was no answer. Lindsey could feel alarm bells ringing in her head. Then she heard a soft bark and then someone saying *Shhh*.

"Nancy? Are you here?" she called.

There was the sound of a door opening in the back of the apartment, and Nancy and Heathcliff appeared. Heathcliff looked like he was going to wag his tail off as he greeted first Lindsey and then Sully. He gave a happy bark and spun around.

"Nancy, is everything okay?" Sully asked.

Nancy gave him a dark look.

"Nancy, do you need me to call Charlie?" he asked.

"No," she snapped. "What I needed was for you to take advantage of the moment and kiss the girl before this one here jumped all over you, but did you? No."

She waved her hands dismissively at him, and Sully looked at her in shock.

"You kept him in the back bedroom just so I could make a move?" he asked.

"That was the general idea, yes," she said.

Sully burst out laughing. Lindsey felt embarrassment heat up her face like a blowtorch on high.

"Nancy!" she protested. "You had us worried sick."

"Sorry, Heathcliff and I were in on it together until you called out, and then he just lost it." Nancy gave the dog a chagrined look.

"Thanks for dog sitting him," Lindsey said. Then, just because she was relieved, she gave Nancy a quick hug. "You're impossible."

"So I've been told." Nancy hugged her back.

"Come on. I'll walk you up," Sully said. Lindsey and Heathcliff led the way, and Sully followed. As they started up the stairs, he added, "Which was what I planned to do anyway, so I could kiss you good night."

Lindsey stumbled on the steps, and Sully caught her from behind, putting her back on her feet.

"Did you catch that, Nancy?" he called down the stairs.

"Yes, and it's about time," she said. "Hurrah!"

Lindsey heard Nancy's door slam as they passed by Charlie's apartment and headed up to hers. If she had felt embarrassed before, now she was quite sure she would die of mortification. It was one thing if they had been on a date and Sully kissed her at the end of it because they both wanted to; it was another to have her landlady trying to orchestrate a good night smooch.

She unlocked her door, and Heathcliff darted in, heading straight for his basket of toys. Lindsey glanced up at Sully, and that was as far as she got before he had her backed up against the wall with his lips on hers. Wow, just wow.

By the time Sully and Lindsey broke apart, Heathcliff had managed to bring out each and every single toy from his basket. They were both breathing hard, and Sully had a wicked twinkle in his eye.

"I didn't want you to have time to overthink it," he said. Then he winked at her, and Lindsey felt her knees buckle. She leaned against the wall, trying to appear nonchalant.

"Well played," she said.

His grin deepened. He picked up two of Heathcliff's toys and tossed them back into the apartment, sending the happy dog off in pursuit.

Lindsey wondered if she should invite Sully in. Was she ready to try again? Was he? Judging by his kiss, she'd say he was.

"I'm going out to the island Monday morning," Sully said. "I can't go tomorrow because the water taxi is booked solid."

Lindsey blinked at the abrupt subject change. "Huh? What?"

"I'm going to go out and see if I can find anything Peter could have used to write emails," he said. "Maybe we missed it the first time, given that we were busy with a dead body, an explosion and a fire."

"Emma is not going to let you do that," Lindsey said. "It's a crime scene, and the house is booby-trapped. You could get hurt or killed or worse."

"So, you don't want to go with me?" he asked.

"Go with you?" she repeated. "You're okay with that?"

"You left your box of books out there, didn't you?" he asked. "I was thinking that would be our excuse to go, as I could help you retrieve them."

"That's genius," she said.

Heathcliff reappeared with his toys, and this time Lindsey scooped up a couple of them and threw them inside.

"I thought you'd like it."

"Are you kidding? If you hadn't already kissed me senseless, I'd kiss you again," she said.

"I really don't see what's stopping you," he said.

He picked up the rest of Heathcliff's toys and tossed them into the apartment. Lindsey laughed as she grabbed Sully by the jacket and pulled him close so she could show him exactly what she meant.

I t was a miserably cold day. Lindsey huddled into her coat, pulling her scarf up over her nose. She glanced at the pewter sky, the barren trees along the coast and the fathomless water surrounding their small boat. Today was definitely the sort of day that signaled winter was not letting New England out of its icy grip anytime soon.

Sully maneuvered the boat through the islands at a slow pace, keeping the boat's wake to a minimum. Lindsey was in the seat beside his while Officer Kirkland sat on the bench at the back of the boat.

Getting Chief Plewicki to agree to let them go back out to the island had required some fast-talking on Lindsey's part along with the latest Deborah Crombie novel. Emma was a crime fiction junkie, and Lindsey had her short-listed for any bestselling police procedurals that came in. Lindsey considered it maintaining healthy interdepartmental relations to keep the chief happy, especially since her broken leg was making her a bit cranky.

Emma had finally agreed to let her retrieve her books on

Monday morning, but only after insisting that Officer Kirkland go with them. The newest officer on the force, Kirkland looked almost giddy to be going back out to the scene of the crime.

"You all right, Kirkland?" Sully called as he made his approach to Star Island.

"Yes, sir," Kirkland said.

"Great, then get up on the bow and prepare to jump," Sully said.

Kirkland's eyes bugged, and Sully laughed.

"On the dock," he clarified.

"Oh, right, on it!" Kirkland bounded from his seat and slid past Lindsey to climb around onto the bow.

As Sully gently slid into the dock, Kirkland hopped down, taking the boat's bow line with him and tying it off while Sully cut the engine. Lindsey hopped out next and tied the boat's stern line, securing the boat for their visit.

Lindsey glanced down the dock and noticed that Stewart's boat wasn't there. She felt a pang of disappointment but shook it off. It was better that it wasn't here, as maybe it meant he was still alive. Then again, if it was here it might mean he was in the house, and she would really like to see him to reassure herself that he was okay.

Officer Kirkland led the way up the stairs to the landing above. It was still crowded with junk. Lindsey exchanged a look with Sully. She was feeling overwhelmed by what they were trying to accomplish, and she wondered if he felt the same.

Officer Kirkland went to step down into the yard, and Sully stopped him with a hand on his arm.

"I think I should take point," he said. "I've been here before and know where to look for the traps."

Kirkland shook his head. "With all due respect, my job is to protect and serve. You're a civilian now, and although I respect your military background, I can't put you in harm's way."

Lindsey shivered as a cold draft shot up the back of her

coat and made her shake. She wondered how long this would go on before one of them gave in.

"I appreciate that, but I have actual frontline training that will be more useful than a few weeks at the police academy," Sully said. He sounded irritated.

"I graduated top of my class," Kirkland argued. "I can handle myself here, and more importantly, my job is to ensure the safety of both you and Ms. Norris—Ms. Norris?"

He whipped his head around the landing, looking at all the junk as if Lindsey might suddenly peek out at him.

Sully glanced over his shoulder, but when Lindsey wasn't there, he did a three-sixty, spinning around looking for her not unlike Heathcliff when he chased his tail.

"I'm over here, boys," Lindsey called from the porch at the house.

As one, their heads snapped in her direction, and she waved. Kirkland looked relieved. Sully looked annoyed. Lindsey didn't care. The house broke the wind, and she was much warmer over here than she'd been over there while they argued.

"Don't move," Sully said. He led the way across the yard, leaving Kirkland to follow. Obviously, the debate was over.

The third step had been boarded over, so that it couldn't collapse on anyone. Still, both Sully and Kirkland stepped over it just as Lindsey had done.

"Just because the police have been here and have thoroughly investigated the house doesn't mean it's safe," Sully said. He gave Lindsey a hard glance. "Stewart could have come back and reset a lot of his traps."

"I was very careful," she said. But she couldn't deny his point. "But I won't take that risk again."

"Thank you," he said.

Kirkland glanced between them and said nothing. Lindsey could tell by the look on his face that he thought this was a relationship thing. She had to fight not to roll her eyes.

She gestured to the spot on the porch where her crate of books had been. It was bare.

"The books aren't here," she said. "I'm pretty sure that's where we left them, although I'm not completely certain."

"What do you think happened to them?" Kirkland asked.

Lindsey shook her head. "Emma confirmed that no one from your department picked them up, so I guess . . ."

"Someone took them, or perhaps they brought them inside," Sully said. "The question is, who?"

CHAPTER

20

BRIAR CREEK
PUBLIC LIBRARY

Lindsey didn't want to say it out loud.

"Stewart Rosen," Officer Kirkland said. He stepped forward as if he would charge the house, but Sully put his hand on his arm, stopping him.

"Or the person who killed Peter Rosen," he said.

"Which could be Stewart," Kirkland argued.

"Either of whom could be in there waiting right now," Sully said.

Kirkland's shoulders sagged. "Right."

Sully took charge. He examined the door and noted that the trap hasn't been reset and there didn't appear to be a new one in its place.

"Stay close and step where I step," he said.

"Ms. Norris, you'll wait out here," Kirkland said.

Before Lindsey could say anything, Sully barked out a laugh. She raised her eyebrows at him, and he looked duly chastised.

"Sorry," he said to her. He turned to Kirkland. "You don't have much experience with librarians, do you?"

"Sure I do," he said. "Mrs. Capshaw was our school librarian, and she was very clear that libraries are places of higher learning. She liked quiet and order, and she read a lot."

Lindsey glanced around him at Sully and said, "It's like he's talking about libraries from the Stone Age."

"What, did I get it wrong?" Kirkland asked.

"Libraries aren't really known for being that quiet anymore," Lindsey said. "Too much going on. And while higher learning is awesome, we're also the place where you can learn how to actually do stuff like knit, fix a car, build an ultralight airplane, you know—whatever you can think of, we can find the directions."

"Ah," he said. "I need to visit the library more often."

Lindsey nodded in approval.

"And although librarians like order, they're also curious like cats," Sully said. "Lindsey, here, might expire from inquisitiveness if we don't let her inside with us."

"Really?" Kirkland asked.

"It's a serious condition." Lindsey nodded.

"Practically a disorder," Sully said. Lindsey frowned at him.

"Well, okay, then," Kirkland said. "But we stay together. This place has all the makings of a B movie horror film."

"Remember, step where I step, and if I say get down, jump up, or put your left foot in and shake it all about, do it without question," Sully said. "Agreed?"

"Yes," Kirkland and Lindsey said together.

Sully gingerly pushed the door open. Nothing jumped out or swung down at them. Still, Lindsey found herself crouching low, half expecting the board with the nails to be coming at her eyes.

The three of them huddled in the foyer. It was cold and dark and so full of boxes and junk that Lindsey had a hard time getting her eyes to adjust to the gloom.

"I'm not sure where to begin looking," she said.

She knew that Sully knew she was talking about a source for Peter's emails, while Kirkland would be thinking she was talking about her box of books.

"We'll just have to take it room by room," Kirkland said.

Lindsey wasn't positive, but she suspected he was chomping at the bit to investigate this house without Detective Trimble or Chief Plewicki breathing down his neck.

She glanced at Sully and saw him looking at Kirkland with the same speculation she was feeling. He glanced at her and nodded. This could definitely work in their favor.

They turned into the first room, and Lindsey felt a surge of claustrophobia kick in. The towering piles of old clothes, yellowed newspapers, stacks of dishes and flattened cereal boxes made her eyeball the piles as if they would topple down at any moment and crush her under their weight.

She had to force herself to keep following Sully, who moved meticulously through the room, scanning the piles from top to bottom. They were halfway through the room when Lindsey realized that somewhere under all of these piles there must be furniture. She wondered how it was holding up under the weight of so much stuff. When she got home she was going to sort her linen closet just to make herself feel better.

"The Rosens have their own power source as well as an electrical line, don't they?" she asked.

Sully glanced back at her over his shoulder. "Yes, the house runs on a combination of sources."

Lindsey nodded. If Peter was using a tablet, laptop, desktop or smartphone, he would need to plug it in at some point, which would mean access to an outlet, which was generally found in the wall. She glanced around the aisle of space they stood in. She couldn't even see the wall, never mind find an outlet.

"I don't see it in here," she said. She was hoping to get their little train moving to the next room, where maybe it wasn't so crowded with stuff.

Sully glanced at her face and reached back and squeezed her hand. She wondered if he could tell just by looking at her that she was having a hard time breathing in here.

"All right," he said. "Let's see what's in the next room."

They moved forward, but it was slow going, and Lindsey knew Sully was still looking for any traps that had been set. Doorways seemed especially worrisome to him, and he paused in front of the entrance to the next room.

He knelt down to examine the doorframe. "Kirkland, do you have a light?"

"Always," he answered, and he unstrapped a small flashlight from his belt.

"Shine it down here, would you?"

"Here, take my spot," Lindsey said, and she and Kirkland maneuvered around each other so that he was behind Sully.

"All right," Kirkland said as he leaned down and aimed his flashlight where Sully directed. He was quiet for a moment and then he asked, "Is that a trip wire?"

"'Fraid so," Sully said.

"Why do I get the feeling that wire will do more than trip you?" Kirkland asked.

"Because it's set up so that if you do trip you land right on the gnome statue holding the spear and impale yourself," Sully said.

"The what?" Lindsey moved so she could glance between the two men's heads. Sure enough, a few feet into the next room stood a three-foot statue of a gleeful-looking gnome, which was doing sentry duty while holding a very sharp, very lethal-looking spear.

"Well, that's not very friendly," Kirkland said.

Lindsey shuddered. She couldn't imagine having the last sight she ever saw be a red-capped, white-bearded gnome grinning at her just before being gutted by him.

"No, it isn't," Sully agreed. "Especially since this wasn't here before."

"What do you mean?" Kirkland asked.

"Emma said that when the investigation team went through the house, they disabled everything," he said. "There is no way they would have missed this."

"So Stewart came back," Lindsey said. She glanced around, hoping to see her wily friend.

"Maybe, or whoever murdered Peter, assuming it wasn't Stewart, came back and set this up, possibly to kill Stewart," Sully said.

All three of them were silent as they thought over this information.

"Can we just step over the wire?" Kirkland asked.

"I'm checking," Sully said. "I'd rather cut it to be on the safe side, but I want to be sure there aren't any other nasty surprises attached to it."

Lindsey held her breath as he checked out the invisible fishing line that was strung just a few inches above the floor from one side of the door to the other. When he rose to stand and took a step over the wire, she felt her whole body tense up.

She pressed her fingers against her mouth to keep herself from shouting for him to stop and instead held her breath, knowing full well that it did nothing to help him, and yet she couldn't seem to force herself to breathe. Not yet.

Once he was on the other side, Sully crouched low and examined the line. He took a pocket knife out of his jacket pocket and opened up the scissors feature.

"I want you two to back up and take cover just in case," he said.

"Whoa, whoa, whoa," Kirkland said. "Can't we just step over it like you did?"

"We can't risk forgetting about it and getting caught by it later," Sully said.

"Good point," Kirkland said.

He and Lindsey moved back the way they had come until Sully nodded. Lindsey noted that Kirkland blocked her with his body, which she thought was unnecessarily gallant of him and a little annoying since she was trying to see what Sully was doing.

She heard Kirkland heave out a pent-up breath, and she figured Sully had just cut the wire. Nothing happened. No knives were launched at their heads, no fireballs flew at them. Instead it was eerily quiet.

Kirkland rose, and Lindsey moved around him to see Sully. He met her gaze and pursed his lips as if to say *phew*. Lindsey felt her heart start beating again, and she sagged a little in relief.

Creak.

The noise came from directly above them and sounded just like a person stepping on a loose floorboard. Lindsey felt the back of her neck prickle with unease.

"I'm thinking we have company," Kirkland said, and he put his hand on his department-issued Glock.

Lindsey glanced up at the ceiling. There was another creak, and this time it was followed by the sound of something being dragged across the floor. Uh-oh.

CHAPTER

21

BRIAR CREEK
PUBLIC LIBRARY

Lindsey felt her heart leap up into her throat. At first, she was giddy, hoping it was Stewart, but then she remembered his boat hadn't been at the dock. Either he was keeping the boat elsewhere or this wasn't Stewart.

She glanced at Sully. His head was cocked to the side as he listened. Kirkland looked about to say something, and Sully put up his index finger, indicating quiet for the moment.

Kirkland nodded, and they all stood still, listening. There was another creak and then the heavy tread of what was most definitely a person stepping across the floor above them.

"There's definitely someone up there," Kirkland said. He looked as if he was about to pull his piece out of its holster, but Sully put his hand on his arm, stopping him.

"Wait," he said. "We don't want any accidents until we know for certain what we're dealing with."

"But—" Kirkland began to protest, but Sully shook him off.

"Trust me," he said.

Kirkland nodded and left his weapon on his hip.

"We have to play this very smart," Sully whispered. "We can't go up the stairs because the path is so narrow with all of the stuff on the steps that if it is the person who murdered Peter, they'll be able to pick us off from above as easy as one, two, three."

Lindsey did not love this description.

"We need to draw them down here, then," Kirkland said.

"No." Sully shook his head. "This is not someone who is going to join the party if he hears us down here. This is someone who is going to jump through a window to get away from us if need be."

"So, we're just going to wait down here?" Kirkland sounded horrified by the idea.

"Consider it a stakeout," Sully said.

Kirkland's frown cleared up at that.

"We're going to need to spread out to cover the downstairs so that he doesn't slip past us."

"What about Lindsey?" Kirkland asked. "She's a civilian. I don't feel right about putting her in harm's way."

"She won't be," Sully said. He turned to look at Lindsey, who had opened her mouth to protest. "No. No arguing. You're going to wait outside and act as a lookout."

"But—" Lindsey argued, but Sully shook her off.

"Remember what happened to Emma," he said.

Lindsey blew out a breath. She would never forget finding Emma under that table or the pain the chief had been in when they had moved her downstairs. Bad pun or not, she knew she didn't have a leg to stand on to argue her case with Sully.

The sound of footsteps moving across the floor above caused the three of them to glance up as one. The sound of something heavy being dragged right over their heads made Lindsey freeze, and she noticed the others did, too.

She wondered what could make such a noise, and then she felt her insides grow cold with the realization that it could be anything in this house, even a body.

Sully put his finger to his lips and motioned for Kirkland and Lindsey to follow him. They wound their way back to the front door as silently as possible. When they got there, however, it looked different.

It took Lindsey a second to realize that the door that they had found unlocked and had left open was now shut. Sully realized it, too, as he motioned for them to stop while he checked the door and the area around it for traps.

The noise from above was fainter here, but Lindsey could still hear the occasional bang and thump. She kept glancing over her shoulder for fear that someone was about to spring out at her, but there was never anyone there.

Satisfied that there was no trap, Sully reached forward and turned the knob on the door handle. It turned, but the door didn't budge. He frowned and tried again. He put his weight into it, but it didn't move. He crouched down to peer through the panel of the old window that had been covered with aluminum foil but that Lindsey had peeled back the last time they were here.

He blew out a breath of exasperation. "It's blocked. Someone blocked it with that old abandoned refrigerator out there."

Sully glanced over his shoulder at them, and Lindsey could see the truth of the situation in his eyes. They were locked in.

A crash followed by muted cursing sounded, and Kirkland jumped. This time when he put his hand on his gun, Sully didn't stop him.

"He could be on his way down," Kirkland said in a low voice. "We can't linger here."

Sully nodded. He scanned the area and took Lindsey's hand in his. He wedged her into a tiny space beside a coatrack that was buried beneath a pile of coats and scarves and carried the pungent odor of the inside of a barn.

"You're the last line of defense," he said. "If he gets past Kirkland and me, I'd like for you to use your phone to call the police and not try to take him out yourself."

Lindsey nodded, and Sully gave her a dubious look. "You've been very lucky in the past with some of the unsavory characters you've run into, but remember that this person murdered a man in a wheelchair. That takes a special kind of sociopath, don't you think?"

Lindsey shivered. Sully was right. Whoever murdered Peter Rosen had no conscience at all. They had likely killed Stewart as well, and now the three of them were trapped in this house with the killer. She could feel her brain spasm with hysterics. She shook her head. Panicking never helped.

"It might not be the killer," she whispered. Sully looked at her. "But I'll behave as if we know for sure that it is."

"Good call," he said.

He squeezed her hands and stepped back, scrutinizing her spot and rearranging the coats until he was satisfied.

Another thump sounded from above, and Kirkland gave Sully a worried look. They moved out of Lindsey's sight, so she leaned back against the wall until she could peek through the coats at what they were doing.

Sully stationed Kirkland just behind the entrance to the sitting room, which was to the left of the stairs and was full of clocks. Kirkland was too big to really be hidden. His crop of fiery red hair was visible as were his knees and elbows.

"Wait here," Sully said to Kirkland. "Remember, we aren't going to do anything until he is all the way down the stairs."

Kirkland nodded and leaned back into the shadows as best he could behind a towering pile of encyclopedias.

It was then that Sully disappeared from view and Lindsey felt her heart clutch in her chest. She didn't like not being able to see him. She wanted to pop out from her spot just to see where he was, but she didn't want to do anything that might put them all in jeopardy.

The sound of something heavy being dragged across the floor above her sounded, and she felt her nerves stretch to the point of breaking. There was another thump and a crash, and she wondered what was happening up there.

Had the killer caught Stewart? Was he tied up right above them, pleading for his life while they hid down here waiting for some indication of what was happening?

She felt sick to her stomach, and the terror that clawed at her insides wasn't helping. It was taking every bit of her self-control to stay in place and not bolt up the stairs and confront the killer.

And then she heard it, a heavy footfall on the top step. She was pretty sure her heart stopped in her chest as she waited for the sound of the next step. *Thump.* There it was. She wondered if Sully and Kirkland had heard it, too. She was sure they must have.

She waited for the sound of the killer making his way down the stairs, but there was nothing but silence. Had he seen Kirkland's hair? Or Sully? Where was Sully? Had he harmed them? Were they in trouble even now while she hid?

Lindsey wanted to peek, but she didn't dare. Sully said she was the last line of defense. She couldn't jump out and ruin their stakeout. Not yet.

The silence felt as if it were being stretched taut like a string about to snap. Then again, maybe it was just her nerves.

She jumped when another thump sounded on the stairs. What could the person be doing that would make such a noise?

Lindsey fisted the fabric of her jacket in her hands. The image of the killer dragging Stewart's limp body down the stairs popped into her head, and she felt her heart thump hard in her chest. She felt dizzy and weak and realized she had stopped breathing. She forced a tiny breath into her lungs to keep from passing out.

There was another bump and then a shout. It sounded like Officer Kirkland. There was a yelp and a crash and the sound of footsteps pounding the floor going in the opposite direction. Lindsey shifted on her feet, torn between leaping out to find out what was happening and staying put to be the backup she was supposed to be.

"Damn it!" That was Sully's voice. "He's getting away!"

"Sorry!" Kirkland yelled. "I thought I had him."

"Go that way," Sully ordered. "I'll go this way, but look out for traps. Be wary."

"Roger that," Kirkland answered.

"Lindsey, stay put. Do not move," Sully hissed.

"Okay," she whispered back.

She heard the two men move away from her and wondered in which direction the killer had gone. Not back upstairs, since neither of them went that way.

Lindsey frowned. It seemed to her that the killer could double back and hurry up the stairs to hide or escape. She leaned forward and tried to see the staircase. She couldn't see it from her spot. She crouched low, hoping that would give her a better angle. No luck.

It occurred to her that it was useless to be the last line of defense in front of a door that the killer wasn't going to use because it had been blocked, undoubtedly by him. Clearly he knew it wasn't viable. The only spot in the area that needed watching was the stairs.

She knew Sully was going to be mad. But it wasn't her fault that he had raced off without thinking things through. The staircase was what they should be monitoring, and she couldn't do it from behind all of this junk.

There was only one thing to do. She stepped out from the pile of coats, keeping low to the floor, and scurried toward the stairs. She heard a crash from the kitchen and almost crab-walked back to her hidey-hole, but instead she lurched forward until she was on the bottom step. She tried to climb the steps quietly, but the hard heels of her shoes knocked on the wooden steps with sharp raps.

She inched her way up the first three steps but then darted up the stairs until she was halfway up and hidden in the shadows. She perched on the step, fretting over what could have made the crashing noise from the kitchen. Had Sully or Kirkland gotten caught in a trap? Or had the killer gotten them?

She wanted to dart down the steps to investigate, but she hadn't heard a cry for help. Surely, if one of them had been injured, they would have shouted for help. She rocked back and forth and hugged her knees while keeping her gaze on the doorways below.

She didn't know what she would do if she saw the perpetrator. Scream, most likely. Maybe throw some stuff at him. She wondered if he was carrying a weapon. She glanced around her at the piles of rubbish. Yeah, this was not going to be a fair fight.

Lindsey listened for any sound of movement downstairs. There was nothing. She couldn't hear Sully or Kirkland moving through the house. She strained her ears, trying to pick up the sound of a step, the creak of a floorboard, the whoosh of a door opening. There was nothing. It was as if the house was empty of any living being except her. Lindsey shivered.

From her vantage point on the steps, she scanned the piles of junk and garbage that filled the room below her. The hair on the back of her neck prickled, and she could swear that someone was watching her. Her head darted from side to side, looking for a person, but the junk below made it impossible to pick anyone out in the shadows.

She fought the panic that clawed at her insides. There was no one there. There couldn't be. Sully and Kirkland were too big for the killer to have gotten by. Unless that crash in the kitchen had been the killer taking out one of the men or maybe both.

Her hands began to shake as fear took hold of her extremities and slowly worked its way up her skin like frost growing on a windowpane. She would not be a victim. She would fight back.

She scanned the stuff crammed along the side of the steps for a weapon. She had seen an assortment of old golf putters out on the porch, but she had no way of getting one. No, it had to be something within reach.

She flipped open the top of the cardboard box beside her. A plume of dust rose up in the air, forcing her to turn away, but not before the musty, moldy cloud flew up her nose, making her want to sneeze. She fought the urge, not wanting to make any noise and give away her position.

She tucked her face into her elbow and looked inside the box. A pile of rusted old door hinges filled the box to the top. She reached in and quietly withdrew one. It was gritty to the touch and heavier than she'd thought. Cast iron and shaped like a fleur-de-lis, it had some heft and a nice sharp point.

Lindsey figured she could either conk someone on the head with it, or, if required, she would stab them with the business end. It wasn't much, but it would have to do.

She held it in front of her, bracing for the killer to run up the stairs at her. But the distinct sound of heavy breathing didn't come from in front of her, it came from behind. It only took her a second, but Lindsey knew with the crystalline clarity born from sheer terror that Peter's killer was standing right behind her.

CHAPTER

22

BRIAR CREEK
PUBLIC LIBRARY

For a nanosecond Lindsey considered not moving, as if she could blend into the piles of garbage like a mannequin or a statue if she just didn't move. Fortunately, her fight-or-flight response kicked in, overriding her temporary paralysis, and she jumped up from her position with a yell, spun around and hurled the door hinge at the person behind her.

It struck true, and the person yelped and then cursed, but Lindsey was already scrabbling down the stairs away from him. She tripped on a box of books, but even the sight of their leather bindings and gilded pages did not give her pause.

She dashed through the narrow pathway that cut across the next room. Her breathing was ragged, and her heart was pounding. She didn't think to slow down for any traps but rather fled like a runaway, knocking bags of clothes over in her wake to keep the stranger from pursuing her.

It didn't work. She glanced back over her shoulder and saw a man in a dark gray puffy jacket with the hood up over his head chasing after her. He leapt over the books and clothes without difficulty.

He was gaining on her. Lindsey turned up her speed and didn't even pause when she launched herself through the doorway into the next room. If there was a trap, she was hoping that by jumping through the middle of the doorway, she would avoid triggering it.

She slammed into a pile of picture frames. They were big and wooden, and one of her legs got wedged in the middle of them. She heard the man behind her. He had stopped at the doorway and was clearly checking for a trap before he came through. It bought Lindsey just a second. She glanced at the path ahead, knowing he would be right behind her, and then she glanced down at where her leg was stuck.

It was a long shot, but she thought that the frames might form a cubby that would hide her away from the killer. She didn't overthink it but let her instincts take over. She ducked down into the old frames. The cramped space smelled of mildew and rotten wood, but she didn't care. She got her foot free and wiggled her way backward. In a matter of feet, the light disappeared completely, and she had to use her hands to feel her way.

She felt an ornately carved wooden leg, followed it up and discovered it was a table. She crawled under it, shoving aside small boxes as she went. The space wasn't as filled in with odds and ends as she had expected, and she wondered how far back she could go.

She heard the heavy tread of the killer pause at the picture frames, and she wondered if he had seen her and would try to come after her. Damn it. Suddenly the confined space seemed claustrophobic instead of cocoon like.

"You can't escape," the man's deep voice hissed after her. "I know every bit of this house. I'll catch you before you find your way out."

She didn't recognize the voice. It was dark and menacing

and made her teeth chatter even as she tried not to make a
sound. She scooted farther under the table. Instead of being
hemmed in, however, there was an opening that went on
through the collection of stuff almost as if it was an inten-
tionally constructed tunnel.

Lindsey didn't hesitate. She moved forward on her hands
and knees. Something squished beneath her fingers, and she
had to press her lips together to keep from crying out. It was
too dark to see what it was, which was probably for the best.
She wiped her hand on the side of a box and moved forward.

She heard a rustle and a bang behind her and realized the
man was coming after her. She crawled faster, but her coat
got caught under her knee, and she fell forward onto her face
with a thump. The ancient carpet beneath her nose was rough
and gritty and smelled of mold. She felt a sneeze build, but
she pinched it off. Yanking her coat up around her waist, she
hurried forward. Deeper and deeper into the recesses of the
broken and rusty piles of refuse she wound her way.

Clearly, this was most definitely a deliberate tunnel built
no doubt to give access to the items in the far corners of the
house. Lindsey felt like a mouse in a maze looking for a piece
of cheese. She heard a knock behind her followed by a curse
and suspected that her pursuer had whacked his head on
one of the table legs.

Where were Sully and Kirkland? Had this man already
killed them? The thought made her sick with dread. She
pushed forward, feeling her way in the darkness. Her fingers
traced the edge of a box, and she realized the tunnel was
turning. She reached out and felt the floor in the opposite
direction in an effort to get her bearings, but it was wide
open. It appeared the path split in two directions, but which
way should she go? What if one of them was a dead end,
which would be a lot more literal if the stranger caught her?

A crash sounded behind her, and she scurried forward,
going automatically to the left, as she assumed it led back

into the house, whereas the right would lead to the outer wall of the room, which could be a death trap.

The tunnel was a little bit wider. She debated pulling items down behind her, but the noise would alert the man to which direction she had taken and might possibly cause an avalanche. She wasn't positive how the items overhead were held up, but when she reached out she felt thick boards above her every few feet, so she suspected that she was in the equivalent of a hoarder's mine shaft. The thought of being crushed to death by the weight of the stuff overhead made her move almost as fast as the sound of the labored breathing behind her.

The tunnel turned again. Lindsey tried to move as quietly as possible, hunching her shoulders in tight to avoid brushing against anything that would make noise. She had gone several yards when she heard the man reach the point where the tunnel split. She froze. She could hear him feeling his way in the pitch black. The sound of his hands as they ran over the boxes scraped across her frayed nerves. She was cold and dirty and scared. She closed her eyes and tried to shrink into herself to make herself as small as possible.

In moments she heard him working his way down the tunnel *away* from her. She silently expelled the breath she'd been holding. She had no idea how far his path would lead, but she resisted the urge to race forward. She didn't want him to hear her moving in a blind panic.

She inched her way forward. Her throat closed up and she gagged when the stink of something dead lingered on the air in its own malignant fog. She wondered if it was a mouse or a rat, maybe even a snake. She refused to picture anything larger, like a body. She shook her head, forcing the image of Peter Rosen's dead body out of her mind. She knew he had been taken to the medical examiner's office. He was not here in this tunnel with her. Still, her skin recoiled at the thought that wouldn't go away.

Lindsey could feel the dirt caked on the palms of her hands, and her nose was running, but she wasn't sure if it was from the cold or if it was her body's natural defense to block the foul smells that filled the cramped space. Tears were stinging her eyes, but she didn't know if it was in reaction to the smell or a bit of panic-induced hysteria. She had a feeling it was the latter.

She pinched herself on the back of her wrist. It was quieter than slapping herself, which she was pretty sure was what she needed. There was no time for a freak-out. She had to keep moving.

As she crawled forward, the opening started to get narrower and narrower, and she had to get down on her belly and scoot forward. She was afraid she was approaching a dead end, but so long as there was a path of any kind, she was determined to follow it.

The going was slow, and she didn't know if the man chasing her had turned around and come back after her. Her only hope was that he was too big to fit in this narrow of a space. She was working her way past an old refrigerator and heap of model trains when she felt a hand grab her ankle.

"Gotcha!"

It was the man's voice. His grip was firm on her leg, and he began to pull her back toward him. Lindsey reached out and grabbed the edge of the freezer, stopping him. With her other leg bent, he wasn't able to grab it, so she began to kick out, making sure he didn't catch her.

She felt a thunk under her heel, and the man cursed. She struck out again and again. Still, his grip on her ankle was strong, and he was pulling her out of the narrow space. Lindsey felt her fingers slipping off the corner of the freezer. Terror motivated her to keep kicking. She struck out three more times, and the third one rang true with a crunch of bone. She was pretty sure she had smashed his hand.

"Uff!" a grunt sounded.

Her ankle was released, and now she burrowed into the narrow space, hoping like hell there was no way he could follow her. The sound of muttering and cursing filled the air behind her, but Lindsey was wriggling forward too fast to listen.

A faint light began to form up ahead, and she realized she was nearing an opening. She moved faster. The sound of items being shoved aside told her that the man was too big to fit into the tight squeeze and he had to move the piles of junk to get to her. She knew she only had seconds to get out before he doubled back and caught her at the exit.

Her breath was ragged, and tears blurred her vision. She wrenched her shoulder, trying to get around an old sewing machine. Lindsey could feel a sob burn in her throat. She choked it down, pushing herself to reach the light before the man caught her again.

The tunnel widened, and she launched herself up to her knees. She crawled under a desk and found herself at an opening into a wider path. She peeked out, looking both ways trying to figure out which direction would get her back to the front of the house, where she hoped to find Sully. She crawled forward, stood and turned to the right. She took three steps when she was grabbed from behind.

A strong arm looped around her middle and picked her up off of her feet. Thinking it was her pursuer, Lindsey kicked and thrashed with all of the adrenaline coursing through her body like rocket fuel.

"Whoa! Lindsey, stop, it's me." She recognized Sully's voice and whipped her head around to confirm that it was him. It was. She stopped fighting. Relief hit her hard, and she sagged against him.

"He's right behind me," she said.

"Excellent!" he said. He looked as if he was spoiling for a fight.

The sound of something scraping and a grunt came from the opening Lindsey had just squeezed through. Sully dropped his arm from around her middle and crouched in front of the opening. He looked like he was going to dive in, but Lindsey grabbed his arm and held him back.

"You can't fit," she said. "I was barely able to get out. He is probably trapped in there and will have to work his way back."

Sully glanced around them and then grabbed a huge framed mirror. He dragged it in front of the small hole and then braced a table between it and the piles of garbage behind it, making it impossible to be moved.

"Now he'll have no choice but to go back," he said. "Show me the entrance."

Lindsey glanced around the path they stood in. She had no idea where she was or how she'd gotten here. She was completely turned around by her time in the tunnel.

"I have to get back to the stairs," she said.

"This way." Sully grabbed her hand and led her to the left.

He didn't pick his way through the paths, so Lindsey figured he'd already been this way and knew it was clear of traps.

They wound their way through two rooms packed with boxes and bags and broken furniture. Lindsey couldn't be happier to put some distance between her and the man who had been chasing her.

"Did you recognize him?" Sully asked as they made their way around the corner and back to the front room.

"No, I only saw him for a second while I was running away, but I'm sure I've never seen him before."

They stopped in front of the stairs. Lindsey glanced at the steps and remembered being terrified and jumping off the steps at a run.

"This way," she said.

She followed the path she had taken with Sully right behind her. They stopped at the stack of picture frames, and she pointed to the hole.

"My leg got stuck, so I climbed in there," she said. "I didn't realize it, but it forms a sort of tunnel."

"Intentional?" Sully asked.

Lindsey nodded. "I think it was built deliberately to give access to the far corners of the stuff."

"I'll be damned," Sully said. He hunched low and studied the opening. "No traps?"

"I was moving too fast to stop and check," Lindsey said. "The path forks. I don't know where the other one leads."

"So, he may not come out this way," Sully said. He began to climb into the tunnel, and Lindsey felt her breath catch.

"Sully, don't go," she said. She grabbed the back of his jacket, holding him in place.

He glanced around at her. His blue eyes were kind when he said, "Don't worry. I'm just going in to listen and see if I can figure out if he's headed this way. I'll return right away."

Lindsey let his jacket slide out of her fingers. It took all of her faith in his ability to handle himself not to grab hold and forcibly yank him out. The thought of anything bad happening to Sully wrecked her. She just didn't think she could bear it.

He disappeared from sight, and Lindsey began to pace in a tight little circle. Listening did not take that long, and when he was gone for more than a few minutes, she knelt down and began to climb in after him.

She had just cleared the picture frames when she bumped into Sully's back. His lack of surprise let her know he had probably either heard her or expected her.

In the faint light, she saw him put his finger to his lips. She nodded. They sat together in the silence. Lindsey felt as if her nerves had been scraped raw. She could hear the rush of blood in her ears, and she really had to pee.

Then they heard it. A muted click that sounded like a door closing, coming from the opposite direction that Lindsey had taken earlier. The intruder was getting away.

CHAPTER

23

BRIAR CREEK
PUBLIC LIBRARY

Sully motioned for Lindsey to back out of their hidey-hole. She stood just outside the pile of frames, and Sully climbed out after her. He stood and glanced around. "Where is Kirk-land?"

"I haven't seen him since you two went your separate ways," she said.

"Speaking of which, weren't you supposed to stay by the door?"

"Yes, but I was worried that the stranger would disappear upstairs, so I moved to block the stairs." She looked at Sully. "But he came down the stairs behind me."

"So, either he's not alone or there are more secret paths that give access to other floors."

"If there was someone else here, I would think that they would have come to help him when he discovered me. No, there has to be another way upstairs in addition to the main staircase," Lindsey said. "They had house staff. There must be a servants' staircase."

"Kitchen," Sully said. "Back stairs are usually tucked in a back corner of the kitchen or pantry."

Sully turned and led the way to the kitchen. It was just as cluttered as it had been when Lindsey had first come in here, but this time there was no body parked in a wheelchair at the kitchen table. She couldn't help but stare at the empty space and the dark brown stain on the floor beneath it.

She felt a shudder start at the base of her spine and shimmy up her back to the nape of her neck. Had it only been a few days since they'd discovered Peter Rosen? It seemed ages ago.

Sully picked his way carefully across the room. The counters were sagging under the weight of dishes and glasses, pots and pans, most of which had a thick coating of dust on them.

How the brothers had lived in such squalor and not gotten dysentery or meningitis, Lindsey couldn't imagine. By rights their house should have been condemned, and if they weren't living on an island all by themselves, it probably would have been. Of course, if they had lived in town, Peter might not have been murdered either. There would have been many more watchful eyes to keep them safe.

Sully reached the far corner of the kitchen and studied the wall. Copper cooking molds hung on the wall in every shape imaginable from fancy round curlicues to one shaped like a turtle and another like a lion. These items also had a coating of grime on them, and the copper had developed a neglected patina.

Sully moved past the display to a built-in hutch. It was crammed with odds and ends, cookbooks and other vintage cooking tools such as a meat grinder and several percolators and no less than four toasters.

"Here," Sully said. He began to examine the hutch, and Lindsey frowned.

"Here what?" she asked.

"This is a secret door," he said.

"How can you tell?"

"There's nothing piled in front of it like the rest of the wall," he said. "Also, the floor in front of it has the wear of a door being open and shut."

Lindsey glanced at the ground. Sure enough, the arch of a door opening and closing was visible on the old wood floor.

"Very clever," she said.

"If only I could figure out how it opens," he said.

He knelt low and ran his fingers around the edges and then did the same with the top. He stood back and shook his head. He then inspected each item on the shelves, as if one of them might hide the door knob.

Lindsey stepped back as far as the stacks of stuff on the floor would allow. She took the hutch in as a whole, looking for some sign of wear or use. It was then that she saw it.

She stepped up to the right side of the hutch and put her hand on a small oval copper mold with a fat pear embossed in the center. She put her hands where the copper gleamed the brightest and tried to move the mold. It twisted to the right with a click, and the hutch swung inward into the wall.

"Well, look at that," Sully said. He grinned at her. "Nice work. How did you figure it out?"

"I read a lot of mysteries," Lindsey said. "And the pear is the only copper mold that isn't covered in grime and still shines a bit, so I figured it had to be touched pretty frequently, and given that it's right next to the hutch . . ."

"It had to be the lever to the secret door," Sully concluded. "Nicely done."

He peered into the dark space the hutch had opened into with Lindsey glancing in over his shoulder. A narrow staircase was visible, and she looked to see if there were curtains of cobwebs hanging down from the ceiling. There were not, and she tried to take comfort in that, at least.

"Why don't you wait—" he began, but Lindsey shook her head.

"No," she said.

He sighed as if he'd known she was going to shake him off all along.

"Stay close," he said. "Don't touch anything. We have no idea if this area is rigged or not."

The open door gave them just enough light to find the handrail above the stairs. Sully switched on a small penlight that he had on his key chain and used it to examine each stair tread before they stepped on it.

The going was slow, and Lindsey found herself listening for any sounds coming from above. They had no idea where the door at the top of the steps would open up to or who might be waiting for them on the other end. She wondered where the man who had been pursuing her had gone, and she fretted about where Kirkland was and if he was okay. Impatience snapped inside of her, and she longed to dash up the stairs, even though she knew it would be a reckless and stupid thing to do. She glanced at the shadows illuminated in Sully's penlight. They were only halfway up the stairs. She wondered if it was possible to die of curiosity.

A soft swoosh sounded behind her, and Lindsey turned just in time to see the hutch shut behind them. The sound of the latch clicking shut sounded inordinately loud in the silence, muffled only by the gasp that slipped past Lindsey's lips. They were locked in.

"Sully." Lindsey said his name more for reassurance than for anything else.

"Right here," he said. "I don't suppose that was you."

"No," she said. Her voice sounded faint, so she cleared her throat and tried again. "No."

"Kirkland would have said something," Sully said. "Come on. If your friend from the tunnels is trying to trap us, he's going to seal up both doors. Our only chance is to get out of the top one first."

Sully hurried up the remaining stairs, and Lindsey followed him. He shone the small penlight all along the edges of the door, looking for a latch. There was nothing.

Frantic that their captor was almost upon them, Lindsey felt along the door where she thought a door handle would be. She found a knob protruding out of the wooden door. She turned it and pushed. Nothing happened. She turned it the other way and pulled. The door gave way, and she toppled into Sully. The smell of stale air evaporated as they stepped into an upper bedroom. A cold breeze was blowing, and Lindsey realized it was the same room where she and Sully had fought the fire when Chief Plewicki had inadvertently tripped one of the brothers' booby traps.

"Thank goodness." Lindsey sucked in a lungful of the cold air. "I was getting just the teensiest bit claustrophobic."

Sully did the same. The room was as cluttered as the rest of the house, but the windows let in plenty of outside light, making it easy for them to navigate through the boxes and bags and piles of clutter.

Sully quietly closed the door behind them. Like in the kitchen, this secret door was built into the wall and disguised as a bookcase. The only clue that it was a door was the fact that there was no clutter blocking it and the traffic pattern that matted the carpet in front of it.

"If we hide, we might be able to convince him that we're still stuck in there," Sully whispered. He took Lindsey's hand and led her across the room.

There was a large wardrobe along one wall, and Sully pushed Lindsey into its shadows while he went and tucked himself in behind the bedroom door. When the killer came into the room, she had no doubt that Sully planned to jump him.

She remembered the feel of the man's hand on her ankle. He had been strong, and although he hadn't used one down in the tunnel, he could very well be armed with a knife or a gun. She didn't like this plan, not at all. She glanced around her looking for any sort of weapon. When Sully jumped him, she could take the opportunity to bash the man on the head, assuming she could find something heavy enough to wield. A quick scan of what was in reach told her that her options were limited to a pile of musty old feather pillows or a broken accordion. Not encouraging.

She listened for the sound of footsteps, the creak of a door or the sound of something being shifted out of the way. There was nothing. It was as if the entire house had gone absolutely still and was holding its breath with Lindsey as she waited.

A cold blast of air blew directly on her from the broken window. She burrowed into her coat and shoved her hands into her pockets for warmth. The end of her nose felt cold, as did the tips of her ears. It was miserable waiting to see what would happen, but she was also relieved that no one had shown up. She began to think the bad guy had gotten scared and bolted from the island.

As the minutes ticked by, she became more hopeful. She was about to lean out from her spot beside the wardrobe and ask Sully if it was time to call it when she heard the distinctive sound of a footfall coming from the wooden floor of the hallway just outside the bedroom. Lindsey felt her hope do a free fall in her chest as dread shoved it aside. She closed her eyes, trying to center herself before . . . *BAM!*

There was a crash, a grunt and the sound of a body hitting the floor.

"Ow! What the—hey, it's me!"

"Oh, sorry."

Lindsey recognized Kirkland's voice and jumped around the wardrobe just in time to see Sully helping him to his feet. He had clearly taken Kirkland out at the knees in a tackle that had caused the other man to crash into an old sewing machine stand that was buried in bolts of fabric.

"Are you all right?" Sully asked. He looked Kirkland over for injuries, but Kirkland waved him off.

"I'm fine. You just surprised me. Hey, whoa!" Kirkland cried out as Sully did a slow fall forward into his arms. Kirkland staggered under his dead weight and slowly lowered him to the ground.

"Sully!" Lindsey cried.

She raced forward to kneel beside him. A nasty knot was forming on the back of his head. She glanced up at the door to see the man in the dark puffy coat who had chased her, standing there holding a statuette of some sort in his hand.

"Nobody move," the man ordered. "Or I'll clobber you, too."

CHAPTER

24

BRIAR CREEK
PUBLIC LIBRARY

Without hesitation, Officer Kirkland snatched his gun out of his holster.

"Drop it!" he ordered. "Do it now!"

"A gun?" the man asked, dropping the statue, which made a loud thunk onto the box beside him. Clearly, it was a weighted piece and would do damage to the thickest skull. "You brought a gun to loot a house? What sort of town is this?"

"Loot it?" Officer Kirkland asked. He looked deeply offended and pulled aside his coat and showed the badge on his chest. "I'm a police officer."

"Oh." The man's eyes went wide. "Oh! Arrest them! They're trying to rob the place."

"What?" Lindsey cried. She was cradling Sully's head in her lap, otherwise she would have gotten up and given the man a piece of her mind. As it was, she snapped at him from her kneeled position on the floor, "I'm not a thief. I'm a librarian."

The man clapped a hand to his forehead with one hand

and pointed to Sully with the other. "What's he then, a fireman?"

"Boat captain, actually," Kirkland answered.

"What are you doing in my family's house?"

Lindsey and Kirkland exchanged a look. She shook her head at him to indicate that she had no idea what the man was talking about. There were only two Rosens, Peter and Stewart.

Kirkland nodded and waved his gun at the man. "Put your hands on your head and keep them where I can see them."

The man complied, and Lindsey felt Sully rouse. She glanced down to find him blinking and slowly shaking his head. He glanced at her and then gently reached up to feel the knot on the back of his head.

"Ouch," he said.

"I'll bet," Lindsey said. "Let me see your eyes."

Sully glanced up, and she checked his pupils to make sure they were even and not dilated, a sign of a concussion. They were good, and for a second she found herself getting lost in his brilliant baby blues.

"Well? How is he?" Kirkland asked.

"He's okay," Lindsey said. She glanced at the man standing with his hands on his head and frowned. "For now. We'll have to keep an eye on him to make sure he stays that way."

"Look, I'm sorry," the man said to Sully. He looked pained, and his features were tight with contrition. "I thought you were looters, and I'm trying to protect my family's home."

"*Your* family? The only two people with a claim on this place are Stewart and Peter Rosen, and you are about forty-five years too young to be either of them," Sully said. He started to rise, and Lindsey took his arm and helped him to his feet.

"My name is Steven Rosen-Grant. I'm their nephew," the man said. He dropped his hands as if to reach for his wallet, but Kirkland gestured at him with the gun to keep his hands on his head.

Kirkland looked at Lindsey, and she turned to Sully. "Can you stand on your own?" He nodded, and she let go of his arm and stepped forward. Kirkland held the gun pointed at the man and said, "Turn around and keep your hands where I can see them or I will shoot you."

The man did, and Lindsey took his wallet out of his back pocket and handed it to Kirkland.

"You can turn around now," Kirkland said. He flipped the wallet open, and they all looked at the Illinois state driver's license, which showed a picture of the man before them and the name Steven Rosen-Grant, just as he'd said.

"IDs can be faked," Sully said. "And the name Rosen isn't that unusual. We'll need more than this for proof."

"Agreed. What do you have there?" Kirkland gestured to the bag on the floor beside the man's feet

The man shifted uncomfortably but kept his hands on his head. "I can explain."

"Criminals always can," Kirkland said.

"I'm not a criminal! My grandmother had an affair with Dr. Rosen and became pregnant with my mother, Gabrielle Rosen, but when he died, his miserable wife cut my grand-mother off without a penny. Whatever I am taking, it is much less than my grandmother or my mother deserved," the man said.

His hood had been pushed back when he put his hands on his head, and Lindsey could see that he looked to be in his mid to late thirties. His face was just beginning to show signs of middle age with a softening of the jawline and wrin-kles at the corners of his brown eyes. He had precisely cut dark hair that framed his ears, which stuck out on the top just a little. Lindsey gasped. His ears were just like Stewart and Peter Rosen's.

She shoved the thought away. Ears that stuck out were

not proof of anything. She glanced at Sully and Kirkland. Their ears didn't stick out. Still, it didn't prove anything.

"Family or not, there is a proper way to go about claiming your inheritance, and robbing the place isn't it," Kirkland said.

"I wasn't—" the man protested but then stopped. He glared at them and said, "Fine, whatever."

Kirkland gestured for the man to turn around. "Let's go. I'm taking you in."

The man sent a panicked glance at the bag, and Lindsey got the feeling that there was something important to him in there.

"We should take the bag," she said. "He must have left fingerprints on some of the things, which would verify his identity."

"And prove that he was robbing the place," Kirkland said. "Grab it, would you?"

Lindsey nodded.

"I wasn't—" the man protested, but Kirkland cut him off.

"Save it for the chief," he said.

Kirkland and their captive led the way out of the room. Lindsey took off her scarf and grabbed the duffel bag that had been on the ground. She knew that it was unlikely that fingerprints would be found on the fabric, but still, she didn't want to risk damaging any evidence if this was indeed the man who had killed Peter Rosen.

The bag was heavier than she expected, and it slipped from her grip. She cried out as an item toppled out of its open zipper. Sully dropped to his knees and caught the loosely wrapped bundle before it smashed on the floor.

Lindsey dropped the bag and grabbed Sully as he listed to the side. She helped him stand, and he propped himself against the doorframe and smiled down at her.

"I'm okay, just a little dizzy," he said. He held out the bundle to her, and Lindsey let the pale blue velvet fabric slide from the object in her hands.

It was a purple satin egg-shaped music box with gilt edges. The top was loose, and when it popped open, a waltz chimed while the tiny porcelain man and woman on the inside spun in a slow circle. Lindsey turned it to get a closer look at it, and a small key fell out into her hand. She held it up to examine it and saw that it had teeth on both sides. She frowned.

She glanced at Sully and saw Kirkland and Steven Rosen-Grant had stopped and turned back and were looking at the key as well.

"That's a safe-deposit box key," Kirkland said. "I take my grandmother to her box at the bank every now and then, and hers looks just like that one."

He turned to look at his captive. "Did you know that was in there?"

Steven closed his mouth. "I refuse to talk without representation."

"That can be arranged," Kirkland said. "Pack it up, Lindsey. Let's go."

Lindsey closed the lid on the music box. The tune stopped playing. She wondered why it sounded so familiar, and she opened the lid again hoping to place the sound. The beginning was unfamiliar, but then she recognized it. It was the exact same tune Stewart Rosen had been humming when he had come to the library the other evening.

"How did you know to take this box?" she asked Steven. "Who told you about it? Have you seen Stewart? Have you talked to him?"

Steven looked nonplussed, but then he turned his head away from her with a snap. But not before she saw a telltale red flush creep into his cheeks. Whatever Steven Rosen-Grant was, he was not a very good liar.

She pocketed the key. She didn't want to risk losing it. Then she rewrapped the music box and put it in the bag. This time she zipped it up before hefting it onto her shoulder.

She took Sully's arm and led him down the stairs. If he didn't really need her help, he didn't say so. Lindsey figured it was probably because he didn't want to offend her, but she was glad, because she was worried about him navigating the stairs with that huge knot on his head.

For that alone, she wanted to put a hurt on Steven, but when she added in the fright he had given her by chasing her through the house, and the fact that he clearly knew something about Stewart, well, it was a good thing Kirkland was escorting him down the stairs and not her. She might not have resisted the urge to take a shortcut, meaning a nice thump to the middle of Steven's back to send him down the stairs more quickly.

When they got to the bottom of the steps, Kirkland cut across the foyer and stopped by the front door.

"Are you responsible for blocking it?" he asked.

Steven shrugged. "I thought you were burglars, and I didn't want you to get away."

"Hmm," Kirkland said. "Well, now you can show us an alternate exit."

"There's a back door off of the kitchen," Steven said.

They followed him through the house. A mudroom was tucked into the back of the kitchen, and it was here that Steven led them. When they got to the door, Sully made them stop while he checked the door and the steps for traps.

"I wouldn't lead you into a trap," Steven said.

Sully stared at him. "The knot on my head tells me otherwise."

"I said I was sorry," Steven said. He sounded irritated. "What are you all doing here anyway?"

"Looking for my cart of books," Lindsey said. "I brought a box full of books out here the day we discovered Peter's . . . er . . . the day that Peter was killed, and I accidentally left it here."

Steven glared at her. "Right."

It was clear that he didn't believe one word she said. Lindsey glared right back. After all, she was partly telling the truth, and at least she hadn't clocked anyone on the head.

With a click, the latch on the back door was released and Kirkland pushed it open. Sully and Lindsey both tensed, as if waiting for another swinging board to greet them with some nails to the face, but there was nothing.

Lindsey felt the breath leave her lungs in a whoosh. Sully leaned down and kissed the top of her head. It was a gesture that reassured, but Lindsey was afraid he'd keel over, and she clutched his arm more tightly.

"I'm okay," he said. "My head has the density of granite."

She glanced up at him and smiled while checking his pupils at the same time. He chuckled, letting her know that he knew what she was doing.

They followed Kirkland and Steven around the side of the house, and Lindsey was relieved that they were on the familiar and trap-free path that led from the house to the dock below.

"So, did you want me to drive the boat?" she asked.

"No," he said. "At least, not until we're away from the island, and only if you want to, not because you have to do it for me."

At the upper deck, Lindsey glanced back at the house. She wondered if she should have locked the back door. It seemed like it, but really, who was going to come out here, and if they did, they had to get past all of the refuse in the yard first.

"It'll be okay," Sully said.

"It just feels wrong," she said.

"Everything about this feels wrong," he agreed.

CHAPTER

25

BRIAR CREEK
PUBLIC LIBRARY

At the police station, Kirkland led Steven Rosen-Grant to an interview room in the back. Emma was moving around in a wheelchair with one leg elevated and jutting out like the prow of a ship. She took out two plastic chairs and the trash can as she made her way toward them across the main room.

"Damn it," she said. "I need a cowcatcher or at least a chair catcher on the front of this thing. Are you two all right? Kirkland gave me the short version on the phone, but I'd like to hear what you two know."

"It's a long story," Sully said. "You have any coffee made?"

"And a bag of ice," Lindsey said and gestured to his head.

Emma's eyebrows raised, and she turned to Molly Hatcher, her administrative assistant. "Are you free to handle that?"

"Giddy-up," Molly said. She winked at Lindsey, who grinned in return. Molly had a thing for cowboys, and she was partial to Lori Wilde's romance novels set in Texas. Lindsey knew without asking to put Molly's name down as soon as the release dates were announced.

Molly rose from her desk at the front of the room, turned and headed toward the back of the station.

"Ice?" Emma asked.

"A precautionary measure only," Sully said.

Lindsey took the opportunity to check his eyes again, but they were fine.

"You don't feel woozy, do you?" she asked.

"No. Hungry? Yes. Woozy? No," he said.

"Come on back, then," Emma said. "Ian brought over a huge pot of clam chowder. I think it was out of pity for me in my wheelchair, but I'm not complaining if it gets me free chowder."

They followed her down a narrow hallway. Although she rammed the side of the wall twice, Lindsey knew better than to offer to push Emma. Because Sully said nothing, she suspected he knew better, too.

"Did you have any luck finding your books?" Emma asked. She glanced over her shoulder at Lindsey as she turned her chair and wheeled into the station's break room.

"Books?" Lindsey asked.

"Yeah, you know, the books you went out there to collect," Emma said.

"Oh. No." Lindsey shook her head. "No luck there."

"But you managed to capture a man who was apparently robbing the Rosen house and says he's a relative," Emma said.

She gestured to a Crock-Pot of chowder, plugged in on the counter. There was a stack of thick cardboard bowls and plastic spoons beside it as well as a box of oyster crackers. Lindsey felt her stomach contract with anticipation.

Molly was just finishing up with the coffeepot, and she handed Sully a bag of ice as she passed them on her way out the door.

"Holler if you need anything else," she said.

"Thanks, Molly," Sully and Lindsey said together. Lindsey pushed Sully into a chair and put the bag of ice on the back of his head. He gave a tiny wince, but she didn't know if it was from the pain of having his boo-boo touched or the chill of the ice. Either way, she didn't remove the bag.

"I'm going to have a chat with our suspect," Emma said. "You eat, and I'll be back shortly."

"I'm due back to the library," Lindsey said.

"I'll try to be quick," Emma said. "If I'm not back here by the time you're done eating, I'll come to the library to see you later. Either way, you both need to eat something. You look like you're going to drop."

"I'm not arguing," Sully said.

"Good. Then you won't argue when the doctor stops by to examine that knot on your head. Also, we need you to file charges for assault."

"Really? I've had worse bumps after a tense night at the bingo hall," Sully said.

"Don't get all macho," Emma chided. "Your charge will give us leverage to hold Rosen-Grant. It's for the greater good."

"Fine, but no doctor," he said.

"Sorry, that's not negotiable," she said. Emma looked at Lindsey. "Right?"

"Right," Lindsey said. At his mutinous look, she said, "For me? So I don't worry."

"Fine, but if I'm playing the invalid, you have to have dinner with me so you can keep tabs on my health," he said.

Emma laughed. "That's our Sully. He never misses a trick. I'm actually less worried about you now."

Sully looked hopeful, but she shut him down.

"No, you're still getting checked out by a doctor."

Sully frowned. Emma grinned at Lindsey before she wheeled out of the room. Lindsey dished two bowls of chowder for them and put one in front of Sully before taking the seat across from him.

"You'd better hurry," he said. "I'm sure she'll be back or send Kirkland for it at any moment."

"For what?" Lindsey asked. She tried to sound innocent, but she knew she had failed miserably when he narrowed his eyes at her.

"The safe-deposit box key in your pocket," he said.

"Remembered that, did you?" she asked.

She took the key out of her pocket and pulled her cell phone out of her handbag. She held the key in her palm and took a quick picture of each side of it before returning her phone to her bag and the key to her pocket.

"What do you hope to gain by having a picture of it?" Sully asked. He dropped a fistful of oyster crackers onto his chowder.

"Nothing, really," Lindsey said with a sigh. "I just thought if Stewart came by the library again, I could show him the picture and ask him about it."

"Makes sense," Sully said. "Assuming that he's familiar with it, he might tell you which bank it comes from."

Lindsey tucked into her soup. It was rich and creamy without being too thick; Mary and Ian made it the proper New England way with cream instead of flour. Her stomach was happy, but even more than that, she felt as if her insides were warm for the first time in hours.

"Do you think Stewart or Peter knew about Steven?" she asked.

Sully shrugged. "It's hard to say. Stewart never mentioned him."

"Steven knew about them, though," Lindsey said. "Obviously, his mother told him all about being a Rosen. He must have felt very bitter about being unacknowledged."

"Which gives him a perfect motive for murder, doesn't it?" Sully asked.

Lindsey swallowed a bite of potato, but it went down hard. Was Steven Rosen-Grant a murderer? Had he gotten to Stewart before they found him? No. Something didn't sit right with that idea. She remembered when he had chased her in the house and had scared the snot out of her by grabbing her leg.

He had been chasing her because he thought she was a looter. Was that normal behavior for a person who didn't care? Of course, he might have been trying to keep her from stealing things he wanted for himself, but she didn't think so. When she took her own panic out of the equation, he had sounded upset by her presence in the house. More than upset, he had sounded protective.

"We didn't find my books," Lindsey said. Which, now that she thought about it, seemed sort of weird. Why would anyone touch a crate of library books when there was so much other stuff out there?

"No, we didn't," Sully agreed. "You know what else we didn't find while we were out there?"

"Any sort of computer," Lindsey said.

They exchanged a perplexed look, but before either of them could comment on the situation, there was a commotion at the door as Emma tried to wheel herself in and crashed against the doorjamb. She backed out and tried again two more times before finally entering the room without mishap.

"That was fast," Sully said, clearly not referring to her entrance.

"He's lawyered up," Emma said.

She glanced up at the Crock-Pot, and Lindsey hopped up from her chair and went to fill a bowl for the chief. Emma looked comically grateful when Lindsey set it down in front of her.

"Thanks," she said. "I wasn't really sure how to tackle the Crock-Pot from down here. I'm sure getting a whole new perspective on our citizens who live life from a rolling chair."

Lindsey knew it was coming, so she decided a preemptive strike was best. She reached into her pocket and took out the key. She laid it down on the table and pushed it toward Emma.

"Ah, Kirkland told me you had this," Emma said. She picked it up and studied it. "Fancy."

"What did Steven tell you before he requested representation?" Sully asked.

"Not much," Emma said. She put the key down and studied them. "Kirkland explained Rosen-Grant's claim to be a relative. To my mind, it doesn't make him less suspicious but more so."

"Any idea what his background is?" Lindsey asked.

"I had Officer Trousdale run a quick background on him. A cursory check shows no priors, but he was raised by a low-income single mother much like his mother was before him," Emma said. "Which is another fact that doesn't help his case."

"How do you figure?" Sully asked.

"If he really is a relative and what he says is true—that the Rosens' mother cut his grandmother off without a cent when there was a fortune that was rightfully theirs—well, that's a pretty big grudge to hold over the years and might make a person prone to murder," Emma said.

"Do you think he killed Peter and planned to do the same to Stewart in an effort to gain the estate?" Lindsey asked.

"I don't want to make any assumptions until I know more, but it certainly is one theory," Emma said. "If we could just find Stewart and learn what he knows . . ."

Her voice trailed off, and Lindsey felt a flash of guilt. She'd had Stewart with her. This mess that was spiraling out of control was largely her fault.

"No, it isn't," Sully said. "Stop torturing yourself."

She glanced at him in surprise. He shrugged.

"Guilt is written all over your face," he said.

"He's right," Emma agreed. "And there's no need. Whoever attacked Milton is to blame. I just wish we knew if they took Stewart or if he ran off on his own. Ah well, tell me your version of what happened today out on the island. Maybe there will be a clue in there somewhere."

Emma enjoyed her soup as she listened to Sully and Lindsey describe the events on the island from their perspective. When Lindsey talked about ducking into the strange little tunnel to escape Steven, she felt Sully tense up beside her. When she got to the part about kicking herself free, he relaxed just a little, but she could tell he was unhappy about what had transpired.

They finished their story just as Emma finished her chowder. She put down her spoon and asked, "Can you think of anything else?"

Sully and Lindsey exchanged a look and said together, "No."

"All right," Emma said. "I have a meeting with Detective Trimble. We're going to try to figure out how to proceed with Mr. Rosen-Grant. It would help us out if you'd both file charges. If he is our killer, I don't want to let him slip away."

"Of course," Lindsey said, and Sully nodded.

"Great, I'll send someone in to take your statements," Emma said. She rolled back from the table and managed to turn her chair around. It only took her two tries to clear the door, and Lindsey heard her muttering mild profanity as she went.

I t was another hour before Lindsey made it back to the library. An enormous bouquet of blue delphinium and yellow roses obscured the children's desk from view. Feeling as if a glimpse of flowers might thaw the frosty edge of fear that still encrusted her psyche, Lindsey walked over and buried her face in the blooms.

"Aren't they amazing?" Beth asked as she popped up behind the bouquet, making Lindsey yelp.

"They are lovely," she said. "Aidan?"

Beth flushed a deep shade of pink. It made her look even younger than her small frame and pixie haircut already did.

"We have another date tonight," Beth said. "I think things are getting serious."

"That fast?" Lindsey asked. She knew she hadn't cushioned the sound of her disapproval well when Beth crossed her arms over her chest and scowled, looking very defensive.

"When it's right—" Beth began but was interrupted by two people who joined Lindsey in admiring the flowers.

"Your friends will be happy for you and approve."

"And until we know it's right, we're tagging along to make sure you haven't picked yourself a clunker."

CHAPTER

26

BRIAR CREEK
PUBLIC LIBRARY

Lindsey turned around to find Violet and Nancy standing behind her. She raised her eyebrows at them and then turned back to look at Beth to see if she was okay with this. Beth sighed, and her shoulders slumped in resignation.

"I suppose it's for the best," Beth said. "My track record is pretty bad."

Nancy moved in to smell a rose. She sighed. "He's looking pretty good so far."

"But a nice bouquet does not a stellar boyfriend make," Violet said. "Mary and Charlene will be joining us as well. Are you in?"

She looked at Lindsey with her most penetrating gaze. It was at moments like this one that Lindsey understood why Violet had been such a successful stage actress. She had no doubt that the woman could pierce the farthest corner of a dark theater with that intense, laserlike stare.

"I wouldn't miss it," she said.

Violet and Nancy nodded as if they had expected no less.

"Tonight at seven at the Anchor," Nancy said. "Charlie is having band practice in his apartment, and you know how Heathcliff enjoys howling with the band."

He certainly did. Lindsey often wondered if her puppy had been a rock singer in a former life.

Lindsey watched the two women walk away and felt sorry for Aidan. The poor man had no idea what he was getting into dating their Beth. Truly, the Spanish Inquisition had nothing on the crafternooners.

Lindsey spent the afternoon on the reference desk. Her inbox in her email was full to bursting, and she had orders backing up, minutes from the board meeting to proofread before sending them on to the mayor's office and about a million other tasks that needed her attention. There was no more putting it off. She was going to have to hire a part-time library assistant ASAP.

She glanced up at the circulation desk and saw Ann Marie talking with a customer. The customer asked for something, and as Lindsey watched, Ann Marie walked the man over to one of the library computers and opened up the Zinio option. The man opened the messenger bag on his shoulder and pulled out a tablet computer. As Lindsey watched, it was clear that Ann Marie was helping him check out magazines to his tablet.

Ann Marie paused by Lindsey's desk on her way back to the circulation desk. Again, Lindsey was struck by Ann Marie's transformation from ponytailed mom in baggy sweaters to the sleek professional in front of her now.

"Hey, boss, I'm going to unload the book drop in the back parking lot," Ann Marie said. "If I'm not back in fifteen minutes, assume I've succumbed to hypothermia and send a rescue dog, preferably the kind who carries a barrel of brandy on his collar."

Lindsey smiled. "Well, here's something to think about, while you're out there," she said. "I'm going to be advertising for a new part-time library assistant in reference, and I want you to apply for it if you're interested."

Ann Marie stared at her. "Huh?"

"I think you'd be perfect," Lindsey said. "You have a great way with people, you know the library and our materials inside and out and I think you could give our adult programming a shot in the arm."

"Me?" Ann Marie asked. "Sit out here?"

"If you're interested," Lindsey said.

"I . . . Yeah," Ann Marie said.

"Great," Lindsey said. "I'll let you know when HR starts accepting applications."

"Okay," Ann Marie said. She grinned then frowned. "You're not pranking me, are you?"

"Not even a little," Lindsey said.

"But what about the circulation desk and Ms. Cole?" she asked.

"We'll hire a new clerk to help her," Lindsey said. "She could probably use some fresh meat, since you don't intimidate so easily."

Ann Marie grinned. "Now that's going to be fun to watch."

Lindsey pursed her lips. "On second thought—"

"No, no, I'm sure it will be fine," Ann Marie said. She backed away from the desk. "No need for second thoughts. I'll help the newb, I promise."

Lindsey watched as she turned and hurried away from the area. She glanced at the desk where Ms. Cole was seated, fine-sorting a cart of books to get them ready to be shelved. Ms. Cole was still frosty with Lindsey, not that she could blame her, and Lindsey had a feeling it was going to get chillier when Ms. Cole found out that Lindsey was considering Ann Marie for the reference desk.

Ah well, the joys of small-town library administration. Lindsey wondered how Mr. Tupper would have handled it, then she wondered if he'd been a drinker, because his nonconfrontational history must have had an outlet some-where. She shook her head. It wasn't nice to think such things about her predecessor. Still, she was curious.

Curious. That reminded her of the safe-deposit key and the contents of the box. She wondered if Emma had figured out which bank it belonged to and if she'd managed to get a warrant to search it. If only they knew where Stewart was, they could ask him, as he was probably the only one who knew.

That thought reminded Lindsey that she had a list of people who had attended Dr. Rosen's funeral, people who had worked for the Rosens. Would one of them know about the safe-deposit key? It had been kept in a music box that probably belonged to Mrs. Rosen. Her maid would have known about it, wouldn't she?

Lindsey darted into her office where she had left the print-out from the microfilmed *Gazette*. She grabbed it from the top of her desk and took it back out to the reference desk. Now the dilemma was, who could she ask about the names?

Being the head of the historical society and a Briar Creek native, Milton was the obvious choice, but she just couldn't get him any more involved in something that had already gotten him hurt. No, she needed someone else.

She glanced out the window at the pier. She could see Sully's boats and his office. The lights were on in the office, as if putting up a small fight against the gloom of the day. Lindsey wondered how Sully's visit with the doctor had gone. She thought he might know some of the names on her list but even better Ronnie, his octogenarian receptionist would know for sure since she had lived in Briar Creek her whole life.

She picked up the phone on the desk and dialed. Ronnie answered on the second ring.

"Thumb Island Tours and Taxi, how can I help you?"

"Hi, Ronnie, it's Lindsey," she said.

"Oh, hi," Ronnie said. "The boss just checked in. His big, blocky head is fine."

"Oh, I'm so glad," Lindsey said. She paused. She wasn't sure how to segue into the next part of her query.

"Was there something else? Do you need the taxi?"

"No, actually, I was wondering if I could ask you about some names."

"Names? Of what?"

"More like who," Lindsey said.

"I'm listening," Ronnie said. She sounded intrigued, and Lindsey imagined her putting down her nail file and leaning in, fully engaged.

"I have to warn you, these are names from the past," Lindsey said.

"That's okay. I have an excellent memory."

Lindsey didn't doubt it. Ronnie ran Sully's office with an efficiency that was unparalleled. Keeping track of taxi pick-ups, drop-offs, tours and her errant captains, she was amazing.

"All right," Lindsey said. She glanced at her list. "Cletus Hargreaves."

"Ah," Ronnie said. "Butler to the Rosens, a mean old goat, he died of pneumonia in the early seventies. No wife or children."

Lindsey took a pen out of the holder on the desk and drew a line through his name. She read off two more names. One was deceased with no family, like Hargreaves, and the other had relocated to South Carolina over thirty years ago.

"Can I ask you something?" Ronnie said.

"Sure," Lindsey replied as she tried to decipher the next name, which was a bit smudgy.

"Where did you get this list and why are you asking me and not Milton? He's the town historian. Wouldn't he be better suited to answer these questions?"

"You're doing just fine."

"But that doesn't answer my question," Ronnie said. "Where did this list come from?"

"From the paper," Lindsey said.

"Which paper?"

"That is way more than *a* question," Lindsey said.

"It's one long, extended question," Ronnie said. "So?"

"Fine, but I would appreciate it if it went no further," Lindsey said. Ronnie grunted, which she took as assent. "I have a list of names from Dr. Rosen's funeral in nineteen sixty-one, and I'm checking to see if any of these people might still be alive and be someone Stewart would have reached out to if he was in trouble."

Ronnie let out a low whistle. "Fifty-four years ago. That is a long shot. Okay, fire another name at me."

"Beatrice Beller," Lindsey said.

"Betty Beller," Ronnie said. "Wow, I haven't heard that name in years. She was the Rosens' housemaid, a beautiful young woman both inside and out. I don't think there was a person in Briar Creek who didn't like Betty, especially Peter and Stewart Rosen. That was back when they would leave the island and come into town and be social. It seemed like whenever that girl left the island to run an errand, she had one or both of the Rosen boys hovering around her like puppies. Huh, I'd almost forgotten how they were back then, so funny and friendly. But Betty left to go marry a doctor, except . . ."

Her voice trailed off, and Lindsey could tell she was slipping into the past, remembering things that had been long forgotten over the past five decades.

"Except?"

"Oh, sorry, I was just remembering that Betty left the Rosen household shortly after Dr. Rosen's death," she said. "We all knew she had a doctor boyfriend in New Haven, and we assumed she had finally decided to marry him. She was young, in her early twenties, but . . ."

"But?" Lindsey asked.

"But I remember seeing her leaving Briar Creek. I was working at Sammy's Fish and Chips, before it became the Blue Anchor, as a hostess, and I remember watching her leave, thinking that she looked sad and a little lost, not like someone about to run off and get married," Ronnie said. "Hmm, I haven't thought of her in years and years."

"So, no idea what happened to her?" Lindsey circled the woman's name. If Betty was sad about leaving, she might have been close to the family and be someone who Stewart would turn to if he needed help.

"None," Ronnie said.

"How about Allison Alston?" Lindsey said. "Oh, and her husband Brent Alston?"

"Ugh," Ronnie said. "Who could forget them? They lived in Manhattan but came up on weekends and for long stretches during the summer. They parked their yacht smack in the middle of the bay and had the loudest, most over-the-top parties."

There was such annoyance in her tone, Lindsey had a feeling it was a resentment born of not being on the guest list.

"They didn't mingle with the locals, did they?" she asked.

"Not at all," Ronnie said. "They clearly thought they were above us. So rude."

"Did they own any of the islands?" Lindsey asked.

"Several, but then there was a terrible scandal involving Mr. Alston and an underage girl. He went into exile in Europe, and the family was forced to sell everything, including the islands," Ronnie said. She was quiet for a moment, and then she gasped. "Huh, I just realized the first three islands that Evelyn Dewhurst bought were originally owned by the Alstons."

"Interesting," Lindsey said. She wondered if it was a coincidence worth mentioning to Emma.

They ran through the rest of the names, and Ronnie was helpful with all but two of them, as she didn't know what had become of George Marzkie or Philip Carver.

Lindsey circled their names and put question marks beside them. She thanked Ronnie for her time.

"You'll let me know if you find any of these people, won't you?" Ronnie asked. "I'd be curious to know what happened to some of them, especially that George Marzkie. If I remember right, he was a hottie."

Lindsey smiled. "I'll let you know."

She stared at the list in front of her. All of these people had been close enough to the Rosen family to attend Dr. Rosen's service. Some were their house staff, some were neighbors, some were people of their elevated social set, but had any of them kept in touch after Dr. Rosen's passing?

Tragedy had a way of making people flee the scene, as if the death of Dr. Rosen or the paralysis of Peter Rosen were contagious conditions that could be spread by human contact. Lindsey wondered if the Rosens had found themselves even more isolated in the aftermath of Dr. Rosen's tragic death.

She glanced at the window that overlooked the bay. She could just see a few of the islands, rising out of the silver body of water as if they could glide across the smooth surface and relocate anyplace they wanted. She wondered if Peter or Stewart had ever wanted to relocate or leave their island. What might their lives have been like if they had?

CHAPTER

27

BRIAR CREEK
PUBLIC LIBRARY

Lindsey walked to the Anchor mentally reviewing the list. It seemed to her that the person most likely to have kept contact with Stewart was the housemaid Beatrice Beller. According to Ronnie, she had been young, so she would only be in her seventies now. Maybe, just maybe, Lindsey would be able to find her.

As she stepped into the Anchor, she saw the crafternooners had poor Aidan surrounded. He was a bit wide-eyed, and Lindsey wondered if he'd feel more comfortable if she tossed him a picture book and a puppet, so he could tame the crowd.

"Now, Aidan, can you tell us a little bit about yourself?" Violet asked.

She was perched on one side of him while Nancy bookended him on the other. The poor bastard had no chance at escape. Mary was standing beside the table with her tray tucked under her arm, while Charlene and Beth sat across from the others. Lindsey noted that Beth was biting her thumbnail.

She gently pushed her friend's hand away from her mouth. When Beth glanced at her, she whispered, "You told me to stop you if I saw you biting."

"Yeah, thanks," Beth said. She tucked her hands under her arms to keep herself from chewing.

"How's it going?" Lindsey asked.

"Well, he hasn't run away—yet," Beth said.

Lindsey glanced across the table and noted that Aidan was discussing his upbringing on a farm in the Berkshires. Both Nancy and Violet were nodding, while Charlene was making notes on the memo app on her phone.

She met Lindsey's gaze and said behind her hand, "I'll be doing some fact-checking later."

"Ever the reporter," Lindsey said.

She glanced at Aidan and saw that a fine sheen of sweat had popped out on his brow. Poor guy. The jukebox in the corner was quiet, so Lindsey strolled over and popped in some quarters. Interrogations were always better when put to music. As a honky-tonk tune about drinking came on, she moved behind Aidan's chair and tapped him on the shoulder.

"Come on, big fella. Dance with me," she said.

The man catapulted out of his chair as if she'd thrown him a life preserver. Little did he know, he had just passed one of Lindsey's tests. Even if the man couldn't dance for beans, the fact that he went willingly to the dance floor was a check in the keeper column. Of course, he was probably just relieved to escape his jailers. Still, he went.

"Lindsey," Violet huffed. "We were just getting to the good stuff."

"You've had your turn. Besides, I'll bring him right back," she said. She leaned close to Beth and said, "Cut in about halfway through the song."

Beth nodded and smiled as Lindsey stepped into Aidan's arms and they began to work their way around the tiny dance floor. Okay, two checks in the keeper column. He was no Joaquín Cortés, but he wasn't squashing her toes either.

"Thank you," Aidan said. "I'm not usually easily intimidated, but the ladies are . . ."

"Intense?" Lindsey asked.

"A smidge," he said, and Lindsey laughed.

"You clearly have a gift for understatement," she said.

He smiled, and Lindsey decided right then and there that he was A-OK. His smile reached his eyes, and in their warm gaze she saw just the sort of good guy Beth deserved to have in her life.

"I know about Beth's ex Ernie or Rick or whatever his real name was," Aidan said.

"Ernie."

"She deserves so much more than that," he said. "I'm trying to convince her to start writing again."

"You are?"

"Yes, she's too brilliant not to be published," he said.

"Done and done," Lindsey said and stopped dancing. Her decision was made. Aidan was perfect for Beth.

"I'm sorry, what?" he asked.

"Excuse me, may I cut in?" Beth asked as she stepped up beside them.

"Absolutely," Lindsey said. "And I'm going to call the dogs off. You've got a good one here."

Beth grinned. "I think so, too."

Aidan looked bemused, and Beth tried to give him a stern look, but it was belied by the twinkle in her eyes.

"But I'm still taking it slow," she said to him.

Now Aidan smiled at her, looking just as smitten, and said, "We've got all the time in the world."

Beth practically swooned into his arms, and Lindsey went back to the table feeling satisfied that her best friend was going to be just fine.

"He's a keeper," she said.

Violet, Nancy and Charlene all nodded.

"After reviewing the facts, we have come to the same conclusion," Nancy said.

They all turned to look at the dance floor where Beth and Aidan were staring into each other's eyes.

"Who is Beth dancing with? Do I need to break that up, or should I say break *him* up?"

Lindsey turned back around to see Ian standing beside their table, looking like he was ready to crack some skulls; well, Aidan's, at any rate.

"No, no, we checked him out," Charlene said. She held up her smartphone. "I even did a background check. He's good."

"Background check?" Violet asked.

"I had a friend on the New Haven P.D. check for warrants, arrest history, et cetera," Charlene said. "He's clean."

"She kind of scares me," Nancy said to Violet.

Violet nodded and then looked at Ian. "Stand down."

"Could I intimidate him just a little?" Ian asked. "You know, set their relationship off on the right note?"

"Of fear and terror?" Mary asked as she joined them. "No."

Ian looked about to argue, but she jerked a thumb at the bar, letting him know where he was needed. Ian wasn't so easily chased off. He paused to plant a kiss on Mary's lips and look into her eyes as a slow smile spread across his face.

Lindsey thought back to the other evening when she and Sully were here and Sully said he had a feeling that Ian and Mary were up to something. She hadn't paid much attention at the time, but now she wondered.

There was a reverence in the way Ian looked at his wife that hadn't been there before. He'd always been besotted with Mary and was quite charmingly vocal about it, but this, this was different.

His hand slid across her flat stomach, and Mary put her hand over his for just the briefest moment. Lindsey gasped.

When Mary turned to look at her, she turned it into a hacking cough, which wasn't much of an act given that she had managed to suck some of her own spit into her windpipe and was choking on it.

"Are you all right, Lindsey?" Mary asked.

Lindsey nodded as her eyes watered up and she forced herself to stop coughing. "Frog in my throat."

"Well, come on and dance it out."

Lindsey turned to find Milton standing there, holding his arm out to her.

"Are you sure you're up to it?" she asked and pointed to the small bandage on his forehead.

"Of course," he said. He waved away her concern as if she was too silly to be taken seriously.

"Where's Ms. Cole?" she asked.

"Still annoyed with me," he said. "I'm hoping some time apart will soften her feelings."

"Well, don't give her too much space," Lindsey cautioned. "One thing men never seem to understand is that when a woman is done, she's done. There's no going back."

"Understood," he said. "I'm giving her space, but I'm also sending flowers and chocolates. I'll woo her back."

Lindsey smiled. Milton had been the town's resident bachelor for years after his wife passed. Ms. Cole was the first woman to give him a challenge instead of chasing him. She didn't doubt that Milton would work his magic on the spinster sooner or later.

He held out his arms in a very formal posture, and Lindsey mimicked him, keeping a few feet between them while they danced.

"And now to my real purpose," Milton said. He lowered an eyebrow at Lindsey in a chastising look. "Why didn't you come to me with your list of names?"

CHAPTER
28

BRIAR CREEK
PUBLIC LIBRARY

"Aw, what? Did Ronnie blab?" she asked.

"It's not her fault," he said. "We met up at our seniors' yoga class, and she asked me if I knew whatever happened to George Marzkie."

"Do you?" Lindsey asked.

"Yes, but that's beside the point," he said. "Why didn't you come to me?"

"Because I didn't want you to get hurt," Lindsey said.

"Asking me questions isn't going to cause me harm," he said.

"Well, I didn't think staying late in the library was going to cause you any harm either," she said.

"I understand," Milton said. "But I am the town historian."

"All right," Lindsey said. "Where is George Marzkie?"

"Last I heard, he left town to go join a commune in upstate New York in the early seventies, and no one's heard from him since."

"What about the other guy on my list, Philip Carver?"

"Dead," he said. "No family left behind."

Lindsey nodded. That seemed to happen quite a lot to the people the Rosens knew. She wondered if that meant something or if she was just getting pessimistic.

"There was one other person that Ronnie didn't know what happened to," Lindsey said. "She said she was a young woman who worked as a maid for the family but left shortly after Dr. Rosen passed."

"Ah yes," he nodded. "Betty Beller, a lovely girl with such a sunny disposition. She grew up in Hotchkiss Grove but lived on Star Island with the Rosens while she worked there. She left the area to get married."

"Do you think there'd be a record of her marriage in the historical society?" Lindsey asked. "I know they used to keep clippings of all the residents' big life events in the genealogical file."

"There might be, because she did live on one of the islands for a time, but there might not be, because she moved away," he said. "I can certainly look."

"Thanks, Milton," she said. "By any chance did Ronnie mention that the first three islands that Evelyn Dewhurst bought were originally owned by the Alston family?"

"No, she was a little fixated on finding George," he said. "I think she's having visions of a grand reunion."

"Oh, well, do you think it's just coincidence that those are the islands Evelyn acquired?"

Milton pursed his lips and then shook his head. "I can't think of any connection off the top of my head, but who knows. I don't generally believe in coincidence."

"Me either," she said.

"I'll do some checking at the historical society," he said.

Lindsey studied him, and her concern must have shown in her face.

"I promise I'll be careful," he said.

"It might be prudent not to talk to anyone about it," Lindsey said.

The song on the jukebox rolled into a slow one, and she glanced over to see Beth and Aidan slow down to continue their dance. Lindsey noticed that Aidan pulled Beth close but in a respectful hold, with his hand on the middle of her back, and he leaned over her, once again in that protective way he had that spoke more than words that he considered Beth something special and dear.

"They make a fine couple," Milton said.

"They really do," she agreed.

They turned to leave the dance floor and found Sully striding toward them.

"I have a feeling your dance card is about to get filled," Milton said with a smile. "I'll be in touch."

Lindsey watched as Milton and Sully exchanged greetings, and then Sully was opening his arms and she was moving into him as naturally as a river rolls into the ocean.

"Are you sure you're up to dancing with that bump on your head?" she asked. "Sheesh, what does it say about me that both of my partners are recovering from head injuries?"

"That you choose rough-and-tumble sorts of men. Don't worry, I won't bust too big of a move," he said. He pulled her close, and she inhaled that particular bay rum scent that was all Sully. "Besides, I have a doctor's note that green-lights me for all activity save maybe skydiving."

"That's a relief," she said. She gave him a quick hug, which he returned, bringing them even closer together and making Lindsey breathless. "I suppose Emma can stop threatening to drag you to the doctor herself now."

"The station was my first stop with my clean bill of health," he said. "Interestingly enough, they had just retrieved the contents of the Rosen safe-deposit box."

"No!" Lindsey said. "How did they find out what bank it was in?"

"Molly has a box in the same bank, and she recognized the key," he said.

"Lucky break," Lindsey said.

"Not really. It's the closest bank to Briar Creek. Just about everyone banks there," he said.

"What was in it?" Lindsey asked. "Love letters? Family jewels? Stocks and bonds? What?"

Sully grinned at her. "You're just a treasure hunter at heart, aren't you?"

"All librarians are," she said. "Books being our treasure of choice, naturally, but we're game for anything, really."

"Well, there were no books, family jewels or love letters," he said. "There was, however, a codicil to Dr. Rosen's will. In it, he states that he is the father of Beatrice Beller's child and provides for her and her child out of the family fortune."

"But she was, oh my . . ." Lindsey's voice trailed off.

"She was what?" he asked. "Do you know who she is, because no one at the station had a clue?"

"She was the Rosen's housemaid. Your family wasn't here yet, so no wonder you don't recognize the name," Lindsey said. "She left the island shortly after Dr. Rosen died, and it was believed that she had a doctor boyfriend in New Haven that she was going to marry."

"Who told you this?"

"Ronnie gave me the bulk of it, and Milton just confirmed it," she said.

"But how did her name come up in conversation? It's been over fifty years since she lived here," he said. He was getting the little vee in between his eyebrows that meant he wasn't happy.

"Funny story, true story," Lindsey said. Sully did not look amused. She sighed. "Fine. So it occurred to me when I was working the reference desk that Stewart might look to someone from his past for support, so I searched back in the old *Gazette* microfilm, and I printed the list of people who attended Dr. Rosen's memorial service. I thought there might be someone from the service that Stewart would seek out. Betty Beller was on the list."

"We have to call Emma," he said.

"Scale of one to ten with one being I'm fine and ten being she's going to lock me up and throw away the key, how do you think this is going to go?" she asked.

Sully blew out a breath. "I think you're looking at a three, but only because your information is very valuable."

"I can live with a three," Lindsey said. "I'll call her now."

They left the dance floor, and Lindsey took her cell phone down the short hall by the back exit to get away from the noise of the restaurant. Sully followed her and waited beside her while the phone rang. No one picked up, and it went to voice mail. Lindsey felt like the universe was giving her a pass.

She left a short and concise message on Emma's voice mail about who Betty Beller was and how she had found out her information. When she hung up, Sully gave her a thumbs-up.

"You got lucky," he said.

"Don't I know it," she agreed.

"Come on. I'll treat you to dinner," he said.

They joined the table where the crafternoon ladies sat. They were all watching Beth and Aidan, who were still dancing, and Lindsey could see approval in their eyes.

"Isn't this wonderful?" Violet asked the group. She raised her glass of beer. "Here's to our Beth finding herself a keeper."

They all clinked glasses.

"No one deserves it more," Nancy said. Then she cast a sly glance at Lindsey and Sully, "It'll be so nice to plan a wedding."

"Stop, just stop," Lindsey said.

Nancy chuckled, and Lindsey shook her head. Her friends were incorrigible, truly. Mary came back to their table and took everyone's order. She went right out to the dance floor and took Aidan's and Beth's orders as well.

Dinner was spent getting to know Aidan a bit better and in a much less inquisitorial way. He declared himself a Patriots fan, and he and Sully began to analyze their team's last season. It was clear to all that as far as Sully was concerned, Aidan was a fine catch for Beth.

It was at the end of the meal when Lindsey checked her phone that she saw she had a voice mail. She knew without checking that it would be from Emma. She gestured to everyone that she had a call to take and went back to the hallway where she could hear the message.

"Lindsey, it's Emma," the message began. "Thanks for the details on Betty Beller. Good work. Really, you should consider a career as a detective."

Lindsey cringed as Emma was not making the least effort to hide her sarcasm.

"Seriously, when questioned, our suspect Mr. Rosen-Grant identified Betty Beller as his grandmother, giving him a solid motive to murder the two men who had control of an estate that according to the codicil, he had a right to. Looks like we've found our murderer. If you could bring that list of names by the station, that would be great. Bye."

The call ended, and Lindsey glanced up to find Sully watching her.

"Was she mad?" he asked.

"More like moderately annoyed, judging by her sarcasm," Lindsey said. "And yet, she still wants the list of names, so I can't have done too badly."

"So, why the long look?" Sully asked.

"Because they're going to arrest Steven Rosen-Grant for the murder of Peter Rosen," Lindsey said. "And I'm not sure he did it."

Lindsey delivered the list of names Emma had requested the following morning on her way to work. The place was quiet with only Molly Hatcher at the front desk. The rest of the cubicles were empty.

"Morning, Molly," Lindsey said. "It's quiet in here today."

"It sure is," Molly said. She was a robust brunette with a big, booming voice and an equally loud laugh, the contagious sort that made you laugh with her even if you didn't hear the joke. But today she seemed subdued.

"Everything all right?"

"Yeah, they're taking Mr. Rosen-Grant to the courthouse for a preliminary hearing," Molly said. She lowered her voice and added, "He hasn't said anything about Stewart's whereabouts."

"Is that the theory?" Lindsey asked. "That he killed Peter and Stewart so he would inherit the estate?"

"It's one of them," she said. She frowned. "He's not very likable. He's bitter and definitely angry, but—"

"You don't see him as a killer," Lindsey said.

Molly shook her head. "Which is stupid, because it's not even based on fact; it's just a gut feeling."

"I know what you mean," Lindsey said.

She thought back to the Rosen house when she'd been running for her life from Steven, but in hindsight she couldn't help feeling like he hadn't intended to hurt her so much as catch her. Upon learning that Kirkland was a cop, his first reaction had been to demand he arrest Sully and Lindsey. If his intentions had been bad, wouldn't he have run or attacked Kirkland or something?

She shook herself free from the thought. There was no way to tell what a person would do for money. Robbery, murder, it was impossible to know what sort of heinous act a person could commit when they felt they were owed a better life and had no qualms about taking it by force. Steven Rosen-Grant could be a coldhearted psychopath and needed to be treated as such.

"I guess it's up to the courts now," Lindsey said. "I have the list of names that Emma asked me to drop off."

She opened her handbag and was digging around its dark interior when the sound of a car backfiring broke the quiet of the office. Only it didn't backfire once but three times in rapid succession and was then followed by the screech of wheels on pavement.

"Lindsey, get down!" Molly yelled, and she grabbed Lindsey's arm and dragged her to the floor behind her desk. At Lindsey's bewildered expression, she said, "That was gunfire."

"Oh, oh no!" Lindsey said.

"Stay down," Molly ordered. She popped up on her knees and peered over her desk. She grabbed the radio from its holder on her desk and spoke into the mouthpiece.

Lindsey held her breath as Molly asked for a response. Shortly after there was a voice, and Lindsey pushed out a breath when she recognized it was Emma's.

"There's been a 10-71 in the parking lot," Emma said. The radio chirped, and a buzz of static sounded. "We're at Code 6. I repeat, Code 6."

"Damn it, I'm still new at this," Molly said. "What's a Code 6?"

"Stay out of the area," Emma said.

"11-40?" Molly asked.

"No, 11-42," Emma said. "We're all okay."

Molly sagged against her desk. "I'll stand by."

"Roger that," Emma said.

"What was all that?" Lindsey asked.

"11-40 is 'advise if an ambulance is needed,'" Molly said. "11-42 means no."

"So, they're okay?"

"For now," Molly said.

In moments, the radio sounded again. Lindsey looked at Molly's hand when she turned up the volume. Her fingers were shaking. Lindsey glanced at her own hands and found they were trembling, too.

"Detective Trimble and I are in the transport wagon with our suspect and headed to the courthouse," Emma said. "Officers Kirkland and Trousdale are patrolling the parking lot. Wait for them to give you the all clear before you leave the building."

"Roger that," Molly said. She put the mouthpiece back in its holder.

"Maybe we should move away from the window," Lindsey said.

"Good idea. How about some coffee? We can wait in the break room."

Lindsey nodded and followed Molly back into the station where they holed up in the windowless break room, sipping coffee and trying to calm their nerves.

From the clock on the wall, Lindsey could see that fifteen

very long minutes passed before Officer Kirkland joined them.

"The parking lot and the surrounding area are clear," he said. He yanked his hat off and tossed it on the table. Frustration poured off of him as tangibly as the steam coming off the fresh cup of coffee Molly handed him.

"Where's Officer Trousdale?" Molly asked.

"Out front, checking the security cameras to see if they picked up the shooter," he said. He looked at Lindsey. "I'll escort you to the library just to be on the safe side."

"We heard three shots fired," she said. "Any idea who they were aiming for?"

"Oh yeah," he said. "They were definitely trying to take out Steven Rosen-Grant."

Molly and Lindsey exchanged a glance. Why would someone try to kill the suspect in Peter Rosen's murder?

"Stewart," Molly said. "Maybe it was Stewart out to avenge his brother's death."

"Well, thank God he's a lousy shot," Kirkland said.

"We don't know that it was Stewart," Lindsey said. "It could be someone else."

"I'm sorry, Lindsey, I know you're fond of Stewart, but who else would have a motive?" Molly asked.

"I don't know," Lindsey admitted.

"Look at it this way. If it was Stewart, at least he's alive and wasn't murdered like his brother," Kirkland said. "Now all we have to do is find him."

"Because we've had so much luck with that so far," Molly said.

"Yes, but it's different now," Kirkland said. "He won't be in hiding if he thinks the man who was out to kill him has been caught, right?"

Lindsey listened to their debate and chewed the bottom of her lip as she thought it over. She wouldn't believe that

Stewart was the shooter. She just wouldn't. It had to be someone else, but who?

Kirkland walked her to the library even though she
insisted she was fine on her own. They were both quiet, and
she noticed that Kirkland was scanning from side to side as
they walked. It was a relief to reach the familiarity and safety
of the library.

"Will you let me know when you hear from Emma?"
Lindsey asked. "I want to know that they're okay."

"Absolutely," Kirkland said. He looked uncomfortable for
a moment but then said, "If Stewart should come to the
library, I know you'll call the station right away."

Lindsey met his gaze, and she knew he was not making
a suggestion but rather giving her an order. She nodded. She
could respect his position.

"I will," she said. At his flat stare, she added, "I promise."

Officer Kirkland left, and Lindsey turned and went into
her office. The adrenaline was wearing off, and she desperately wanted to put her head on her desk and take a power
nap. She was just sinking toward the desk's surface when
there was a knock on her door.

Milton stood there, looking concerned. "Is it true? Was
there a shooting at the police station?"

Lindsey gestured for him to enter. "It's true. No one was
hurt, and the shooter got away, but the police believe that
he was aiming for Steven Rosen-Grant."

Milton's gray eyebrows shot up on his forehead. Lindsey
knew he was thinking the same thing that had occurred to
her and Molly, but like Lindsey, he rejected it.

"It wasn't Stewart," he said. He sat in one of the chairs
opposite her desk.

"I don't think so either, but it would sure help if Stewart
would appear so we knew he was all right and so we could
prove that he's innocent."

"The shooter has to be someone who would gain by Steven's death," Milton said.

"Could it be someone from his life in Illinois?"

Lindsey glanced at the door to find Sully there with his arms crossed over his chest, studying her. There was a look of relief on his face that told her more than words just how much he cared about her well-being. She smiled at him.

"It's possible, but I don't know how we could prove that," she said.

"You could check the Illinois newspapers," he suggested.

"Are you suggesting I butt in?" Lindsey asked him in surprise.

"You won't listen to me if I tell you not to," he said. He pushed off of the doorframe and took the seat beside Milton.

"If you can't beat 'em, join 'em, eh?" Milton asked.

"Something like that," Sully said.

"I'll check the papers in Illinois to see if he's mentioned, but I can't help but feel like this is connected to Steven being a Rosen," she said.

"In what way?" Milton asked. "I thought we agreed that we didn't think it was Stewart."

"I don't, but isn't it convenient that Peter Rosen has been murdered, Stewart Rosen is missing and possibly dead and now the only other heir to Star Island was almost shot and killed?"

"So, you think it is someone who wants the island," Sully said. "And they're willing to kill to get it."

CHAPTER

30

BRIAR CREEK
PUBLIC LIBRARY

Lindsey shrugged. "I'm just saying it's possible."

"Who?" Milton asked, and then he blinked. "Wait. That makes more sense than you know."

Sully and Lindsey both turned to him.

"After we talked about how odd it was that Evelyn Dewhurst had bought the three Alston Islands first, I did some research on the Alston family," he explained. "Turns out one of the reasons Alston lost his fortune was because of Mrs. Rosen."

Sully leaned forward. "Do tell."

"She was the one who outed him for his relationship with a thirteen-year-old girl. He fled the country with the young girl, leaving his wife penniless. She had to sell everything just to survive."

"How does that tie the islands to Evelyn Dewhurst?" Lindsey asked.

"I can't prove anything," Milton said. "There was no documentation, and we'd have to use other sources to verify, but . . ."

He paused, and Lindsey gestured for him to continue.

"Alston's wife was named Allison *Evelyn*," he said.

"So, we're thinking long-lost relative?" Lindsey asked. "There seem to be a lot of those cropping up. I'd feel better if the name was more unusual, like Philomena or Clarissa."

"Maybe it was just coincidence that Evelyn picked those three islands, or maybe there is something about those islands and the Rosen island that she is fixated on," Milton said. "Like size or shape or location."

"That's a good angle," Sully said. "I can't think of a similarity off the top of my head. They all have different houses, they're in different locations . . . No, I'm not seeing a connection."

The three of them were silent for a moment. Lindsey could feel an idea forming in her mind. It was a bad idea. It was fraught with risk and danger, and she had promised herself she would not do anything that might get someone hurt. Still . . .

"I think we need to draw the shooter out," Milton said. Lindsey glanced at him. He was reading her mind.

"If they shot at Steven thinking he was the last heir, then all we need to do to tip their hand would be to announce that a new heir has been found," Sully said.

"How'd you know that's what I was thinking?" Milton asked.

"Because I'm betting that's what all three of us were thinking," Sully said. He raised an eyebrow when he glanced at Lindsey. "Am I right?"

"Looks like great minds do think alike," she said. "The gossipy article you mentioned got me to thinking: if we could get something into tomorrow afternoon's issue of the *Gazette* about a newly discovered heir to the Rosen estate, we might be able to pique the killer's curiosity."

Milton pulled out his cell phone. "I'm calling Saul, the editor, now. I'll tell him I've uncovered information at the historical society leading to another Rosen heir."

"Wait!" Lindsey cried. "We haven't worked out all the details yet. I'm not sure this is the best idea. It could put you in terrible danger."

She thought about how upset Ms. Cole would be and actually flinched.

"I appreciate the concern," Milton said. "But whoever this person is—or, more accurately, whoever these persons are—they knocked me down, they abused my trust, they shook my faith in my fellow man. How can I not do everything in my power to bring them to justice?"

"Hear, hear!"

Lindsey turned to the door to find Ms. Cole standing there. Dressed all in shades of yellow today, she had a sort of pudgy banana thing going, but the pride that shone on her face as she looked at Milton made her positively radiant.

"Eugenia," Milton said. He rose from his seat. "You understand why I must do what I can?"

She nodded. "I don't like it, and you have to promise me you'll be careful, but I do understand, and I'm, well, proud of the warrior within you."

Milton hugged her close, and Sully and Lindsey both glanced away, catching each other's gaze and smiling in mutual embarrassment as they waited for the clinch to break up.

"So, I hear there's more snow in the forecast," Sully said.

"Really? More, you say?"

A flash of yellow caught her attention, and Lindsey turned to see Ms. Cole approach her desk.

"I owe you an apology," she said. "It wasn't your fault Milton was attacked, and I'm sorry I was not as understanding as I could have been."

"That's quite all right," Lindsey said. "Emotions were running high, and these things happen."

Ms. Cole gave her a brusque nod and turned and left the office, pausing beside Milton to whisper something in his ear that made his bald head glow like a beacon.

It was agreed that Milton would be in the historical society office the following evening after the news story came out. Lindsey and Sully would also be there, but in hiding, to bear witness to whoever came in to query about any more Rosen relatives.

It was as the men were leaving her office that Lindsey felt her first surge of hope and doubt.

"Lindsey, isn't that . . . ?" Sully pointed to an object behind her office door.

Lindsey moved around him and glanced down. "My box. It's my box of books."

They exchanged worried looks, and Lindsey knew Sully was thinking the same thing she was. This was either a message from Stewart that he was okay, or someone was messing with her head. Of course, if Stewart had been here, he could very easily have been in the parking lot of the police department earlier, shooting at the man he believed was responsible for his brother's death. Lindsey blew out a breath, trying to ignore her sudden feeling of unease. It couldn't be Stewart, she was sure of it, mostly.

Sully and Lindsey arrived at the historical society an hour before the *Gazette* was available. Milton ushered them through the back door, and the three of them went over the plan in a windowless office in the center of the one-story brick building.

"I'll stay in the main room while you two keep out of sight in the file room," Milton said. He opened a door off of the main room that housed two rows of large steel file cabinets full of clippings about the town and its residents for more than the past century.

"We're assuming that the person—" Lindsey began, but Milton interrupted.

"Persons," he said. "There have to be two people involved, remember? One to draw me out and one to whack me from behind."

"You're right. We're assuming the persons responsible for Peter's death are going to see the *Gazette* article right away," Lindsey said. "It could be that they don't see it at all."

"Oh no, everyone is going to see it," Milton said. "Saul told me that the front-page story is the arrest of Steven Rosen-Grant and the shooting in the parking lot. He said they've doubled their print run anticipating the demand."

Lindsey smiled. "Saul must be in his glory."

Saul Potts had been a big-city newsman all his life. He'd retired to Briar Creek several years before but had been muscled into taking the job as the editor of the *Briar Creek Gazette* when his wife, Jeanie, threatened to leave him if he didn't find something to do besides follow her around.

"He's positively giddy," Milton said.

"As soon as the person arrives asking about the heir, we will call the police," Sully said.

"You have to make sure you play it very carefully," Lindsey said to Milton. "They've already killed at least once. If they think you suspect a connection, they might harm you . . . Oh, I don't think we should do this!"

"Lindsey, it'll be okay. I'll knock twice on the door to let you know when someone enters the building," Milton said. "I know what I need to do. Trust me."

Milton closed his eyes and did some pranayama breathing while Sully closed the door behind them as they ducked into the file room. Lindsey's last sight of Milton showed him with his head back and his eyes shut, looking the picture of peace or, as her dark side kicked in, a man about to meet his doom. A feeling of dread filled her, and she felt her heart rate kick up and her hands began to sweat.

"We should call the police right now," she whispered to Sully. "To put them on alert."

"There's nothing to report yet," he said. He reached over and squeezed her shoulder. "It's going to be okay. I won't let anything happen to Milton."

"I wish I knew who we were dealing with and why," Lindsey said.

"We will soon enough," Sully said.

He was wrong, so very wrong. An hour and a half passed. They could hear the occasional "*Om*" as Milton practiced his yoga. Lindsey would have joined him, but the file room only had a narrow aisle running down the middle. There was barely enough space for the two of them to sit, never mind practice yoga.

They agreed to spend their time going through the files. It was a long shot, but they focused on the late fifties and early sixties hoping something about the Rosens would pop.

She was amazed at how long they worked without speaking. She would have thought it would be awkward, but instead it was companionable, as if they understood each other well enough for no words to be necessary.

Still, it was cramped. They kept the light on in the small room, which helped to keep it from feeling claustrophobic. They had both switched the sound off of their phones to keep from having a text or a call come in at the worst moment possible. Still, Sully checked the scores to the Celtics game on his while she checked the time on hers every fifteen minutes or so.

The *Gazette* was distributed to homes and the local businesses by an intrepid group of paperboys and girls, and Saul Potts usually dropped a stack off in the library on his way home from the *Gazette* office. Lindsey knew he took great pride in making the weekly paper a periodical with substance and not just birdcage liner or fish wrap.

When she glanced at the clock on her phone for the umpteenth time, she realized the paper had been out for over an hour now. She really hoped that whoever had shot at Steven Rosen-Grant was reading all about their handiwork and that

Saul had featured the information Milton had given him prominently in the story.

Lindsey was beginning to fear that they would be here well past dinnertime, and the hankering for a piece of fried fish with a pile of fries and a mound of coleslaw was beginning to be all she could think about. Her stomach growled, really loudly, and she glanced up to see Sully smiling at her.

She felt her face heat up, and then she whispered, "When we get out of here, I am ordering the biggest pile of fish and chips you have ever seen."

In answer, Sully's stomach growled as well. It surprised a laugh out of Lindsey, and he gave her a rueful glance.

"I'm with you on that," he said. "I swear I could eat a pile of broccoli right now, and I despise broccoli."

"I loathe zucchini," she confessed. "But, yeah, I'd eat a plate of it right now."

"Brussels sprouts," he said. They both made gagging faces.

"Peas," she said.

"Peas?" he asked, looking alarmed. "Who doesn't like peas?"

"Me," she said. "They're gross. The texture is nasty."

"Well, that settles it, then," he said. "You can never get seriously involved with the Englishman, since I think mashed peas are a staple of the English diet."

"Bleck," she said. He grinned, and, like always, her heart cartwheeled in her chest. "Besides, there's a more important reason why I can never belong to Robbie."

"Do tell," he said.

"My heart belongs to another. It always has," she said.

They sat silently staring at each other, and then Sully was leaning in close, and she knew he was about to kiss her.

Knock, knock!

Sully jerked back, and Lindsey felt her eyes go wide. That was the signal. The two knocks that they had agreed Milton would tap on the door when a person was spotted coming into the historical society.

They both sat motionless, afraid to make even the slightest rustle of clothing, lest they alert the person to their presence. Lindsey strained to hear, and she knew Milton was facing the door between them when his voice was as clear as if he were in the room with them.

"Why, Mr. Hodges, good evening," he said. He sounded as surprised as Lindsey felt.

Then again, she supposed it was silly of them to think that no one else from town might stop into the historical society that evening, especially Hodges and Perkins, who were probably still scouting for collectibles while waiting for Emma to give them the go-ahead to leave town, which she would have thought Emma would have done once they caught Steven Rosen-Grant.

She glanced at Sully. He was frowning, and she suspected he was thinking the same thing she was. She had a moment of panic that whoever was looking for the heir to the Rosen estate would come in and Hodges could find himself in the middle of something he hadn't anticipated, but maybe they would get lucky and his request would be a small one and he'd be on his way quickly.

"Hi, Mr. Duffy. Please call me Calvin," he said.

"Milton," he returned. Lindsey wondered if they were shaking hands. "Where's your partner, Mr. Perkins?"

"Kevin is back at the bed-and-breakfast, packing our things," he said. "It seems we've finally been given the okay to leave town."

"Excellent. I'm sure you're eager to get back to your shop," Milton said.

"More than you know," Calvin said. He gave a chuckle that sounded forced.

Lindsey glanced at Sully and saw his eyebrows go up. So he heard it, too.

"So, was there something I could help you with?"

"Yes, actually," Calvin said. He cleared his throat before

he continued. "There was an item in the *Gazette* this evening that caught my attention."

"I'm sure Saul, the editor, will be pleased to hear it," Milton said.

"Have you read it today?" Calvin asked.

Lindsey heard someone, Milton, she suspected, cross the room to the window. There was the sound of the drapes being moved aside.

"No, I'm afraid not. There's my box of *Gazette* issues out on the steps. I'll have to remember to get them before it snows. What was of special interest to you?"

"Actually, there was a bit of information in the cover story about Peter Rosen's murder that I am hoping you can verify."

"I'll do my best," Milton said.

"It said there was another heir to the Rosen estate in addition to Stewart and Steven Rosen-Grant. I need you to tell me who it is."

CHAPTER

31

BRIAR CREEK
PUBLIC LIBRARY

Lindsey reached over and grabbed Sully's hand and squeezed it hard. It was the only thing she could think to do to keep from crying out.

Calvin Hodges, the collector? He was the one who had been trying to get rid of the Rosens? But why?

"Oh, that," Milton said. Lindsey heard him walk around the room, and she suspected he was positioning himself so that his great big desk was between him and Hodges.

Sully had pulled out his phone and was firing off a text to Chief Plewicki. It was the only way they could think to let her know what was happening without making any noise. He also sent one to Ms. Cole. She was their backup. She was to call the police and make sure Emma got the text message from Sully.

"Yeah, that," Calvin said.

"I'd really like to help you," Milton said, "as I'm sure a man in your occupation is interested in who owns a house packed to the rafters with odds and ends, some of which are

undoubtedly worth a fortune, but I can't give out that information. I have to respect the person's privacy. I'm sure you
understand."

"I do. I definitely do," Calvin said. "But I'm afraid I'm
going to have to insist that you tell me."

There was a tense silence coming from the room. Sully
slipped his phone into his pocket and put his hand near the
doorknob. Lindsey knew he was getting ready to jump out
and assist Milton if it was needed.

"What's it to you?" Milton asked.

It was the first time Lindsey could ever remember hearing
him sound like an ornery octogenarian.

"It is everything," Calvin said.

There was a note of sheer desperation in his voice. What
could be so important about the Rosen house that would
make a collector from Chicago sound terrified?

"I'm sorry," Milton said. His voice was almost kind now,
and Lindsey knew he was reacting in his usual soothing way
to the fear that was pouring off of Calvin Hodges like a sour
smell.

"Not at the moment, you're not, but I imagine you
will be."

It was a new voice, a woman's. Lindsey felt Sully's gaze on
her and turned to look at him. He mouthed the name she
had suspected all along. *Evelyn Dewhurst.*

"I ask you to do one thing, Hodges, one thing. Lord, you
are incompetent. No wonder you're about to lose your business," she said.

"I was handling this," he snapped. "And you can stop
acting so high and mighty. You wouldn't know anything
about anything if I hadn't told you the night we met at the
Anchor."

"Oh, but I *am* high and mighty, and you know it," she said.
"Milton, I want the name of the remaining heir to the Rosen
estate, and I want it now. I don't have the time or inclination

to play games with you, so give me the information and I won't have to have Hodges hurt you . . . much."

"It was you two," Milton growled. He sounded so angry Lindsey almost didn't recognize his voice. "You're the ones who knocked me down outside the library. You were trying to get to Stewart, weren't you?"

"What did you not understand about me not having time for this?" Evelyn asked. "Tell me who the remaining heir is before Hodges beats it out of you."

"Wait, I never agreed—" Hodges protested.

"Oh, do shut up!" Evelyn snapped. "What did you think was going to happen tonight? You know what the endgame is. Now stop being such a sniveler."

"I never agreed to hurt anyone," Hodges argued.

"Didn't you?" Evelyn asked. "Didn't we both?"

There was the sound of rustling, and then Milton let out a yip. Lindsey had her hand on the knob and was about to turn it when Milton shouted, "A gun, Evelyn? Really? How unladylike."

Sully put his hand over Lindsey's and stopped her. Milton's shout had been to alert them to the new level of danger on the other side of the door.

"If we startle her, she might shoot him by accident," Sully breathed in Lindsey's ear.

She nodded that she understood, but she was terrified that something would happen to Milton before they could get to him.

"Wait for it," Sully said. Lindsey knew he was using all of his naval combat training to pick the right moment to bust out of the file room.

"It is a bit brutish," Evelyn conceded. "But it got your attention, didn't it? Now the name, please."

"No."

"Then I'm afraid you give me no choice," Evelyn said. "Shall I start with your kneecaps and work my way up?"

That was the first time Lindsey ever understood the term *all hell breaking loose.*

In one motion, Sully was up, the door was shoved open and he sprang past Lindsey into the room, where he took Evelyn down at the knees, grabbing her gun as she went.

Lindsey raced into the room after him and hurried to Milton's side.

"Are you all right?" she asked. She hugged him tight.

"I'm fine," he said. He hugged her back. "Just fine."

Sully rose to his feet, pulling Evelyn up after him and shoving her into a chair. He had the gun, and he motioned for Calvin to take the chair beside her.

"You killed Peter Rosen, didn't you?" he asked.

Evelyn looked away while Calvin shook his head from side to side.

"No, I had nothing—"

"Shut up, you idiot," Evelyn said.

"Did you kidnap Stewart and kill him, too?" Lindsey demanded.

"No!" Calvin answered. "I swear!"

"SHUT UP!" Evelyn shrieked, and she hit him with her right fist like a hammer to the sternum, making Calvin double over and suck in a breath.

"Where is Stewart?" Sully asked. Evelyn stuck her chin up in defiance and turned her head away.

"I don't know," Calvin wheezed. "We tried to grab him that night at the library, but he was too fast for us."

"Who shot at Steven today?" Milton demanded.

Evelyn continued with the stony silence, and Lindsey felt her patience snap.

"Judging by the fact that she owns a gun and clearly knows how to use it, I think it's a safe bet that it was Evelyn," she said.

A tick of her lips was Evelyn's only response, but it was enough.

"I imagine she is the one who killed Peter Rosen as well,"

she said. "Really, Evelyn, all to own an island? And what did she promise you, Calvin, all of the contents if you'd just help her get rid of the current residents?"

Calvin was still clutching his chest, but his face became mottled with a red rash of shame that bespoke his guilt more clearly than a confession.

"You killed my brother?"

The voice was soft, no more than a whisper, but everyone heard it. All eyes turned to the doorway where Stewart Rosen stood, holding a shotgun that was aimed right at Evelyn and Calvin.

"Stewart!" Lindsey cried.

He looked rumpled and disheveled, but otherwise he seemed okay. In fact, compared to the last time she'd seen him, he looked surprisingly fit with a healthy color to his skin and not nearly as exhausted, plus he wasn't humming.

"I'm going to kill you," Stewart said. He lifted his shotgun and pointed it at Evelyn and Calvin. It was the first time she lost her composure, and she did it spectacularly.

"You can't! It would be murder!" She glanced at the others in the room. "You're witnesses. If he kills me, it is murder and he'll go to jail for the rest of his life."

"What does it matter?" Stewart asked. "You've taken away my brother. Who do I have left?"

"I didn't," Evelyn said. "I didn't take him away, I swear."

"You killed him!" Stewart yelled. There was a crazy light in his eyes, and Lindsey felt her heart seize up in her chest. He was going to shoot Evelyn, and there wasn't a thing they could do about it.

"No!" Calvin said. "He shot himself. He committed suicide."

"You're lying," Stewart said. "Why would he do that? Why would he shoot himself through the chest?"

"Because he was trying to hurt himself," Calvin said. His voice broke when he continued, "Because he wanted to die slowly and painfully to punish himself for killing his father."

The silence that descended upon the room had the density of a shroud. For Lindsey, it was the final turn of the screw that made everything fit right and tight.

"So, that's what happened," she said. She glanced at Stewart.

"No, it didn't! It was a boating accident. It wasn't his fault," Stewart said. "My brother would never take his life. He would never leave me. He was my best friend."

"I know this is hard, Stewart, but we have to be honest here. Too many lies have caused too much damage, don't you think?" Lindsey said.

He looked at Lindsey, clearly desperate to understand why his brother would commit suicide.

"Your brother was in love with Betty Beller, wasn't he?" she asked.

Stewart's lips tightened, and he nodded. "We all were. She was so different from . . ."

His voice trailed off, and Lindsey assumed he meant his mother but didn't have the heart to say it.

"Stewart, I don't know if you've heard, but Betty was involved with your father, and she had a child, a little girl named Gabrielle," Lindsey said. "She grew up and had a little boy named Steven, Steven Rosen-Grant. He would have been your father's grandson."

"No, he wouldn't," Stewart said. Lindsey opened her mouth to protest, but Stewart shook her off. "No, my father wasn't his grandfather. Peter was."

"What?"

Steven Rosen-Grant stepped into the room followed by Chief Plewicki, on crutches, and Detective Trimble.

Stewart started at the sight of him. Standing across from each other, the resemblance was uncanny.

"Drop the gun, Stewart," Emma said. She glanced at Sully and added, "You, too."

Sully turned the handgun so that the handle faced out,

and he held it out to Trimble, who checked the safety and put it in his coat pocket.

Stewart was not nearly as cooperative. His hands shook as he kept the shotgun trained on Evelyn and Calvin. But he glanced out of the corner of his eye at his grandnephew.

"My father couldn't have children," he said. "When we were kids, we had the mumps and my father caught it. He had wanted more children, but he was infertile after that. Naturally, he blamed my mother. When Betty arrived, he took a shine to her, and it was clear that he thought she was his for the taking.

"He planned to prove his fertility by getting her pregnant. He pursued her relentlessly, right in front of my mother. It soon became clear that he and Betty were having an affair. When it was discovered that she was pregnant, my mother had an episode. She was convinced my father would divorce her and leave her penniless while he started a new life with Betty. But then, my father discovered Peter and Betty in bed together . . ."

His voice trailed off as he revisited what had to be a horrible, horrible memory.

"What happened?" Steven asked. His gaze was intense upon his uncle's face, as if the next words uttered would determine the course of his life forever.

"My father went a little crazy," Stewart said. "Even though a storm was coming, he demanded that Peter take the sailboat out with him so they could discuss this like real men."

Stewart flinched, and Lindsey could only imagine how terrified he must have been for his brother.

"I went to try to talk my brother out of going," Stewart said. "I wanted him to hide until my father's rage passed, but when I got to his room, my mother was there. She told him that the only way they could have what they wanted was for my father not to come back. She told him, 'You know what you have to do.'"

"Oh no, no, no," Steven cried, and he sank to his knees. "I didn't know that. He never said . . . I didn't know that he was my grandfather. I thought he was my granduncle. When Grandma Betty died last year, I found his name in her address book, so I wrote to him to let him know. I thought, uh, I thought he might care enough to get in touch with me, and he did. I didn't tell him who I was, at first, and when I did, he told me not to use the name Rosen on my return address or his brother would get suspicious. I thought he was trying to keep me away to deny me my heritage."

"But you kept corresponding with Peter and discovered that the Rosens owned a very exclusive piece of real estate that was a treasure trove of stuff, so you enlisted the help of Perkins and Hodges to evaluate what you decided was your rightful inheritance." Lindsey knew she sounded harsh, but the story being revealed was just one bit of reprehensible behavior after another.

"Yes, Steven emailed me, saying he was Peter Rosen," Calvin said. "By the time I figured out who he really was, we were already here."

"How did you figure it out?" Steven asked Lindsey.

"You're both from the Chicago area," she said. "How else could Perkins and Hodges have heard of this place? Besides, neither Peter nor Stewart used computers or cell phones or tablets. How could they have emailed Perkins and Hodges? It had to be you, Steven, pretending to be Peter."

"I just thought it was time to collect what was rightfully mine," Steven said. "Peter told me about the key in the music box and that his mother had hidden papers at the bank, papers about Grandma Betty. I thought if I could get to the safe-deposit box, I could prove I was a Rosen and that part of the estate rightfully belonged to me."

"Well, it seems your desire to redo the past is something you have in common with Mrs. Dewhurst," Lindsey said.

"You don't know what you're talking about," Evelyn said. "I am leaving now."

She made to get up, but Emma shook her head. "Sit down."

"But I . . ."

"Shut it," Emma said. She glanced at Lindsey and said, "Explain."

"Evelyn has been buying up all of the islands, but the first three that she bought originally belonged to the Alston family," Lindsey said. "A scandal, revealed by Mrs. Rosen, cost the Alston family their fortune. I take it Allison Evelyn Alston was your grandmother?"

"Lies, all lies! Besides, you can't prove anything," Evelyn said.

"Not yet, but I really don't think it is going to be that hard to prove that you are an Alston," Lindsey said. "DNA swabs being what they are nowadays and all."

Stewart spoke up. "You don't need to do that. Allison Alston knew her husband had squandered the family fortune, and she knew he was having an affair with a child. She tried to blackmail my mother, saying that she was well aware that Betty carried my father's child and she was going to go public if my mother didn't give her a large sum of money. You don't threaten my mother." Stewart smiled rather grimly. "She went right to the authorities and told them about Alston's thirteen-year-old lover. I have the entire account in her diary . . . somewhere." He looked at Evelyn with contempt. "And you look just like her."

Evelyn paled.

"Is anyone else getting a headache?" Emma snapped.

"Sit down. You'll feel better," Trimble said.

"I'm not sitting down," she argued. "Stewart, lower your weapon or I'll shoot you myself."

Stewart turned to look at her, and his face was one of utter despair. "Maybe that would be for the best."

"No, please, no," Steven cried. He looked beseechingly at his uncle. "All of this is my fault. Mine. Peter told me that he was responsible for his father's death, that he could have saved him when he fell overboard but he chose not to. I thought he had robbed me of my grandfather. I was so angry. I told Calvin, thinking we could use it as leverage to force him to give us items out of the house, but then Calvin came to town and met Evelyn, and she . . ."

"Convinced you to use his guilt against him, to drive him to suicide, leaving only Stewart, who would also die from, what, a horrible accident? Then the property would be yours," Emma said. She looked at Steven as if he were a worm that crawled out of her apple.

"No, I never meant for him to kill himself. I never meant for any of this to happen," Steven protested. "I just wanted to finally belong somewhere, to have a piece of what was supposed to be my life."

"It's true," Calvin said. "Driving Peter to commit suicide was her idea." He jerked a thumb in Evelyn's direction. "She badgered him and berated him until he was a sobbing mess, and then she put the gun in his hand. I didn't know until after he killed himself that that had been her plan all along, and by then, it was too late." He gestured to the gun Sully had handed to Trimble. "That's the gun he used to end his life. She had me take the gun so it would look like Stewart murdered his brother. She thought that would be a nice way to get rid of the two of them. One dead and one in jail."

"It should have been two dead." Stewart lifted the shotgun and pointed it at his own head.

"No, Stewart, don't!" Milton yelled.

"Why not?" Stewart asked. "What do I have to live for?"

"You have a nephew," Milton said. "And he needs you. If you do this, you'll destroy the one thing Peter left behind for you."

Stewart glanced at Steven, at the face so like his brother's. He studied the younger man as if looking for a sign. Steven rubbed the tip of one of his ears just the way Lindsey had seen Stewart do when he was stressed.

Lindsey held her breath, hoping Stewart saw it, too, and recognized something in the gesture that reminded him of himself or Peter.

Stewart nodded and slowly lowered the shotgun. Lindsey let out a pent-up breath as Emma hobbled forward and gently took the gun from his hands. Sully's hand was at her back, and Lindsey sagged against him as she realized all of the danger had passed.

"I think it's time to move this over to the station," Trimble said. "Clearly, there is still much to be sorted. Kirkland. Trousdale."

The two officers came into the room from outside. They cuffed both Evelyn and Calvin and led them from the room. Emma and Trimble gently led Steven and Stewart in their wake.

At the door, Emma turned around and looked at Milton, Sully and Lindsey.

"Go get yourselves something to eat and then report to the station. We have a lot to discuss."

They watched as she turned away, and Milton said, "Is it just me or did she not seem that mad? Maybe we're not in that much trouble."

"Oh yes, you are!" Emma shouted over her shoulder right before the door slammed shut after her.

CHAPTER

32

BRIAR CREEK
PUBLIC LIBRARY

It was Beth's turn to bring the food for their Thursday crafternoon. Since she had been a bit scatterbrained lately, Lindsey had her phone and was ready to call in a couple of pizzas for express delivery. She needn't have worried.

When she arrived at the room, it was to find Beth not wearing her usual story time outfit but rather a pretty blue cardigan over a matching shell with a gray flannel pencil skirt and knee-high black leather boots. Lindsey gave her an impressed look, and Beth grinned.

"Dinner date after work," she explained.

"Is it officially getting serious?" Violet asked.

"You mean have we popped out the big *L* word yet?" Beth asked. All of the ladies gave her their undivided attention. "No."

"Whew," Nancy said. "I am delighted that you have found a nice man, but there is no need to rush things."

"Agreed, you want to enjoy the salad days as long as you can," Charlene said.

Lindsey listened to the women advise her friend while she went to check out Beth's spread. The huge loaf of soda bread with raisins and caraway seeds drew her to it with a power that was almost magnetic. Several wedges of cheese, some rolled meats, a selection of fruit, vegetables and dip rounded out the offering.

"I just have to ask, who chose *Anna Karenina* for our book this week?" Beth asked. "I mean, are you trying to scare me off of relationships?"

"I thought a romance would be a nice change up since we did a mystery last time," Violet said. "Besides, it is such a romantic story when Anna chooses Count Vronsky."

"But the ending," Beth protested.

Mary joined Lindsey at the table. "So, how are you since the hullabaloo last week?"

"I'm fine," Lindsey said.

She had been so busy giving statements and such after everything had been revealed at the historical society the previous Wednesday that she hadn't had much time to catch up with her friends. Still, she remembered that evening at the Anchor and how attentive Ian had been to Mary.

"I think the question is how are *you?*" She met Mary's gaze and noticed that her friend looked away quickly before looking back at her.

"You know, don't you?" Mary asked. She glanced at the others to make sure they weren't listening.

"I suspect there are glad tidings coming from you and Ian whenever you choose to share them," she said.

Mary smiled. "Does Sully suspect?"

"He thinks you're up to something, but I don't think he has a clue what it is, yet," Lindsey said.

"We're just waiting for the twelve-week mark," Mary said. Her eyes twinkled. "Just a few more weeks to go. You don't mind keeping it quiet, do you?"

"Keeping what quiet?" Lindsey asked with a wink. Then she grinned and gave her friend a tight squeeze. "I'm thrilled for you."

"Thanks," Mary said.

"Hey, you two, what's going on over there?" Nancy asked. "Were you planning on joining us?"

"Sorry, I was just wrestling the butter away from Mary," Lindsey said.

"Well, do tell us what your thoughts on *Anna Karenina* are while you're at it," Violet said.

"Love is a train wreck," Lindsey said.

The ladies all laughed, and she was relieved not to have given away Mary's wonderful news. A baby! How amazing. Now she could go out and buy all of her favorite children's books, and maybe she'd even try her hand at knitting again and make a baby blanket.

"Do we have enough brown paper for our craft project?" Charlene asked.

"Yes, I brought a roll of it, donated from the hardware store," Nancy said. "When Shelley heard we were making a blind date display out of the books, she was more than happy to help."

Since the paper flowers had proven so popular in the library, Lindsey had strong-armed the crafternooners for another library project. This time they were wrapping books in brown paper and writing short descriptions on them, with a drawing if they felt so inclined, and then they were going to put them on display in the library in a "have a blind date with a book" display. Beth had come up with the idea, and Lindsey thought it was charming and the perfect antidote to the end of February winter blahs.

"So, did I tell you who I saw in town at the post office in daylight?" Violet asked. She waited barely a second before forging ahead. "Stewart Rosen, with his grandnephew, Steven."

"They've been in to the library quite a bit as well," Lindsey said. "I think they are enjoying getting to know each other, and Kevin Perkins has stayed on to help them sort the house."

"I'm so glad he had nothing to do with the whole sordid mess," Violet said. "I like him."

"What's going to happen to Evelyn and Calvin?" Beth asked.

"Emma says they are facing multiple charges of trespassing, harassment, assault and attempted murder. It was Evelyn who shot at Steven," Nancy said. "I don't think this is going to end well for her. The town council is already trying to see if they can force her to sell her islands."

"Can they do that?" Charlene asked.

"I don't know, but they're sure going to try," Mary said.

The conversation moved from the recent events that had captivated the town, back to *Anna Karenina*, over to whether it was supposed to snow, and on to Beth gushing about Aidan and the plans they had for their shared story times.

After the meeting, Lindsey wheeled their cart of brown paper–covered books out to the display area she had cleared off for them in the high-traffic area by the front doors.

She was happily arranging them, admiring the work the crafternooners had done in writing their intriguing descriptions to entice readers to choose the books, when she saw someone approach out of the corner of her eye. She turned with her what-can-I-do for-you smile firmly in place when she recognized the red blond hair and twinkling green eyes.

"Robbie," she cried. "You're back!"

"I am," he said. He opened his arms and hugged her close.

"How was the trip? Do you want some tea?" she asked. Just the sight of him made her realize she had missed him more than she thought, and she was genuinely pleased to see her friend. She squeezed his arm and asked, "How are you?"

"Funny you should ask," he said. He tilted his head to the side and gave her an almost shy smile. "I'm divorced."

The Briar Creek Library Guide to Crafternoons

Sharing a book, a craft and some delicious food with good friends is the basic recipe for a successful crafternoon. Lindsey and the girls like to mix it up by reading all sorts of different books, from classic to contemporary, from literary tomes to bestselling genre fiction. They also enjoy trying out new crafts and new recipes. Attached are some suggestions to kick-start your own crafternoon, but remember, the most important part is to have fun!

Readers Guide for
The Daughter of Time
by Josephine Tey

1. The title *The Daughter of Time* comes from a quote taken from Sir Francis Bacon that reads, "Truth is the daughter of time, not of authority." What did he mean? Do you agree with this idea? Why or why not?

2. Tey's premise in the book is that historical facts, such as Richard III murdering his brother's children the Princes in the Tower, often become warped over time and by political agenda. Do you agree or disagree? Can you think of any historic events that later proved to be false?

3. The hero Alan Grant, a Scotland Yard detective, is known for his skill at physiognomy, the ability to read a person's character by their appearance. To relieve his boredom during a hospital stay, he is taken with a portrait of Richard III and decides that the man in the portrait was kindly and not capable of the murders he was rumored to have committed.

Do you believe that a person's character can be ascertained by their facial features? Give examples for why or why not.

4. It is clear that through the detection done by her protagonist Alan Grant, Tey set out to make the reader rethink what has always been accepted as fact, that Richard III was evil. As an avid reader, is it possible for a work of fiction to change the way you think? Give an example.

5. Lastly, having read Tey's book, do you believe Richard III guilty of murdering his nephews, or do you think it was a malicious rumor spread by the Tudors to discredit the last Plantagenet?

Craft: Paper Flowers Created from Scrap Paper

Scissors
Scrap paper, preferably with words on it
Colored markers
Hot glue gun
Florist wire
Buttons

Cut the scrap paper into the petal shape of your choice. They can be round, oval, teardrop shaped, anything you choose. Cut a variety of sizes, four large, four medium, three small. Using any colored marker, color the outer edge of the petals. Once the glue gun is primed, glue the large petals together at their bases, leaving a small opening for the florist wire to be fed through. Next repeat the process with the medium- and small-sized petals. Once you have all three done, take a button and feed one end of a length of florist wire through it. Now use it as the center of your flower and string first the small, then the medium, and lastly the large petals onto the wire. Use the glue gun to make the petals secure. When the glue is dry, shape the flower by folding the outer edge of the petals back to make it look like the flower is wide open.

Recipes

BETH'S IRISH SODA BREAD

2½ cups all-purpose flour
½ cup sugar
½ teaspoon baking soda
¾ teaspoon salt
½ tablespoon baking powder
½ stick unsalted butter, softened
1¼ cups buttermilk, shaken well
1 large egg
1 cup raisins
1 tablespoon caraway seeds
1 tablespoon melted butter

Preheat oven to 350°F. Butter and flour a large baking sheet.
Whisk together first six ingredients.

Mix buttermilk and egg in separate bowl then add to flour mixture until dough is moistened but still lumpy. Add the raisins and caraway seeds to the dough and knead on well-floured surface about 8 times to form a soft and less sticky dough. Pat into 6-inch round dome on baking sheet.

Cut a ½-inch-deep X on top of the loaf with a sharp knife, then brush the loaf with melted butter. Bake in the middle of the oven until golden brown, 40 to 45 minutes. Transfer loaf to rack to cool completely.

SERVES 8.

CHARLENE'S SHEPHERD'S PIE
Easy Shepherd's Pie
(Cottage Pie in the U.K.)

1 pound lean ground beef
1 teaspoon Worcestershire Sauce
Salt and pepper to taste
1 cup frozen mixed veggies (corn, carrots and peas)
6 medium potatoes, peeled, boiled and mashed
1 cup shredded cheddar cheese

Brown ground beef. Drain grease if necessary. Simmer beef and season with Worcestershire sauce, salt and pepper. While simmering, add frozen vegetables. When vegetables are warmed through, pour mixture into a 2-quart casserole dish. Spread mashed potatoes on top (should be about an inch thick). Sprinkle with cheddar cheese and bake at 350°F until cheese is browned on top, about 30 to 35 minutes.

SERVES 4.

Turn the page for the never-before-published
bonus short story . . .

AN UNLIKELY MEETING

"Lindsey, we've started crafternoon without you," Beth Stanley said. "Oh, sorry, I didn't realize you were still in interviews."

"We would be if our candidate were here, but as it is you're not interrupting anything," Lindsey said.

Lindsey Norris, director of the Briar Creek Public Library, glanced at the three people in the room with her and then at the clock. It was fifteen minutes past the start time of the final interview for the day. She glanced at Herb Gunderson and asked, "Should we call it?"

He frowned. Herb was a very cross-the-t's-and-dot-the-i's sort of guy, and Lindsey knew he was wondering what timeline the human resources department would give for abandoning the interview of a no-show. Was there a designated limit? Fifteen minutes? Twenty? A half hour?

"Let me make a quick call," he said. "Maybe you should check your messages and see if the person"—he glanced at the papers in front of him—"this Paula Turner, called. Maybe she's withdrawing her application or something came up and she has to reschedule."

Lindsey nodded. That seemed reasonable. "I'll be right back."

She followed Beth into the hallway, noticing for the first time that Beth was not in her usual story time outfit. The interviews had run later than she'd expected, and their weekly crafternoon, a lunchtime book club where they did a craft while they discussed the book, was well under way.

"Going well?" Beth asked. "Any stellar candidates?"

"It's a misery. I had no idea how hard it was going to be to replace Ann Marie on the circulation desk with Ms. Cole. It has to be someone who can handle her and who works well in a library environment," Lindsey said. "The candidate pool has been underwhelming, and I was really holding out hope for this last one."

"Maybe she'll still show. It's been raining for four days now. The roads are a mess, and I hear a couple of bridges have been washed out because of the floods. When I came in this morning, the wind was so strong it was blowing the rain sideways. The weatherman said it won't let up for another day or two," Beth said. "It could be she got held up in traffic."

"I suppose," Lindsey said. Still, she couldn't shake off her disappointment. She knew she was probably being inflexible, but if Paula Turner really wanted the job, she needed to get to her interview on time, bad weather or not.

They entered the main part of the library, and the automatic doors swooshed open. Lindsey glanced over, hoping to see a woman looking prepared for a job interview, but instead it was her downstairs neighbor Charlie Peyton, a young musician who occasionally pet-sit her furry black puppy, Heathcliff.

"Lindsey, thank goodness!" he cried. Charlie was soaked. Despite the raincoat he wore, his pants and shoes were sodden, and his long black hair was hanging in thick strands that dripped water onto the rubber doormat.

"Charlie, are you okay?" Lindsey asked.

"I'm fine, except . . ." His voice trailed off as if he had to go and gather his next words before spitting them out. "I lost Heathcliff!"

He lifted his hands, and Lindsey saw the familiar collar and leash clutched in his fingers, and she felt her heart free-fall from her chest to her feet.

"What do you mean *lost*, exactly?" she asked. Her voice came out shrill, and she tried to cough it back to its normal register.

"I took him out to do his business," Charlie said, "and we were headed back to the house when all of a sudden, he started putting up a fuss. The next thing I knew, he'd popped his head out of his collar and was running down the street as if he was being chased by a knife-wielding clown. Oh, wait, I think that's my issue. Well, you get the point. He ran off. I thought he was coming to you. No?"

"No," Beth said. She shook her head. "I've been working the front desk all morning. I would have seen him."

Lindsey scanned the library, but there was no furry black puppy wriggling his way through the stacks. She hurried to the circulation desk where the library's old-school librarian was checking in materials.

"Ms. Cole, excuse me, have you seen my dog?" Lindsey asked.

Ms. Cole lowered her reading glasses on her nose and studied Lindsey. "No dogs are allowed in the library."

"I know that." Lindsey blew out a breath of exasperation. "But it seems that Heathcliff got away from his dog walker, and he thought he might have come in here."

"When Mr. Tupper was the director—" Ms. Cole began, but Lindsey cut her off.

"Yeah, yeah, dogs weren't allowed, I get it. If you see my

dog, please call me," Lindsey said. She turned to Charlie and asked, "Where else have you looked?"

"No place, I came right here," he said.

"All right, I'm going to get my jacket and go out and search," she said. "Maybe he just got distracted by a ripe garbage can somewhere."

"I'm coming, too," Beth said.

She followed Lindsey into the workroom, where they kept their coats and umbrellas. They zipped up their fleece-lined jackets with the extra-large pockets, grabbed umbrellas and hurried back into the lobby.

When they arrived they found the rest of their crafternoon group, Nancy Peyton, Violet La Rue, Charlene La Rue and Mary Murphy, all wearing coats and carrying umbrellas, looking ready for action.

"Charlie told us what happened," Nancy said. "I sent him into the crafternoon room to dry off, warm up and get something to eat."

"Good," Lindsey said. "Sorry, I should have sent him there myself, but I'm a little . . ."

"It's all right," Violet said. "We know how much Heathcliff means to you."

Lindsey felt her throat get tight, and she nodded, since no words were small enough to squeeze past the lump blocking her throat.

"I am sure he's fine," Mary said. "He's one smart pooch. Probably, he's hiding out waiting for the worst of this downpour to pass."

"Absolutely," Charlene said. "Now does everyone have their phone? We can text one another as soon as one of us finds him."

They all checked their pockets and nodded. They were all so sure that Heathcliff was out there just waiting for them that Lindsey felt her spirits lift.

"How do you want to tackle the town?" Nancy asked. "What are Heathcliff's favorite spots?"

"The pier for boat rides with Sully, the bakery where they give him treats and the playground because he likes to play with the kids," Lindsey said. She paused to compose herself as she was flooded with images of him frolicking with the children who adored him, riding on the bow of Sully's boat and wagging his tail off at Kristen the baker, who always saved him a doggie bagel.

"Okay, that's a good start," Violet said. "Nancy and I will take the pier; Mary and Charlene, you hit the bakery; Lindsey and Beth, you start at the playground."

They moved as one toward the doors.

"Lindsey, where are you going? What about the interviews?" Herb Gunderson came out of the glassed-in room they'd been using.

"They're going to have to wait, Herb. My dog is missing," she said.

"But what if our last candidate shows up?" he asked. "I checked, and we're technically supposed to wait for at least thirty minutes."

"Tell her to have a seat, and I'll try to be back in thirty minutes with my dog," she said. With that, Lindsey led the way out of the building into the cold, wet afternoon.

Within minutes, Lindsey's shoes and pants were soaked. She didn't care. The end of her nose was frozen, and her cheeks felt hardened from the cold. Still, the only thing she could think about was Heathcliff. Lindsey glanced at Beth. She looked equally as miserable and determined.

They hurried through Briar Creek's small side streets, pausing to call, "Heathcliff, come here, boy!"

But no wiggly black dog answered their call. Lindsey couldn't even be sure he could hear them over the wind, which seemed to grab their words as soon as they left their lips and smash them to the ground as if they were no more significant than the raindrops it used to pelt them repeatedly.

When they reached the park that Heathcliff loved, it was

full of puddles but no laughing children and no gossiping caregivers sitting on the surrounding benches. The swings swayed back and forth with each gust, giving the abandoned park a ghostly feeling. Lindsey shivered.

Beth grabbed Lindsey's arm and pulled her under the large climbing apparatus. Lindsey stepped in a puddle and cringed at the cold that filled her shoe, not that she could get any wetter. The big plastic fort over their heads gave them some shelter from the wind, which was a welcome respite.

"I don't see him," Beth said. She wiped the rain from her face.

"I don't either," Lindsey agreed. "If he were here, he would have come to us, unless . . ."

"Unless what?"

"He's injured." Lindsey could barely choke the sentence out.

"He's not!" Beth insisted. "He's a smart dog. Something must have caused him to run off like that. Maybe he saw a hot female dog and just couldn't help himself."

Lindsey had to give her friend points for trying. "He doesn't really have a full boy-dog operating system at his disposal, so I'm not sure that would cause him to dash off like that."

Beth looked unhappy to have her theory squashed. Their phones hummed at the same time, and they gave each other a startled glance.

"Maybe someone found him," Beth said as they both grappled to pull their phones from their pockets with their cold, clumsy fingers.

Two texts were waiting, one from Violet and one from Charlene. No one had seen Heathcliff, and the other two pairs of searchers were going to separate and see if they could cover more ground.

"I think that's a good idea," Beth said. "I'll text them and let them know that the park is a no-go."

Lindsey felt the crush of disappointment weigh on her.

She shook her head. She was not giving up, not even close. While Beth tapped out a text, Lindsey felt her phone buzz. She checked the screen and saw she had incoming texts from Mike Sullivan, whom everyone called Sully, and Robbie Vine. Both men had heard that Heathcliff was missing, and they were out looking for him, too. She texted them back a status report and a thank-you and felt a surge of hope. Surely, with all of his favorite people looking for him, her sweet boy would be found.

"I hate to leave our shelter," Beth said, "but I think we'll have more luck if we split up like the others. I'll take Grove Road into the neighborhood and knock on doors. Which way do you want to go?"

Lindsey glanced at the area. When she and Heathcliff came to the park, they took a walking path along the marshlands back to their house. There was a big gray cat who hung out in the area, and Heathcliff liked to bark at her; although he never stood a chance of catching her, he sure enjoyed giving chase. The cat seemed to enjoy it, too, which Lindsey found odd. The dirt path was a favorite of Heathcliff's. Maybe he had gone that way.

"I'm going to search along the path that cuts through the marsh," she said. "We use it all the time, so it's familiar to him."

"All right, stay in touch," Beth said. She went to leave their spot but then turned back to Lindsey and gave her a quick hug. "Don't worry. We'll find him."

"Thanks," Lindsey said. She felt tears sting her eyes, but she blinked them away. She refused to get upset until all hope was lost.

As Beth took off in one direction, Lindsey set out in the opposite. She searched two short neighborhood streets and the back of the churchyard as she went.

The wind rendered her umbrella useless, but she kept it in hand just the same. She crossed the street to the main park in town. She blinked the rain out of her eyes and squinted at the gazebo at the far end. She didn't see her boy taking cover there or under any of the benches that sat at the edge of the green, offering a view of the bay and the Thumb Islands beyond.

She felt a panicked sob well up in her chest. Heathcliff had come to her a little over a year ago during an epic nor'easter. Some horrible person had shoved him, a young puppy, into the library book drop. He could have frozen to death but, no, instead he had wagged his way into Lindsey's life with a zest and enthusiasm for living that was unrivaled.

His furry black face was the first one she saw in the morning, usually when she was trying to get him up and out of her bed. She still wasn't quite sure how he managed to carve out that territory as his own, but that was his charm. He won over hearts with his bushy eyebrows, perky ears and fuzzy tail. Lindsey didn't know anyone, barring Ms. Cole, who could resist his handsome face and happy-go-lucky personality.

She crossed the park, feeling as if she was fighting the wind for every step. A big gust knocked her back two steps, but she redoubled her efforts, lowered her head and forged on, refusing to turn back.

"Lindsey! Lindsey!"

She paused. Was it wishful thinking that made her think someone was calling her? She turned in the direction of the sound. A blurry figure stood at the edge of the park, covered from head to knee in a bright yellow slicker. Lindsey narrowed her eyes. She didn't recognize the person and was about to turn back when they started waving.

Maybe it was someone who had seen Heathcliff. She hurried across the sodden ground. Her shoes sank into the soft soil, making the trek even more difficult. When she got close, she saw that it was Jeanette Palmer, owner of the Beachfront Bed and Breakfast.

Jeanette was eighty-plus years old, but it didn't show. She wore her snow-white hair in a topknot, which was covered in a clear plastic bonnet, and she had a well-muscled, petite figure that seemed to be in perpetual motion. She also had a fondness for the steamier novels that the library carried. Lindsey hoped she wasn't being flagged down for a status update on the latest Jennifer Ashley novel.

"Lindsey!" Jeanette grabbed her hands in hers. "I saw him. I saw Heathcliff!"

"You did?" Lindsey was so excited she actually jumped for joy. It was a bad plan, as she landed in a puddle, soaking her shoes even more. "Where?"

Jeanette's face crumpled with concern. "He was in the road, and a man on a motorcycle was chasing him."

"What?" Lindsey cried.

"Heathcliff barked at the motorcycle, and the motorcycle rider tried to hit him, then Heathcliff ran and barked, and the motorcyclist tried to hit him again. It was horrible. I tried to get to him, but I was too far away and couldn't move any faster in this damn wind." Jeanette sounded distraught, and Lindsey squeezed her hands in hers to let her know it was all right.

"Then what happened?" Lindsey asked.

"Oh, honey, I am so sorry," Jeanette said.

Lindsey felt the world go still, and her breath stalled, her blood stopped pumping and she felt her chest collapse in on itself. She couldn't bear to hear that her baby had been hit by the motorcycle. She just couldn't.

"Is he . . . Is he . . . ?" She couldn't say the words.

"I don't know," Jeanette said. "I saw him lie down on the road right in front of the bike. I didn't think he'd been hit, but now I think he must have been. Then the motorcycle driver picked him up and put him on his lap and took off."

"What?" Lindsey asked. She sucked in a huge gulp of air, and her heart started to pound hard, as if to make up for missed beats. She was dizzy but fought to stay in the moment. "Where did they go?"

"I'm not sure, but it looked like they were headed toward the old marsh road," Jeanette said.

Lindsey didn't pause to think about it. She squeezed Jeanette's hands and kissed her cheek. "Thank you!"

"Lindsey, you can't go after them," Jeanette cried. "You could be abducted by some sadistic biker gang and be tortured or worse!"

Worse than torture? Lindsey didn't think she imagined the thrilled note in Jeanette's voice. The woman really needed to wean off of the racy reading material.

"I'll be careful, I promise," she said.

Then she took off running. The path that she and Heathcliff liked to walk ran parallel with the old marsh road, which skirted the wetlands on this side of the bay. If she was very fast, and very lucky, she might be able to catch them.

She darted into a copse of trees. The smell of damp earth and wet leaves filled her nose, which at any other time she would have stopped to take in and savor, but not now. The bare-limbed canopy of branches overhead didn't diminish the rain, but the thick trunks of the grove did cut the wind. She hurried, running blindly along the well-worn path, trying to keep from tripping on the uneven ground and exposed roots in her effort to catch up to her dog and whoever had taken him.

The path led down into a small ravine. Lindsey slipped down the muddy trail and would have landed in the large puddle at the bottom if she hadn't hooked her arm around a nearby white oak. The bark was cold and wet, but the young tree felt strong. Lindsey pulled herself upright and moved to the side of the path where the ground was higher and less wet. She picked her way along the damp leaves, trying to avoid another fall.

Scrambling up the opposite bank proved just as tricky, and she had to shove thin branches out of her face while she pulled herself up the rocky incline. Her breath was steaming out of her lips into the cold afternoon air, which caused her lungs to burn. She paused for just a moment to catch her breath before continuing on.

The sound of the rain hammering the ground was her only companion. She didn't hear the rustle of critters or the chirp of birds. It seemed as if everyone had the good sense to take shelter from the storm, everyone except Heathcliff. She thought about what Jeanette had told her. She couldn't imagine why Heathcliff had taunted the person on the motorcycle. That wasn't like him at all.

There was no arguing that his barking at the motorcyclist and then running away had definitely been a ploy to get the driver's attention, but why? Why would he have run away from Charlie? Heathcliff loved Charlie, so much so that when Charlie's band practiced in the apartment below Lindsey's, Heathcliff liked to howl along, almost as if he considered himself their lead singer.

What could have triggered Heathcliff to run away like that? She couldn't imagine. And what had the motorcyclist wanted with her dog? Maybe they thought he was lost and they were going to take him to an animal shelter.

She wondered if she should text Beth to go ahead and call the shelters if she got back to the library first. She started to reach for her phone when she heard a yip. She froze, straining her ears against the weather's forceful presence to see if she heard it again. There was nothing. Had she imagined it?

She moved quietly forward, almost as if she was afraid her movement might chase the sound away. There! She heard it again. It was hard to tell which direction it had come from, but she realized that she was near one of the old fishing sheds that dotted the shoreline. Could the person who took Heathcliff have taken him there? But why? Not for anything good, she was sure.

Lindsey jogged up the path, feeling newly invigorated by the sound of her boy's bark. She knew it was him, she just knew it. The path wound around a large section of forest and then leveled out. A dirt road crossed the path and led back into the marsh where the fishing sheds began. Lindsey turned onto the

dirt road, hoping that it wasn't just the power of wishful thinking that convinced her she'd heard that familiar bark.

The road was wider and smoother than the path had been.
She glanced over the dried grass and tall stalks of phragmites
and could see the roof of her house on the opposite side of
the marsh. Lindsey lived on the third floor of the captain's
house, which was one in a line of old houses that had been
built when Briar Creek had found its footing as a resort town
in the late eighteen hundreds.

Most of the large houses were now three-family homes
with the various floors being rented out to tenants. It was a
particularly lovely area, as the yards were big, the driveways
were paved with crushed shells and picket fences divided the
properties in a politely charming manner.

Could Heathcliff have gotten away from the motorcyclist
and headed for home? Was he barking all the way there?
Was that what she had heard? He was known for grumbling
under his breath when he wanted a walk, a snack or a belly
scratch. For a guy who didn't speak the language, he sure
got his point across.

Again, Lindsey felt her chest get tight, while her throat
constricted and tears stung her eyes. She just didn't think
she could stand it if something bad happened to him.

She decided to go farther down the road just to rule it
out. She had only gone about one hundred yards when she
saw it. Parked on the edge of the road was a big black motorcycle.

Lindsey began to run. She yelled, "Heathcliff!" Her voice
came out desperate and hysterical, not inaccurate, but not
very intimidating either, so she cried out again, this time
lowering her voice, "Come here, boy!"

If the person who had taken him was about to cause her
baby harm, she wanted them to know she was coming. Not
only that but she wanted them to know she was not afraid
to kick some biker ass either.

When she reached the motorcycle, she put her hand on the body of the vehicle. The engine was still warm. It felt good against her chilled fingers, but she didn't linger. It was clear that whoever rode the motorcycle had arrived recently, so they were probably nearby.

She glanced around, trying to determine where to go. The dried reeds to the right were flattened in one section, as if someone had recently stepped on them. She forged ahead, stepping carefully into the phragmites, feeling a bit like she was stepping into a cornfield maze as the reeds closed in over her head.

"Heathcliff!" she called.

This time there was no mistaking the sound of a dog's bark, and it was coming from the direction of the marsh up ahead.

"Heathcliff!" she cried again.

This time he answered with a frenzied bark, as if her little guy was in trouble. Lindsey broke into a run, slamming through the reeds, not caring that they yanked off her hood and snagged her hair and lashed her face. She had to get to her boy.

She broke through the tall grass and stepped into a clearing. A short dock led to a dilapidated fishing shack made of weathered wood; well, what was left of it anyway. She assumed the past few days of rain and wind had shoved it off of its perch and dropped it into the soggy marsh. Only a few feet of the top and the roof were visible where they stuck up out of the mud. It looked like the mucky marsh was slowly sucking the shack into its mouth like a snake swallowing a rat.

"Heathcliff!" she cried.

A sharp bark answered from inside the shack. Lindsey hurried forward. She climbed onto the broken weathered boards that made up the haphazard dock. She slipped once, pinwheeled her arms to get her balance and then moved a little bit more carefully. Heathcliff was inside. He was safe. If she didn't crash into the side of the structure like a rampaging elephant, he would likely remain so. She inhaled slowly through her nose and let it out.

None of this made any sense. Why had the motorcyclist kidnapped Heathcliff? To hold him for ransom in the shack? If so, why was their bike parked back on the road? Where were they? Lindsey had no answers. She just knew her dog was in there and she would full-on brawl to get him out if she had to.

She inched her way along the rain- and mud-slicked boards until she got to the front. The shack was small, maybe seven by seven. She hunkered down beside the opening that had probably once held a door. She peered around the edge, hoping to get a glimpse inside.

She blinked into the gloom. It was too dark to see, but she could hear someone breathing. It was a raspy panting sound, and she felt the hair on the back of her neck stand on end.

"Well, don't just stand there gawking. Help me!"

Lindsey started. She heard Heathcliff whine, and she leaned into the opening. "Why did you take Heathcliff? If you've harmed him . . ."

"Heathcliff, huh? Is that because you're a *Wuthering Heights* fan or because this fine young dog fits the description 'half covered with black whiskers; the brows lowering, the eyes deep-set and singular. I remembered the eyes.'" It was a woman's voice, low and earthy, and full of humor.

"I am a Brontë fan, which I gather you are, too," Lindsey said. She studied the woman. "But you didn't answer my question."

"I'd say he was the one who took me. I was on my way to an appointment when he lay down in front of my motorcycle," she said. "Darnedest thing I've ever seen. I had to pick him up to get him to move. I figured I'd take him with me and hope someone recognized him, as I'm not from around here. I went to turn onto the street I needed and he bolted, barking at me over his shoulder like he was demanding that I follow. I hesitated for a second, but he was clearly in distress, so I followed him and he led me here.

"I don't understand," Lindsey said. She blinked into the gloom. "Why would he want to come here?"

A pitiful mewling sound was the only answer Lindsey got before a bedraggled Heathcliff slopped his way toward her, clearly being pushed by the person inside the dark shack. Lindsey reached out to grab him, and it was then that she saw he carried a tiny gray kitten by the scruff of its neck in his mouth.

"Oh my goodness!" she exclaimed. She took the kitten, and Heathcliff turned and darted back inside.

"Yeah, we've got a whole litter in here, and your boy was determined to get them out," the woman said. "Judging by the weather, I'd say we were just in time. I think we can get them out one at a time, but mama cat is pretty unhappy. Can you hold the kittens for me?"

There was a yowl as if the mother in question was protesting the woman's choice of caregiver.

"Yeah, sure, I can do that," Lindsey said.

She plopped the kitten into one of her large coat pockets. Her eyes were adjusting to the gloom, and now she could just make out the woman inside. She was up to her thighs in mud and water. Her teeth were chattering despite the heavy leather jacket that she wore.

Mother cat and kittens were on a ledge just above the waterline. Lindsey had no doubt that if the storm kept up overnight as it was predicted to do, they all would have drowned. Several boards had been used to build a makeshift ramp, and Lindsey realized the woman must have done this in order to help Heathcliff get the cats out.

"Sort of wish I had an 'Eat Me' cake right about now," the woman said. "I could rip the roof off this place and just scoop the cats out of here."

"*Alice in Wonderland*?" Lindsey asked with a laugh. "That

would help you grow big enough for the moment, but you'd also need the 'Drink Me' potion to shrink back to your original size."

Heathcliff slipped and scrambled across the boards and plopped another kitten, a black-and-white one this time, into Lindsey's hands.

"Aw, aren't you just the saddest-looking thing?" Lindsey asked. "What are we going to do with you?"

"Careful," the woman said. "'You become responsible, forever, for what you have tamed.'"

"*The Little Prince*," Lindsey identified the book quote. "Nice."

The woman leaned closer to the door, and Lindsey caught a glint of light on the woman's hair, which appeared to be a big fat braid of deep purple that hung halfway down her back. Interesting. She seemed very well read for a biker.

"Who's your favorite author?" Lindsey asked.

"Now that's like asking mama cat here who her favorite kitten is," the woman said. "I could never choose a favorite book. There are far too many that have meant too much to me over the years."

"I feel the same way," Lindsey said.

Two more kittens were dropped into her hands. She had to double up the two smallest kittens in her oversized pocket and hope they weren't too squeezed in there.

"Okay, now I need to try and get mama out," the woman said.

Lindsey heard the mother give a plaintive yowl. Clearly, she was unhappy that her babies had been taken, and the rising water was only adding to her stress. Lindsey leaned into the shack to get a look at the situation. Her eyes had finally adjusted to the dim light, and when she saw the mama cat, it all started to make sense.

"That's your friend, isn't it, boy?" she asked Heathcliff. She glanced at the woman and said, "Heathcliff might be able to help. He's been chasing this mama cat around the marsh for months. I think he considers her his friend."

"That makes sense," the woman said. "Let's see if he can coax her out."

Heathcliff seemed to understand, as he jumped onto the ledge where the cat had curled up into a defensive ball. She hissed and spat and tried to swat him with her claws, but there was no heat behind the attack.

Heathcliff patiently put his nose forward until she rubbed her face against his. Then he licked her head as if to assure her that it was going to be okay. Lindsey felt as if she were a proud mom watching her firefighter son come out of a burning building having just saved a family.

The woman inside kept talking to the two animals in a low, soft voice that soothed. Lindsey watched as she slid off her jacket and held it open like a makeshift bag. After some adjusting of his position, Heathcliff picked up the mama by the scruff of her neck and dropped her into the jacket. Before the cat could maul her, the woman bundled her into the coat.

"Lead on, hero," the woman said to Heathcliff, and he climbed up the ramp and outside to stand with Lindsey. The woman handed her coat through the opening to Lindsey.

Mama cat blinked against the bright outdoor light as her pupils contracted. The pretty gray cat had fur as soft as crushed velvet and green eyes that seemed above average in intelligence.

"You may want to pick better places to have your litter next time," Lindsey said. The cat blinked and began to lick her shoulder.

The woman tried to haul herself out of the shed, but the muck held her fast with its suction-like grip. Lindsey put the cat down and reached into the doorway to give the woman a hand. Lindsey leaned back as she pulled, bracing herself with her feet. It was harder than she'd anticipated to fight the muck, which seemed intent on keeping its prize.

The woman's white blouse was soaked and adhered to her skin, making it almost transparent. Lindsey could see a colorful sleeve of tattoos decorating her arm; they were renderings of books in flight against a starry background.

"Tell me if I'm crazy," Lindsey said as the woman burst through the door with one big heave, "but your name wouldn't be Paula Turner by any chance, would it?"

The woman rose to her feet. She was covered in mud from her armpits to her boots. She turned her head and gave Lindsey a sidelong look and raised one eyebrow.

"Who wants to know?" she asked.

"Lindsey Norris, library director," Lindsey said and held out her hand.

Paula nodded as she shook her hand. "I think I missed my interview."

"Yes, you did," Lindsey said. She led the way off the dock, carrying mama cat. Once on shore, she pulled the kittens out of her pockets and returned them to their mother. She and Paula watched as the family nestled deeper into Paula's coat.

Lindsey glanced at Paula and noted that she looked defeated but not surprised.

"That's too bad," Paula said. She hunkered down to inspect the cats. "Library clerk sounded like the perfect job for me."

"Oh, you got the job," Lindsey said as she crouched beside her.

"What?" Paula gasped. She looked genuinely stunned. "But you don't know anything about me or my past, which is—"

"I know what's important," Lindsey interrupted. She met the woman's gaze. She liked what she saw there. She was operating on instinct now, but then this whole day had been a lesson in following her gut. "I know enough. Welcome to Briar Creek, Paula Turner."